Sandcastle
of PIRATES
BEACH

BOOK ONE OF THE WAR OF THE SKY LORDS SERIES

Sandcastle of PIRATES BEACH

D. EDWARD WILLIAMS

Clovercroft Publishing

Sandcastle of Pirates Beach

©2019 by D. Edward Williams

All rights reserved. No part of this book may be reproduced or transmitted in any form or by any means, electronic or mechanical, including photocopying, recording or by any information storage and retrieval system, without permission in writing from the copyright owner.

Published by Clovercroft Publishing, Franklin, Tennessee

Copy Edit by Christy Callahan

Cover and Interior Design by Suzanne Lawing

Illustrations by Ruben Carral

Printed in the United States of America

978-1-948484-65-7

CONTENTS

Chapter 1	THE LEGEND	9
Chapter 2	SURPRISE IN THE SAND	19
Chapter 3	CRAB TALES	35
Chapter 4	CLAMMING	57
Chapter 5	BLAST OFF	71
Chapter 6	WHAT LIES BELOW	81
Chapter 7	TO THE RESCUE	103
Chapter 8	THE KEY	131
Chapter 9	TURTLE TALES	161
Chapter 10	RIVER'S END	171
Chapter 11	CRABS AND GULLS	185
Chapter 12	A BIG FEAST	213
Chapter 13	THE HUNT BEGINS	243

CHAPTER 1

THE LEGEND

Rainbows

Red, Orange, Yellow, Green, Blue, Indigo, and Violet (often called Purple by the Sky-Lords). Each mighty color has capabilities that can be used, if only one knows how.

LORE OF THE SKY-LORDS

Once a generation, all of the sand crabs living near Pirates Beach gather together in the great hall of the sandcastle, to hear the legend of the Lords of the Sky and the terrible Breaking of the Rainbow. Crabs consider this story to be very important, as it has long been foretold by the Questions (crabs who can occasionally see into the future) that this particular crab colony would play a special role in returning the missing Rainbow to its glory among the clouds.

HEY THERE! HOLD ON. STOP. WHAT IS GOING ON HERE?

Crabs, you say? What are sand crabs doing in this story? How can crabs have a meeting to discuss these very important things that usually only humans talk about? You are asking some critical questions—and I don't mean "Questions" like the crabs who can see into the future. These are just regular questions that really do need to be answered, before we proceed. So that said, let me explain a couple of things to help out.

Now, I know that many of you reading this story are not really familiar with Crabs, especially the ones living in Galveston, Texas, on Pirates Beach. These are very smart crabs that love to play, including games with people or other creatures found near the shore. They also like to share stories, go on adventures, and act in a generally civilized way. This particular tale involves not only human children that play on the beach, but also the creatures (both good ones and bad ones, including some very, very, very bad ones) that live there. So, with that little bit of advice, let's get back to our story.

Oh sorry, almost forgot, one more thing: there may be very real Pirates involved here. So, watch out—they can be very dangerous. You have been warned! OK, no more interruptions. Here we go, back to our story (again).

"GATHER ROUND, GATHER ROUND," boomed the Crab storyteller, whose name was Crex. "Youngsters to the front, elders to the rear. Hurry up now, we are about to begin." All of the young crabs living in the colony were there, as well as a good number of the adults. Storytelling was a very popular tradition for this particular colony of crabs, no self-respecting sand crab would miss it—unless they just had too.

Cracker was there, of course, along with all his friends. These kinds of stories were his personal favorites. In fact, the only younger crab not to be seen that day was Orion. Although his pals were all in the gathering, no one seemed to notice Orion's absence—except for Cracker—as everyone else was so excited to hear the always wonderful tale of the Sky-Lords and the Breaking of the Rainbow.

Settling down quickly, with pincers crossed in front of them, every one of the crabs in the large audience hall now focused their attention on Crex. This is what they heard him say:

"When the Lords of the Sky were children—those many, many long years ago—they liked to play a game called Kick-the-Cloud. A small group of young Lord-lings would often play all day long. It was their very favorite thing to do! By the rules of the game, whoever lost the previous round had to be 'It' for the next one. Today's story is about one particular Lord-ling, a mean-spirited (not very nice) young Lord, he was nicknamed by his fellow playmates, 'Putrid'—Lord of Boogers and Bad-Smelling Things."

At this point, the young crabs who were listening intently to the story, suddenly roared with laughter. Hearing any adult say *Booger* was always very funny, especially coming from the leader of the Colony—as Crex well knew. A few of those youngsters added their own special noises, some sounding like a whoopee cushion—*pphhttthhtt*—just for a few extra laughs.

After allowing things to settle back down, Crex continued with his tale. "Young Lord Putrid always seemed to be 'It.' And of course all the Lord-lings loved to tease him by saying, 'Putrid's It, Putrid's It, Putrid plays like an id-e-it.' Then they would all roar with laughter at Putrid's expense. 'Ha Ha Ho Ho He He.' To make matters worse, Putrid had a very bad (almost terrible) temper; he often left the game in a huff because he was so mad at having to be It, over and over again. The constant teasing by his fellow Lord-lings, didn't help matters either, of course.

"One day, after trying to win at Kick-the-Cloud and losing (again), Putrid got so mad he left the group to go sit alone on his favorite mountaintop. In his great anger, he caused a horrible stench (*pee-yew*, one might have said) along with a mighty thunderstorm to erupt, seemingly out of nowhere. Because the storm blew up so quickly, half of the sky was still in bright sunlight while the other half was inside a raging downpour. This caused a most beautiful rainbow to appear—perhaps the largest, most beautiful ever.

"All of the Sky-Lords loved rainbows of course, the bigger, the brighter, the better. This one, created purely from Putrid's anger, was exceptional—big, bold, and brilliant—and vibrant with distinct colors that seemed to be almost alive, something truly special to behold.

"Driven by his rage, Putrid knew with complete certainty, that the other Lords would absolutely love this Rainbow—they were likely admiring it even now—which made him hate it all the more. Putrid's losing Kick-the-Cloud, being laughed at by all the others, and now seeing something he knew was making those same Lords happy drove Putrid completely mad. In fact, the bigger, more beautiful this rainbow became, the angrier Putrid got, which in turn just made the rainbow even more spectacular to behold.

"Then, suddenly, right in the midst of his terrible rage, Putrid got a horrible, a totally terrible idea, which he immediately loved. Focusing his fury completely on this new inspiration, he thought, I will show those stupid Lords that they shouldn't make fun of me. *I will destroy this beautiful rainbow, just tear it apart while they watch!*

"Putrid couldn't stop there of course. Now that his idea for revenge had taken shape, he only wanted to make things worse. Talking out loud to himself he said, 'Once I've ripped this rainbow into individual pieces of pure color, I can use their strength, their power, to create my mighty Objects that will bring misery to the world below. I will spread them across the wide lands, causing all kinds of problems for the beasts, birds, and the people living down there. This will make those stupid Lords upset. I will show them! Then, they won't make fun of me anymore!'

"With that last evil thought, Putrid's sneer changed into a big smile, which slowly grew across his face, one so big he could barely contain it without laughing out loud to himself. Along with the smile came a truly wicked gleam to his eyes. Looking around one last time, making sure that none of the other Sky-Lords could see what he was up to, Putrid gave a final, 'Hmmpphh!' then set to his awful task. Hidden behind the clouds on his mountain perch, Putrid ripped that most beautiful rainbow right out of the sky. Grabbing it with his big stinky hands, Putrid used every ounce of his rage driven strength to break it apart into the rainbow's seven distinct colors: Red, Orange, Yellow, Green, Blue, Indigo, and Violet (which Putrid called Purple).

"Then, still standing high on the mountain's peak, hidden for a brief time by the last remaining storm clouds, he put forth all his lordly abilities, combining them with the raging hate and anger he felt toward his fellow lords, to transform the seven mighty colors into his awful Rainbow Objects. Red for Ruling, Green for Gloom, Blue for Bickering, Purple for Power, Orange for Oblivion, and Indigo for Ill—Putrid turned all these beautiful colors into simple objects that earthly creatures would be very easily drawn to. Only the strongest of will or purest of heart would be able to resist the call and influence of his foul Objects.

"Putrid's evil purpose, deeply embedded into each one, insured that using any Object would increase one's wealth and power, even allowing for conquest; but, using them would never grant one satisfaction or happiness. Possessing such a thing would only lead to the desire to gather more of them. All this Putrid saw clearly in his mind, with each dark Object coming to life in his hands. As he finished each one, Putrid would stand up, whisper some dark secret or curse upon it, then toss the Object far off his mountaintop—for the future pain and suffering of those living on the earth below.

"When he finished his sixth object, Putrid paused to survey what he had accomplished. All that was left of what had once been the most glorious of rainbows, were now simply scraps of each individual color, some even beginning to fade as he watched, lying on the ground beneath his feet.

"Fortunately, some of the elder Sky-Lords figured out what was happening soon after the Rainbow they were all admiring was suddenly torn from the sky. Rushing to the mountaintop to stop Putrid, they were, unfortunately, mostly too late. Saving only a single color—Yellow—from Putrid's evil scheme, they placed it straight into the Sun, so that all living things on the earth would have new hope each day when the Yellow sun rose then crossed over the sky, bringing light and warmth to all beneath it.

"Working quickly to save what they could, the Sky-Lords took each scrap of color that they found lying on the ground, to create their own mighty works—they called them the Rainbow Colors—to fight against Putrid's dark creations. Red for Reason, Green for Glory, Blue for Bravery, Purple for Peace, Orange for Optimism, and Indigo for Inspiration; the Sky-Lords combined the Rainbow's remaining power with their own strength, compassion, and the ability to work together.

Just as Putrid sent his Objects down to earth, the Sky-Lords did so as well with their Colors.

"Unfortunately, what was finally left of that most beautiful rainbow after all the frenzied activity was, well, absolutely nothing at all! Not a single shred or scrap of the Rainbow was left over. The Lords, seeing this, sadly realized that there would be no more rainbows. At least not until all of the Rainbow items (both Objects and Colors) were brought back together again under the Yellow sunlight, to return to their glory in the sky.

"Putrid, as punishment for what he did, was imprisoned by the Sky-Lords in a very special cell for many, many an age (a very long time even by a Lord's standards) where he could be mean and make bad smells all by himself. Many of the younger Sky-lords often called him Putrid the Tooter—for obvious reasons. He would remain there until he apologized properly for his actions, including collecting up all the awful Objects he had made, or was somehow able to open it and escape!

"As they finished their work, the eldest Lord said, 'There will be many problems across all the lands resulting from this horrible breaking of the Rainbow. I can already feel the ill spreading from those terrible Objects that Putrid has created.'

"Another Lord responded, 'You are right, my lord, but our creations will surely help, won't they? Besides, you never know how things will turn out. Maybe some good will also come of all this, in the end.'

"The eldest Lord answered, 'Yes, of course they will help, but one never knows how these items will be used. I doubt Putrid realizes that these creations of his will increase in strength if they are ever used together. Bringing the Objects together will also very likely change what can be done with them. If these evil Objects are all brought under the control of one creature, while the items for good we made are scattered elsewhere, terrible, terrible things may result!'

"After a moment's pause he finished, 'But, we cannot interfere, things must be worked out by the living creatures below. We have done what we can.' The other Lords shook their heads sadly in agreement, slowly going back up to their own homes among the clouds.

"Putrid, left alone, almost forgotten in his special cell for many an age, could be seen—if anyone bothered to look—smiling, as he thought over and over about what he had done, perhaps what he might still do those on the earth once he was released or, better still, once he escaped."

Every one of the listening crabs was completely silent for a moment, as the story ended with the speaker's voice dropping to little more than an urgent whisper, slowly finishing those last words, *or, better still, once he escaped,* leaving a lasting image of the wicked Sky-Lord Putrid plotting some sort of awful revenge.

For just a moment, it seemed no one in the great hall was even breathing, so compelling was the story, until the entire audience suddenly burst forth into huge applause! The cheering easily drowned out Crex's captivating conclusion. Continuously cracking, clacking crab claws created considerable commotion within the large assembly, showing just how much everyone appreciated the tale about the Rainbow Objects and Colors.

Wearing a big smile, the storyteller enjoyed watching all the crabs in the hall relax after his tale had finished. Crex, as head of the colony, knew the importance of repeating the story on a regular basis, which he did every year or two. This way, everyone living in the colony—including the young ones—knew about the Breaking of the Rainbow, along with the various Objects and Colors, created as a result of that terrible act.

Some of the younger crabs immediately spoke up with questions. One of them asked, "Crex, do you know what form all of the Objects and Colors take, are they really big or are they small?" Orion's friend Skitter followed by asking, "Yes, and what do they do, especially those that Putrid created?"

Crex responded to the group, "These are some very good questions. I certainly don't know everything about them. In fact, I doubt anyone really does, other than the Lords who made them. Over time, I do know that the creatures living here on the beach have taken to calling

Putrid's evil creations the Rainbow Objects, or just 'Objects' for short."

"What about the good creations, Crex? You know, the ones created by the Sky-Lords, what are they called and what do they do?" one of the youngest crabs, Cracker, asked quickly.

"Those are known as the Rainbow Colors, or just the 'Colors,'" answered Crex. "Since you are all so curious, I will tell you that I know a little bit about three of each type. The three Objects we crabs know something about are the Purple Patch of Power, the Red Rock of Ruling, and the Blue Bowl of Bickering. I don't know what form the Orange, Green, or Indigo Objects appear as."

Speaking up again, not letting Crex finish, Cracker asked, "But what about the Colors, Crex? Tell us about those too, please."

Smiling at Cracker, Crex continued, "Yes, yes, Cracker, I was getting to them. As I said, we crabs also know about three of the Colors—the Purple Prism of Peace, the Green Gauntlet of Glory, and the Red Ring of Reason. All I will say about what they do is that the Colors we know of—help defend against those using the Objects. You see, each Object or Color has different powers that can be used by those in possession of the item. Of course, to wield them properly, the owner must have both knowledge and the will to use them."

A number of the younger crabs all started asking lots of questions at this point. Crex did not answer any more of them though, as it was getting very late. Instead, he stood up telling the entire group that story time was over. They needed to get to sleep.

As the crabs slowly left the great hall, going back about their business, Crex pulled a box out from under his seat. Inside the box, which was lined with a soft red velvet, sat what appeared to be a sea-green metallic glove, looking very much like those worn by medieval knights as they went into battle. Smiling, Crex lightly touched the Green Gauntlet for just a moment before closing the box, which he then put swiftly away.

It was a long-standing tradition of the sandcastle crabs, for the storyteller to acknowledge the Green Gauntlet in such a manner, after each telling of the tale of the Sky-Lords and the Breaking of the Rainbow.

CHAPTER 2

SURPRISE IN THE SAND

> ***Purple Patch of Power***
>
> *One of the legendary Rainbow Objects, known simply as the Purple Patch, it encourages its wearer to seek riches and influence in any way possible. Over time this lust has caused the Patch to also become synonymous with theft, often being used by Pirates and thieves to help obtain their desires. The Patch also aids its wearer in recruiting others, helping him or her in thieving efforts.*
>
> LORE OF THE SKY-LORDS

"Hunter, Come See! Look at this cool log I found, see how big it is? It's also really strong, I bet, not rotted out like so many of them!" shouted Devin to his cousin (and best friend) Hunter, as he was grabbed the log by one end to then slam the other down onto the sand, testing in truth how tough the log actually was.

Devin and Hunter are both twelve-year old boys who just love vacationing at the beach. They could spend their entire day running through the soft sand, playing in the surf with boards, tubes, boats—whatever was at hand—and most importantly, discovering new exciting things to see and do.

"Wow, Devin, you're right, that's a really great piece of wood. Not what we normally find laying around here, that's for sure. It looks stronger than normal driftwood. I think we should build something with it," suggested Hunter as he looked at the log more carefully.

"I agree, let's go find some more logs. There's plenty laying around here, so we can make something cool, maybe even build ourselves a fort!" Devin pointed to other driftwood laying around the beach.

The boys ran back toward the sand dune, where most of the driftwood ends up after washing ashore. Suddenly, just as they got near the dune, a large brown bird with a dirty covering of feathers, one good eye, an evil grin, and an odd purple patch covering where his second eye should have been, flapped his wings, startling both boys. Taking off right in front of them, the bird looked like a small pterodactyl from ages ago.

"Isn't that weird? I tell you, I think that bird was watching us, Devin. Can you believe it?" commented Hunter, pointing toward the slow-flying bird.

"Really? Why would he do that, why?" wondered Devin out loud.

"I don't know, but look, he is still circling around, watching us," responded Hunter, continuing to point at the strange bird now gliding, with wings outstretched, just over the water's edge.

"Let's go get some wood and build our fort, then we can have a battle with that big bird," suggested Devin, laughing and smiling as he said it. The boys quickly forgot about their future foe, going to work by the sand dune, trying to figure out what to add on to their newly found log.

Meanwhile, the dirty brown bird landed on a dark stump of wood, perhaps left over from an old pier or landing dock that had long ago fallen into the sea, now just sticking up, all alone, out of the ocean. Rather than look for fish or some other meal as birds normally do, this bird simply sat on the stump, continuing to gaze at the boys with its one good eye. The purple patch the bird was wearing also seemed to be watching the boys, with a strange shimmer of its own, as if the Patch itself was somehow alive.

The sand dune Devin and Hunter were playing near was covered with grasses and other plants that could survive the windy salty conditions of the beach. Just below the edge of the dune, where the tide only occasionally rises to, all sorts of things had washed up from the sea, to accumulate on the dry sand. Logs, seaweed, occasionally a fish skeleton, old rope, shells, even a rare shark's tooth, and other interesting items were to be found there.

The driftwood log Devin had found was almost five feet long, with a smooth feel all along its length. The ends of the log were smaller in width than the middle, although the thickness was the same throughout. While smooth now from years of weathering, each end looked like it might have been broken off somehow in the past. All that was left on this day was the main piece of wood, which had found its way to this beach after a long, maybe even interesting, journey.

"Hey! Look! Here are a couple more logs," said Hunter, dragging two of them together over toward his friend. "Maybe we can use these to build our fort?"

"Oh yes! Those will be great!" shouted Devin excitedly, while looking at Hunter's additions to their wood collection. "Let's move them all into a pile right now."

"OK."

Hunter was a bit bigger than Devin. Already having reached five feet tall, he had wide broad shoulders to go with a sheepish smile that was highlighted by a small gap between his front teeth. Both boys were quite strong for their age, with Devin having a thinner, more wiry build. Devin's twinkling, mischievous deep-blue eyes went well with his infectious laugh and charming smile, when he chose to use it, which was not very often.

Working hard for fifteen to twenty minutes, the boys dragged a few more of the smaller pieces of wood, while rolling some larger ones over to where they had placed their first log so that they could start their construction project.

"How are we going to build our fort, Devin?" Hunter wiped his right hand through his short, recently cut light-brown hair. "Some of these logs are really heavy; it will be hard to stack them up. I don't think we have any way to hold them together, do we?"

Looking at their little collection of logs, then checking out the rest of the beach to see what else might help them, Devin finally responded by pointing to the sand just a few yards away. The beach where Devin was pointing to was not smooth like everywhere else. Here, the sand appeared dug out, as runoff from a recent storm created a channel in the beach, all the way from the dune almost to the ocean, where recent tides smoothed the beach out again. This channel was about a foot below the rest of the beach. "I think we can use that area over there, where the sand drops down, Hunter. Maybe we lay some of our logs across the sand, you know, use them as a base or platform? Then we figure out a way to prop up the others somehow. What do you think?"

"Sounds great! I like it! Let's get our fort started right now!" Hunter smiled, moving toward the logs they had gathered to move them across the sand. He grabbed the original piece of wood, then pointed to one side of the old log, where it looked like someone had carved numbers or letters into it, right smack in the middle. "Hey, what's this?"

With just a quick glance at the log, Devin answered, "Looks like two sevens to me, one forward and one backward. What do *you* think it is?"

Hunter looked at the symbols a bit more carefully from the other side (upside down). "I'm not sure, but to me they look kinda like letters, look—a *J*, maybe followed by an *L*."

"A J with an L. Hmmm," thought Devin out loud, now growing more curious himself. "Why were those initials put there? Where is the K? Why not JKL?" Devin laughed at his own little joke. "Why do you think?"

"I don't know, maybe a *Pirate* carved them for some reason. Wouldn't that be so cool? I mean, *look* at it. I don't think this is really just a simple log at all, but maybe a piece of wood that was once used for something important," said Hunter innocently, but with real excitement growing in his voice. "Well, whatever it used to be, we should use it for our fort now, I think."

The boys quickly moved their piece of wood with the initials on it over to the area where the beach dipped down, into a narrow channel in the sand carved out by runoff from a recent rainfall.

Devin pressed one end into the higher side, with six inches or so embedded into the beach, while Hunter pushed the other end down into the sand on his side, a bit lower but still leaving a small gap beneath the log. "Hunter…Hunter! Look, now we can easily add the other pieces of wood, either we should make a platform with them or maybe even build up the low side, make it higher. What do you think?"

"Let's build a platform," Hunter shouted. "We can always dig out some more sand…to make an entrance or something else if we need to. Let's use up the logs we have, then we can get some more wood, rope, and other stuff to make our fort bigger and stronger."

Working with the other driftwood they just collected, the boys attacked the sand, building their fort. Leaving their first log—the one with the JL in the middle—facing the front, so that it could act as the entrance to their fort, they started constructing the platform. Putting the other pieces of wood behind the first one, the boys soon had a roof over a small opening in the sand. If the tide eventually got that high, it would go in through the front, flow through, and not simply wash away whatever they eventually got built—or so the boys hoped.

Moving the sand around to help strengthen their growing platform, it took both boys a few more minutes to stabilize the structure. Finishing their work, the boys decided to open up the rear of the fort by digging up the beach like dogs. Soon sand was flying everywhere as both Devin and Hunter were bent over, using their hands to fling sand between their legs.

Tiring quickly from their crazy digging, the boys slowed down once they had dug out a larger channel under the logs, clearing the sand away from the rear of the structure. As they finished with the back, neither boy bothered to do much to the front, whose opening stayed much smaller, maybe ten inches high at its tallest point. The front of their fort still faced the ocean. It started with a small gap between the logs and the sand below that grew wider and deeper under the logs as one went from the front to the rear, ending in a much larger exit at the back, opening out toward the sand dunes.

Devin finally stood up, his body now covered with sand, including his pastel-orange swim shirt and his sky-blue swimsuit, to look at their handy-work saying as he brushed off the sand, "Looks good to me, Hunter. I think it's really a fort now. We can even keep adding on to it as we find more stuff; you know, make it really big…if we can get the right pieces of wood. Let's go look for extra logs, maybe some rope or even some netting to hold things together."

Hunter responded excitedly, "OK, let's find out what else is around here. Come on, let's go."

Standing up to implement their new plan, Hunter also had to brush away some sand from his shorts. That day he was wearing a baggy red swimsuit with a mostly green T-shirt. As little sand had gotten on his shirt, Hunter only brushed the suit a time or two without worrying much about anything else. Thinking, *this is going to be a truly great day*, Hunter took a deep breath and looked around for a moment. The sun was shining brightly in the sky, no chance of rain or cold, and best of all, he could spend his entire afternoon just hanging with his cousin on the beach!

Both boys started searching for more driftwood or any other materials they could use as part of their makeshift fort. As he walked back, away from the ocean toward the sand dune's edge, Hunter noticed a number of small holes about the size of a quarter or a half-dollar, a few even larger, that had appeared in the sand. "Hey, Devin, look at this. What are these holes for?" he asked, pointing down.

"Those are ghost crab holes!" Devin answered excitedly. Crabs were lots of fun. He never passed on an opportunity to play with them. "If we look around maybe we will see a crab digging out some sand. It's really cool. They throw the sand out of their tunnels, making a little pile to one side of the hole. Look for holes with piles of fresh sand next to them."

"How can you tell if the sand is fresh? And why are they called 'ghost' crabs? Do you know?"

With a smile, Devin explained to him, "Look for the dark-brown sand, which means it was dug out recently. It's dark because it's wetter below the surface. That's where the crabs are digging. Once the sand gets up on the beach, it dries out in the sun, making it lighter. Pretty cool, huh? As to why they are called 'ghost' crabs, it's because of their color, almost the same as the sand, so they are almost like ghosts. I think they are also called sand crabs. I just like saying the word *ghost* better."

"Look, look, over there!" shouted Devin, pointing with his left hand. "See that crab?"

A small sand crab, about the size of either boy's cupped hand, had just poked its head out of one of the holes. The crab was looking toward Devin and Hunter with its two small black eyes sitting atop his head. After staring at the boys, completely motionless for a few seconds, the crab darted back down into its hole.

"Hunter! Let's stay right here and watch. I bet you it will come back out. Maybe we can even catch it," Devin whispered energetically. "But we will need to be very still."

They both froze in their tracks, staring at the crab hole. In less than a minute they saw the crab return, as a small bit of wet dark-brown sand that looked like a tiny cylinder suddenly flew out of the hole they were watching. The sand landed on the beach a few inches from the hole it had come out of, next to at least a dozen others. After a few seconds, the crab's head followed the cylinder of sand. It simply popped out of the hole, looked around—seeming to stare right at the two boys again—almost as if he was telling them something. After a brief pause, the crab ducked right back into its hole once more.

"Did you see that?" asked Hunter. "That crab threw some sand out of the hole, just like you said. I wonder if he's digging a tunnel somewhere."

"Yeah, let's go see if we can find out. Maybe we can find even more crabs. Maybe the crab is digging for something!" replied Devin with a laugh. "You know, I've always wondered what they do down there? Maybe it's something really cool!"

The boys scrambled over to the crab hole, which happened to be very near the upper edge of the beach right next to the sand dune. They noticed that there were a lot more holes in the sand as the got closer to the dune, some a lot larger than the one they had just watched the crab disappear into. Both boys thought to themselves that there must be a lot of sand crabs nearby.

Suddenly, another slightly larger crab with a bit of pink on its otherwise sand-colored body immediately dashed away toward the dune, as if it had seen the boys approach. Hunter quickly leaped after it. The crab zigged away from Hunter, right toward Devin's bare feet. Startled, Devin let out a cry of happy surprise. Jumping back to avoid the crab, he tried to catch it by reaching out with his hand, but the funny-looking, although very speedy, crab just zagged right toward another crab hole.

Unfortunately for the crab, Hunter got to the hole first, forcing it to move off in another seemingly random direction. The boys were unknowingly driving the crab toward a peculiar bend in the dune, where instead of running along parallel to the beach, it curved out toward the sea for a bit, to go around a house that was built nearer the water than others along the shore. This curve might just help trap the crab, then the boys could catch it.

Right in the middle of the bend, the dune's grasses—an odd mixture of browns, greens, and yellows—appeared to grow longer here than anywhere else on the beach. Strangely, the plants all seemed to bend forward, even lie down, rather than grow up toward the sun. The effect of this odd growth was that the long grasses completely covered over the dune's edge, where the sand dune met the beach. It was right toward this spot in the bend that the scuttling crab was now heading.

Hunter shouted to Devin while pointing toward the sand, "Look, look, there he goes, under the grass. Let's try to catch him. You stay on that side; I'll stay over here. That little crab will have nowhere to go."

"Great thinking. Will do!"

The boys were so excited at the thought they were actually going to catch a crab, that they didn't even realize it had simply scuttled right under the overhanging grasses, then completely disappeared.

"Hey, Hunter, where did the crab go?" asked Devin suddenly. "I don't see it on the sand anywhere. Why can't we see it? Why?" He looked around with a confused wrinkle in his brow. "Crabs never run into the grass, never, and I have caught a lot of them. This is so weird. He should be right in front of us!"

"I don't know where he went," answered Hunter, pointing to various spots on the sand dune. "He was just right here, then he ran under the grass over there. Let's look underneath this stuff anyway. Maybe it's just covering him up, or a crab hole is hidden there. I'll bet that's where he is, trying to hide from us."

Devin, following Hunter's direction, went straight over to the dune's edge. With his right hand, he reached under the overhanging grasses, preparing to pull the long-overgrown blades away from the sand, to see exactly where the crab had gone.

Hunter ran right up next to Devin, ready to search for the crab too. Plus, he was in better position now to catch the crab if it tried to escape once its grassy cover was removed. Both boys were crouched down, eager, anxious, ready for the crab when Devin pulled back the grass, only to see…

"Ohmygosh! Doyouseethat? Whatisit? Wherediditcomefrom?" Devin's words rushed right out of his mouth so fast that he had to pause for breath as he lifted up the overgrown blades to look directly at what they had previously hidden.

With both his mouth and eyes wide open in surprise, Hunter responded, "I don't know, but it looks just like…like a giant miniature sandcastle!"

Before them, perfectly etched into the side of the sand dune—perfectly hidden by the overhanging grasses until Devin had pulled them back—was what appeared to be the front of a wonderfully elaborate, incredibly complex castle made entirely of sand. There were many levels to the castle, starting on the bottom with a large door, whose turrets on both sides grew up at least two levels above it. Connecting the turrets, right above the door, was an arch with beautiful markings across the top.

Just like a real castle, this sandcastle had a lower wall that went out from both sides of the main door with a tiny walkway at the top. In front of the walkway were a number of openings in the wall, allowing whoever lived inside the castle to look out onto the beach in front of them. Rising above this first level were other levels, complete with intricate windows, balconies, and on some of the highest rooms, even turrets, that could be used to place a very small flag—if the sandcastle had been real (which it couldn't be, could it?)

"Can you believe this?" Devin almost shouted, completely forgetting the crab they had just been so eagerly searching for, in his excitement. "I mean, I've been to real sandcastle building contests that adults have to create these things. This one is absolutely the coolest ever!"

"It looks so real. I mean, how far under the sand dune do you think it goes?" Hunter wondered. Waiving his finger back and forth to point at the sandcastle's width, he added, "It looks like this structure goes along the dune a couple of feet from each side of the door. Could there be real rooms inside, to go with all this?" With a flash of insight Hunter finished, "I'll bet that the crab we were chasing tried to get in there somehow! Do you think that's even possible?"

"You're right, I'd completely forgotten about our friend, the crab. Let's look closer and see. I wonder if there might really be an inside to all this. What do you think? Besides, how could a crab get in?" Pausing for a moment to think, Devin squatted down to point his right hand at the structure. "Why would someone even do all this, then hide it under these grasses anyway? Why not build it out on the beach where everyone could see it?"

Continuing to talk as much to himself as well as to Hunter, Devin proceeded to get down on his hands and knees, right in front of the sandcastle, to have a good look at it. "I don't see any way for a crab to get in. There aren't any crab holes or openings here at the entrance. I will say it again though, this sandcastle is really really cool."

Hunter looked up to see if anyone else had spotted what they were looking at. No one on the beach appeared to be paying any attention at all to the boys, but he did notice that a large one-eyed brown bird, the same one who had been watching them earlier, was just now spreading its wings, taking off from the wood stump in the ocean. Rather than head out over the sea, the bird headed back in toward the sand dunes, appearing to stare directly at Hunter as it approached the shore. Hunter turned back toward Devin to get his attention—and to point out the now rapidly approaching bird—just in time to see his friend crouch down, ready to look right at the front door of the sandcastle.

What Devin saw as he gave the entrance a closer examination was quite surprising. He was looking directly at a very impressive, yet oddly detailed entryway made of some kind of wood, not just sand. This door, strange enough to be in a sandcastle, had an even stranger upper half. A beautiful silver frame had been placed squarely in the middle of the door, halfway up between the wooden handle and the top, right where a peephole might have been. In the middle of this frame, some sort of cut stone or crystal of the purest purple had been set. Whether it was the sun catching the stone at just the right angle, or Devin's gaze looking right at it, there was a sudden explosion directly in Devin's eyes, creating a blindingly beautiful brilliant blazing bright ball of the purest purple light and…just like that Devin disappeared!

"Devin! Devin!" yelled Hunter in complete surprise. Blinking rapidly a few times, he clearly was not expecting to see Devin simply vanish in a flash of light before his eyes. Hunter even forgot for a moment why he had turned back toward the sandcastle to tell him about the strange bird who was at that moment flying straight toward them, by this time having almost reached the shore. As Hunter crouched down to search for Devin, his eyes somehow seemed to be drawn straight into the heart of the now-pulsing crystal jewel.

Losing sight of everything around him, Hunter's gaze was caught tight by the strange purple light, which seemed to glow a bit stronger with each additional pulse. Now looking straight into the purple stone, he noticed there were many, many different reflections inside it, like some sort of purple prism. Focusing harder, Hunter thought he could almost hear talking, as if someone or something were calling out to him when, all of a sudden, there was a silent explosion, as if a camera's bulb had gone off right in front of his eyes, with the same beautiful brilliant bright purple flash—just as before with Devin. When it was over, Hunter had disappeared from the beach as well!

"Hunter, Hunter, come on, get up, get up, quick, come on!" Devin shouted as he shook his dazed, slightly confused friend.

"What, what happened to us? What's going on? Where are we?" Hunter asked from his kneeling position on the ground.

"I don't know, but look, see the door to the sandcastle now?" Devin pointed directly in front of them, at an entrance big enough for each of them to easily walk through.

Centered above the door's middle, set in a beautiful frame, was the slowly pulsing purple crystal. It was obviously not a pretty stone set in some wood door. No, at this size the stone appeared to be a much larger purple prism of some kind.

"Isn't that cool, Hunter? Somehow this prism has brought us down here? Why do you think we are this size now? Why Hunter? Why?" Devin continued with a flood of questions without any apparent concern over their new smaller appearance. Instead, he focused with genuine curiosity at the very unusual events that had just happened to both of them.

Hunter and Devin were, of course, now looking directly at the front door of the sandcastle, which just seconds ago had been only as big as one of their hands, maybe five or six inches high. Now the wooden entryway was life-size, easily big enough that they could just walk right in had the sandcastle actually been real, with a working front door.

Astonishingly, to both boys' delight and surprise, that is exactly what started to happen. The door to the sandcastle suddenly began to open slowly outward, toward them. Even more extraordinarily, once the door finished swinging open, the crab—the one with the pink tint whom they had forgotten about in all the excitement—had returned. It seemed to be waiting for them just beyond the opening doorway. The boys had been right all along—the crab really had gone into the sandcastle. Even more amazing was that it was now standing there yelling at them in a way they could both hear and understand!

"Come inside, come inside, quickly now!" ordered the crab, obviously trying to get them to move forward, and into the sandcastle.

"Why?" asked Devin, startled at the crab's talking to them.

"Hurry now, no time for questions!" urged the crab, waiving his claw like a hand to encourage them to come inside.

Devin never hesitated, immediately heading straight through the door, curious to see what was hidden behind the walls of this crazy sandcastle. For some reason, he felt very comfortable with this talking crab.

Still on his knees and feeling a bit confused by what had just happened to them, up hopped Hunter, who, hearing hurry, half hesitated. Hoping he had heard Devin speaking—certainly not expecting the crab to talk—he completely ignored the warning uttered by the crab now standing in front of him. Rather than follow Devin into the sandcastle, Hunter turned back toward the sea to view the beach from his now much smaller perspective. Instead of seeing lots of sand with a bit of surf in the distance—as he expected—Hunter was completely shocked to see a large open mouth, coming straight down from the sky, aiming directly at him.

"GET DOWN!" shouted the crab, as he quickly scuttled out, bumping directly into Hunter, immediately knocking him off his feet, face-first into the sand. The crab's timing was perfect, as the brown bird Hunter had been watching with great interest earlier came flying across the beach, trying to scoop Hunter up with one quick bite.

The bird, now skimming very low to the ground, just barely missed his target as Hunter was knocked down into the sand, directly under the bird but away from its mouth. Snapping its large beak tightly shut where he thought the boy would be, the bird came up with nothing but salty air in its mouth. It passed close over the top of the falling boy, whose short hair stood straight up in the wake of the breeze created by the bird's passing.

Hunter's nose wrinkled in disgust from the nasty, stinky fish breath—a most unpleasant smell, one that he would never, ever forget—coming from the bird's snapping mouth. Sand covered much of Hunter's face from his fall to the beach. As soon as the bird passed safely by, it rapidly pulled back up into the air to avoid the approaching dune, Hunter scrambled to his feet. Running as fast as he could, now following the talking crab, he raced straight through the open door, hopefully into safety.

Once they all passed the threshold of the sandcastle, the door, with the jewel now emitting a constant bright purple light, swung immediately shut behind them. As the bird flew away, not returning to try again, the purple glow from the door softened to just illuminate the inside of the sandcastle, where the two boys with the crab were now looking around.

"Whew!" The crab exhaled. "Thank goodness we are safe from that awful bird. I think it's OK to relax now," he added, breathing heavily.

"Hi, I'm Devin," said Devin directly to the crab. Then he pointed a finger at Hunter. "That's Hunter. Thanks for saving him from that mean bird. What's your name?"

"My name is Cracker," returned the crab, cracking his big pincer a couple of times. Turning to look at Hunter, Cracker continued, "Are you OK, Hunter? That was really close."

"Oh yeah, I'm OK. Thanks for knocking me down. You might have saved my life! Why do you think that bird was trying to get me?" Hunter stood in the entryway, brushing the remaining sand off his face and clothes as he talked.

"That's old One-Eye the Pelican." For that is what the large brown bird was—a nasty, dirty Pelican. "He tries to eat all of us crabs when he has a chance. I guess he thought that since you are now our size, maybe you would taste good too," stated Cracker. "I don't really know, but we all have to keep on guard when that bird or any of his pals come around. Anyway, we are all safe now. He won't try to get into the sandcastle, so don't worry about him anymore. Let's go introduce you to others here in our colony. Welcome, my new friends, to the Sandcastle of Pirates Beach!"

CHAPTER 3

CRAB TALES

> ***Purple Prism of Peace***
>
> *A very powerful multifaceted Rainbow Color created by the Sky-Lords after the Splitting of the Rainbow. Made of crystal, mounted in a sparkling silver frame, the Purple Prism normally emits a soft, peaceful tinted light—except if viewed directly. Then it may explode in a blindingly bright beacon of purple. The Prism brings creatures together, both in size and communication, so that they may live in harmony. A strong deterrent to aggression, those who seek Power cannot get past it. The Purple Prism's primary purpose provides powerful protection, preventing persons possessing Rainbow Objects from harming those within its influence.*
>
> LORE OF THE SKY LORDS

Cracker, it turned out, was a young crab himself. He knew of the legends told by his family, along with the stories often shared by the older crabs, that the purple jewel in the sandcastle's door had amazing magical properties. But today's events were unlike anything he, or likely any other crab living in the colony for that matter, had ever seen take place.

This day had started like any other. Cracker had gone out to find some entertainment on the beach. After getting tired of playing tag with the two boys, Cracker had slipped back inside the sandcastle, which on a normal day would have been the end of his time with them. Usually, he went immediately to find his friends and laugh about his exploits, after playing with people. This time was different. For some reason he decided to hang around a bit, maybe to enjoy watching the boys wonder what happened to him. To his great surprise, instead of watching the boys get frustrated, then leave as humans typically do, he watched as the two boys discovered the sandcastle, something people had not done in a very long time.

Even more amazing to Cracker was that one of the boys was looking right into the jewel in the doorway, causing the Purple Prism to suddenly spring to life. As the jewel's light burst forth, that boy instantly became part of the sandcastle's world! Cracker knew instinctively that something very important was going on. Rushing back to open the castle door, he looked out, just in time to see old One-Eye the Pelican flying in low across the beach—directly at him. Clearly, the Pelican was coming in after the boys. Cracker was not sure why, but One-Eye appeared determined to snap them up, before they could get to safety inside the sandcastle, if he possibly could.

"Guys, now that you are here," Cracker began, "I think we should go straight away to see the head of our colony. I'm sure there will be a lot of things you will want to know about that he can help with. I'm also pretty sure he will want to see you both for himself." Cracker was not all that surprised he was now actually talking to people. Living in the sandcastle, he knew communicating with other creatures was possible, even thought this was his first time talking with humans. "Once you have met our leader, his name is Crex by the way, maybe then we can go out and have some fun. It's clamming season, you know, and we have some of the best clamming runs anywhere. I know you will just love it. C'mon, let's go." Cracker turned away, toward the inside of the sandcastle, where he obviously expected the boys to follow, then headed down the main hallway deeper into the castle.

"Hey, Devin, what do you think 'clamming' is? Any idea?" asked Hunter quietly. With just a hint of growing nervousness in his voice he added, "Do you really want to follow Cracker in there? Aren't you at all scared? I mean, how will we get back to our normal selves??"

With a smile slowly growing on his face, Devin whispered back with confidence, "I don't know anything about 'clamming,' but I'll bet its lots of fun." Devin paused for a moment. "I'm not sure why, but I think we should see what's going on down there. It can't be just a coincidence that we are now five inches tall and able to talk to a crab, can it? It's possible that we are both dreaming and none of this matters, or we have found a truly amazing secret, something well hidden from most people. Either way, I think we should follow Cracker. We can ask questions as we go." In a louder voice that Cracker could also hear, he finished, "Come on, let's go with Cracker…check this place out."

Cracker, after waiting on the boys to join him, commented, "You will like it down here, I promise. Most all of the crabs are friendly, and there is so much to do, you will see."

As they caught up to him, Devin had some questions for Cracker. "Why are you not surprised that we are now your size and able to talk to you? For that matter, why are Hunter and I here in the first place?"

Hunter added a very important question of his own, "And how will we ever get back?"

Squatting down for a moment, Cracker answered, "I don't know for sure, but it has to do with the Purple Prism you see in the doorway. There have been many stories about various creatures, not just humans, that the prism has brought into the sandcastle. You are certainly not the first, which is why I am not too surprised. In all of them, once here, everyone is relatively the same size, like you are to me now, and can just as easily communicate with each other. Getting back happens to be pretty straight forward too. All you do is return to the prism, and as you go out, it will reverse things. You will be your normal size once again. We will have to ask the adults for any more details, as I have never seen such a thing happen in real life. Just heard some of the legends."

Devin turned to Hunter. "You good to go?"

"Yeah, I guess so. You think it's really that simple, getting back, I mean? Should we try it, just to be sure?" Hunter answered, implying that knowing he could get back to normal would make him feel a lot better about their current situation.

"Can we, Cracker?" Devin asked, knowing how important this was to Hunter. "Just go test things out…make sure we can get home again if we need too."

"Of course, you can. Let's do it right now," Cracker answered.

Returning to the sandcastle door, Hunter went first. Opening the door, he looked into the purple jewel which began pulsing once more. In a purple flash of light, Hunter was once again standing on the beach, back to normal and waiting for Devin, who returned to his side just moments later.

"Satisfied?" Devin asked with a big smile. He certainly was.

"You bet I am!" answered Hunter, clearly happier now and sounding genuinely excited to go on a real adventure under the dunes.

Both boys, all reluctance now gone, quickly dropped back to their knees, looked directly into the prism, and almost immediately found themselves once more in the land of the sand crabs!

Cracker was waiting for them at the door as the boys returned. Resuming their trek into the sandcastle, the boys followed Cracker down a long slightly sloping pathway that had smaller passages going off to each side, seemingly at random. Every once in a while, another crab would pop out of one of the tunnels to look inquisitively at the newcomers. If a younger crab saw them, he or she would almost always follow, just behind Cracker's trio, joining up with them like a little parade. Soon, there was quite a group of young crabs following Cracker and the two boys.

After a couple minutes, they came to a large fork in the pathway. The main passage went on straight, while also descending slightly. The second tunnel split off, turning right to go back up, the other way.

Cracker turned to the right, pausing while the boys caught up with him. "Isn't this exciting?" he said. "This is the first time in many generations that 'Bigs' have been down here."

"What's a Big?" asked Devin almost immediately.

With a little chortle, Cracker pointed at Devin. "Why, YOU are a

Big. So is Hunter. That's what we call humans, 'cause you are so BIG when you are out there on the sand." Cracker cracked his big claw a couple times, laughing at his own cleverness.

Devin added quickly, "I guess that was just a 'little' joke there, huh, Cracker?"

All of them were suddenly laughing, enjoying the strangeness of the conversation, yet also understanding these were new friends.

Continuing up this new trail, Hunter turned to Cracker. "What's in all those other tunnels?" He pointed to the numerous small openings that went here and there, just off the main path they were on—the ones where no crabs came out to look at or to join them.

"Lots of different things," the crab replied. "Some lead to crab holes where we can sleep, others are used to store things or as gathering places, and the rest are just used to connect things together. You see, we like to dig, so there are lots of holes and tunnels down here."

"Don't you ever get lost with all those tunnels?" Devin asked. "There are so many of them."

"No, not really. We crabs can find our way around pretty well once we are out and about, crawling around. It's a pretty useful skill. We always seem to just 'know' the right path to take to get somewhere," said Cracker. "You have only seen a few of our tunnels so far. Just wait till we get to go out to play! There are lots and lots of great places to go, with some really fun things to do here in the sandcastle."

Hunter was very curious about this strange place. "Why isn't it dark in here? I don't see the sun or any other light source, but it's still bright enough to see. How can that be?"

"I'm not exactly sure how that works," Cracker replied. "It has something to do with the sand here. Sunlight, or for that matter moonlight, reflects through the sand, keeping things down here lit up whenever there is enough natural light outside. It's different when there is real rock, not just sand, above you. Once you get completely under true rock, then it's usually totally dark, but as I said, if it's mostly sand above you, then there should be enough light to do whatever you need to."

"Wow, that's really cool!" Hunter replied. "So, what you are saying is, we can go exploring all over the place, and as long as we stay underneath the sand on the beach, we will be able to see things? That's just crazy, I tell you!" Hunter, already thinking about going out to look for hidden treasure, quickly realized it would be a lot easier to find buried stuff from underneath the ground, rather than digging from the top.

Devin changed the subject as he pointed all around. "Why doesn't all this just fall down, Cracker? I mean, it's just sand holding things up, isn't it?"

"The sand holds up pretty well if the tunnels are built right," Cracker answered. "We crabs dig things out really well, so everything stays up, most of the time. Every so often there will be a cave in, it happens. If the roof falls in, then we just repair things. Really, there is nothing to it. It's interesting that the tunnels here within the sandcastle hold up better than most. I think it has to do with the Purple Prism in the doorway, but Crex or someone older will have to explain it better…if you really want to know."

Devin had lots of questions about how things got built down here—his favorite word growing up had always been *why*—the passageway rapidly widened into a very broad open space, which included a large group of crabs talking together near the center of a very big room.

"Where are we?" whispered Hunter and Devin in unison.

"We are in Crex's audience chamber. Now, before you ask, as I know you are about to, as I told you before, Crex is the leader of all the sand crabs here on this beach. He is very smart and seems to know a lot of the things you will both be interested in…like how you got here, maybe. Let's go see him, shall we?" Cracker broke into a big smile.

Cracker then led Devin and Hunter, along with an ever-growing band of young crabs following them, right to the middle of the chamber. Standing there was an enormous crab, with a pincer on his right side easily larger than either Hunter or Devin, talking to a few other adults from the colony. As the group made its way across the room, the older crabs all turned at the same time to look at the approaching youngsters.

Crex, immediately recognizing there were two boys with the younger crabs, waived his larger pincer as if to beckon them to come closer, while his eyes—large black orbs on the top of his head—swiveled around to look at them directly.

"Hmmm, what have we here?" rumbled Crex in a rolling low-pitched voice that reflected both strength and wisdom. At least it seemed that way to the two boys.

Cracker answered excitedly, "Look, Crex, I found these two Bigs on the beach today. Somehow, they got the Purple Prism to bring them down to us!" He cracked his main claw with a *crack, crack*. "I was there. I saw it happen! Really, I did! It was so cool!" Trying unsuccessfully to calm himself down, Cracker continued, "Their names are Devin and Hunter," pointing his large pincer at each boy. "And do you know what else? I just saved them from old One-Eye, not twenty minutes ago, I tell you! He was trying to snatch them up, right at our front door. But I got them inside, before he could!"

All the crabs—those following the boys as well as the adult crabs already in the chamber—went silent for a moment as if Cracker's news, especially the parts about the Purple Prism and One-Eye the Pelican, had some extra importance, which they needed to take in. The silence was broken as Crex turned to say something to another adult crab next to him. It seemed that Crex's action was a signal to the rest of the crabs, as everyone in the hall started talking among themselves, all at once, about these new developments.

Crex returned his gaze to the entire group. Finally, in a loud, deep voice that got everyone's attention, he rumbled, "Really? Hmmm, old man Pelican tried to get these two boys right when they got here. Very, very interesting indeed." He pointed his smaller claw directly toward Devin and Hunter. "Well, boys, welcome to the realm of the Sand Crabs. It's been a long time since one, not to mention two, of your kind has been here in the sandcastle."

Before the boys could respond to Crex, or anything could be said by anyone, four new female crabs—each one looking very different from the others, yet they all seemed to have a rough outline of a question mark on their shells—came out from a large dark tunnel behind and slightly to the left of Crex. As they approached, they could be heard saying, "Who, what, where, why…who, what, where, why," over and over again.

Cracker spoke urgently, "Devin, Hunter, this is amazing. These crabs are called the Questions. They only come out together when something important is happening or going to happen. Most of the time we don't understand what they are saying, as they usually speak in riddles, but it is always very important when they come out." Cracker paused, as if remembering something important. "Listen, if they ask you a question, you must answer it. Or every single one of the crabs living here will ignore you until you have left - if you don't."

By the time Cracker finished talking to the boys, the Questions had arrived at the growing collection of crabs in the center of the chamber. As they had marched right up to the gathering, any crabs in their way quickly moved aside. Standing in a straight line, looking directly at the two boys, they spoke in turn.

"Who are you?" demanded the first crab to Devin.

"What are you doing here?" questioned the second to Hunter.

"Where will you go?" wondered the third crab back at Devin.

"Why will you disappear?" asked the fourth, finishing with Hunter.

Then in unison they chanted:

"Who, what, where, why—
We are the questions.
Answer us,
You must try.
Who, what, where, why—
You have the answers.
Speak them now,
Do not lie."

With that, the four crabs settled down, with all eyes looking at the two boys, clearly waiting for them to give their answers.

Suddenly, what had just been a very lively place, with groups of crabs talking and asking questions about why the Bigs were there, not to mention One-Eye's unexpected involvement, now became perfectly silent. Every crab's attention was now directed straight at the boys, awaiting their response to the Questions' questions.

The boys themselves were clearly not sure what to do. Devin looked at Cracker, while Hunter looked at the questioning crabs, giving them one of his famous big grins. They really were so funny looking after all.

Cracker broke the silence, whispering urgently to Devin, "You must answer the Questions. They rarely speak, but when they do, it is always very important. Even Crex must answer them. Go on, tell them the answers as best you can. There really is no right or wrong, but they can tell if you are not being honest. Personally, I think how you answer, not what you answer, is the real test. By the way, they may respond to your answers too, so listen carefully. They usually give good advice… if you can make sense of it."

Devin turned toward the Crabs, answering the first question, *Who are you?*, with a smile on his face, "Hi there, my name is Devin. This is my friend Hunter. Very nice to meet you."

The four Questions rose up on their six legs, bowed, and responded in very polite voices, "Devin, hello, welcome to our palace in the sand. Hunter, hello, we are glad to have you in this land." Then they all squatted down again—waiting.

Without pause, Hunter, seemingly inspired by Devin, answered his first question, *What are you doing here?* "We are explorers." He grinned proudly. "Once we discovered the sandcastle, the Purple jewel in the doorway somehow made us small enough to get in. Of course, escaping from the ugly Pelican who was trying to get me is what got us to come inside."

Again, the four Questions rose on their legs, bowing in unison. "Hunter, you made the right choice, coming in here. Devin, beware, it is not just the Pelican whom you should fear."

Not knowing exactly what the last response from the Questions meant, Devin continued on, answering *Where will you go?* by saying:

"We thought we would hang out, maybe explore a little, with Cracker and his friends. It sure sounds like a lot of fun to Hunter and me."

For the third time, the Questions rose to look straight at the boys. Again, in unison they said, "Devin, hanging out with Cracker, fun indeed, for you three. Hunter, not all here will be your friend. When you have to make a choice, follow what you can see."

With a slightly puzzled expression, Hunter gave his answer to the last question: *Why should we disappear?* "That makes no sense... unless something is going to happen to us? Is it? Do you know? I guess if we disappear, it means we must be going home?"

For the last time, the Questions rose, bowing to the boys, then responding together, "Hunter, you may come and you may go, leaving is not always through the front door. Devin, remember to help others if you can, for three will not always be as good as four!"

Just as suddenly as they came, the Questions whirled around to march right back into their tunnel. Chanting their chant, they disappeared with a last, barely audible, "Who, what, where, why."

Then they were gone.

There was a short period of absolute silence after the Questions had retreated back into their tunnel. Then the surprise at their sudden appearance, along with the mysterious messages given to the newcomers, seemed to wear off, all at once. Suddenly all the crabs in the chamber began to speak to each other, snapping their pincers while creating quite a racket around Crex, Devin, Hunter, and Cracker. The younger crabs were wondering what the hubbub was all about as the adult crabs were asking each other questions about these new Bigs, especially what the boys' arrival, One-Eye's involvement, and of course, the Questions' messages might mean for the colony.

Changing the subject a bit so that everyone could settle down, Crex spoke up. "Hunter, Devin, after all that excitement, I'll bet you boys might want something to drink. Are either of you thirsty or perhaps a bit hungry?"

Hunter spoke first. "I am a little thirsty, Mr. Crex." He paused for just a moment, his face tightening in thought. "But what was that all about? I mean, they said not all would be my friend. What does it mean to 'follow what you can see'? I'm not going to follow what I can't see, and—"

"Just Crex will do," Crex answered calmly. "Understand, you both have just experienced something that only rarely happens here in our colony, so you will have to be patient. You see, the Questions can look into the future in some way none of us really understand. They give hints and clues to what may come, almost riddles, but it is never clear what they are really trying to say to you…usually until the exact moment you truly need their help."

Crex continued, "My advice is to remember what you have heard. When the time is right, their words may guide you in some way, maybe help make the right decision when you are not sure what to do." Then he turned to a crab to his right. "Ginger, can you find some water for our new friends here?"

The crab named Ginger immediately scuttled off to one of the side halls, returning almost immediately with two small very white shells filled with fresh water. "Rain water, the best kind," she said as she stood before the two boys. "We catch it when it comes down, then save it for when we are thirsty or have guests."

As both boys drank the refreshing water, the other crabs continued to talk about the Questions.

Devin rapidly lost interest in their conversations, as the crabs were now talking about things in the colony—not about him or Hunter. Instead, he began to look around the large chamber they were in. He noticed that the walls were all decorated with clam and oyster shells, many of which had cracks or chips in them. Some of these shells also had a crab claw hung directly above it. The shells and claws seemed to be mounted all around the room, as if they had some special meaning.

"Crex, excuse me, but why do you have all those shells and claws hanging from the walls?" Devin asked.

"That is a very good question, young man. You are very observant." Crex focused once more on the boys. "Perhaps you have heard of the game Crabs and Gulls?"

"No sir, I've never heard of Crabs and Gulls," answered Devin. "What is that?"

Crex leaned forward. "Well, well, never heard of Crabs and Gulls, have we? I think you are in for a treat then." With his booming voice, Crex shouted out to all the crabs in the chamber, "Gather round, everyone. Sit, sit, please, make yourselves at home." Speaking to the boys, he said, "You are new here and don't have much experience with us crabs. I think it might be good for both of you to learn a little about the history of the sandcastle. Let me tell you the story behind one of our favorite games, Crabs and Gulls."

"Aww, Crex, I know all about that," Cracker interjected. "I could just as easily show them how to play that kids game. Besides, I want to go clamming with them today, not hear stories about Crabs and Gulls. Clamming is where the fun is!"

Crex looked at Cracker, his black orbs swiveling around from Devin to look at him directly. With a smile, he answered kindly, "Yes, Cracker, you know how to play Crabs and Gulls, but now I am going to tell you the real story of where the game actually came from. It wasn't always a game, you know. We adult crabs still take it quite seriously; in fact, we have even improved on it since those days…if I do say so myself. Besides, learning a bit from our past will be good for everyone, including you."

Turning to Devin and Hunter, Crex asked, "What do you think? Would you like to hear a little bit of Crab lore before you go out to explore? It might even be of help someday."

Both boys answered, "That would be great."

Devin said, "We don't know anything about this sandcastle, so a good story sounds like just the thing." Smiling at Cracker, he added, "As long as it doesn't take too long."

With that, Cracker, Devin, Hunter, and the other young crabs (who by now had grown into a large enough group to be considered a real audience) sat down around Crex to hear the story.

"Many, many years ago, before Bigs came to this area, each crab in the colony would go out on the beach to dig our holes, look for food, or just to scuttle around for a bit of fun." Turning his gaze to Cracker, Crex continued seriously, "This was in the time of one of your oldest forebears, young Cracker. Did you know it was one of your family member's efforts that was the basis for the game? This is really his story."

Cracker looked a bit surprised—as did all the other young crabs—as he had not known about this particular twist, but no one said anything.

Looking back toward the two boys, Crex resumed, "Known to all Crabdom as Pincer, because of the very large pincer he had on his right arm"—Crex held his own magnificent pincer up, snapping it a couple times for effect— "Cracker's ancient relative loved to go out onto the beach early in the morning, before any of the other crabs were awake or before any other creatures got to the beach. Pincer loved the sunrise, especially on days with a low tide, as then there would be lots of beach to explore.

"Usually on those early mornings, the only thing Pincer had to worry about were the birds that also got up early—gulls, Pelicans, things like that—since one of their favorite breakfast treats was, and still is, crab." Crex asked the boys, "In fact, did you two know, a seagull's favorite saying is, 'The early gull gets the crab'?"

Devin and Hunter looked at each other, laughing at Crex's words. Both of them were thinking, *The early bird gets the worm.* That's what the adults they knew said about getting up early, not, *The early gull gets the crab.*

Crex, laughing with the boys, returned to his story. "One fine summer day, Pincer was out in the early morning, climbing through some fresh seaweed that had washed ashore the previous evening. There were no birds in sight when he climbed out of his crab hole, so Pincer had dared go a bit farther away from safety than usual. A mass of seaweed lay before him, just sitting in thick clumps on the sand, right where the last high tide had pushed it earlier, before sunrise.

As the water pulled back with the receding tide, the seaweed, now stranded on the beach, was mostly brown with golden tips. It seemed to call out to Pincer that he should explore it. Within those fresh clumps, Pincer knew there would be quite a number of tiny fish, shrimp, and other smaller sea creatures trapped there without any water. They would soon, hopefully, make a most delicious start to his day.

"Climbing through the fairly thick seaweed, seeking his morning meal, Pincer was unaware that a large Seagull named Peck had spotted him crossing the sand. Thinking to himself that the little sand crab would make a nice breakfast treat, Peck changed his flight path slightly, so that he could easily pluck Pincer off the beach.

"Skimming rapidly across the water, the Seagull Peck watched Pincer climb to the top of a large clump of seaweed. With an expectant smile on his beak, the Gull surely thought, *The early gull gets the crab…and there is mine!*

"Peck flew low across the calm ocean waters, while coming in fast with the rising sun now directly behind him. He did not think the crab could possibly see him, even if he happened to look up. This approach to catching a crab was common for many ocean-going birds, as their crab victims usually never knew what was happening to them, even when the birds attacked!

"Aiming his beak straight at Pincer, with wings spread wide while he glided in with the breeze, Peck flew directly toward the crab. Racing in off the ocean, smiling and saying to himself, *Soon this Crab will be mine…soon,* Peck opened his beak wide, just as he crossed over the edge of the water's breaking surf. Eagerness filled the Gull with anticipation, as he swooped in, ready to pluck Pincer right up off the beach, then go drop the crab hard on some hard rocks near the dune."

Looking around during a short pause in Crex's narrative, Hunter saw that all the younger crabs were completely focused on the story, with wide eyes and all their antennae pointing at Crex. There was, however, one exception. Hunter's attention was drawn to a younger crab who had entered the chamber just as Crex was starting to speak. This crab was standing at the back of the listeners, looking directly at Hunter, not really paying any attention to the "Crabs and Gulls" tale. Watching this crab for a few seconds, until the other crab gave him a slight smile along with a quick wink, Hunter—slightly embarrassed for no real reason—gave a quick smile in return, then looked back to see what Devin was doing.

While Devin appeared to be just as interested in the story as all of the other young crabs, he was still able to interrupt Crex, to use his favorite question—a couple of times anyway. "Why would that Gull want to drop Pincer on some rocks? Why, Crex, why?"

Crex answered, "Young Devin, that is also a very good question. You may not know it, but that is one of a Gull's favorite ways to eat a crab—by dropping him on the rocks to kill him first. It breaks apart the shell you see, so then the Gull can eat him more easily."

"Oh, I'm so sorry. I didn't know. That sounds just awful," Devin replied in a quiet voice, looking at Cracker sadly.

"Now, don't be sad," said Crex. "This story has a long way to go, and the ending may not be exactly what you are currently thinking." Crex turned back to his audience. "Now, where was I? Oh yes, just as Peck was about to grab Pincer, the seaweed clump Pincer had climbed onto suddenly gave way under his weight. Down dropped Pincer, straight onto the sandy beach, a few inches below the seaweed. The crab's unexpected rapid drop caused Peck to barely miss his target. The Gull squawked loudly in frustration as his snapping beak passed just over the crab below. Flying above the top of the pile of seaweed, Peck wheeled himself around in midair, flapping his wings hard to quickly climb back up into the sky, ready to come back for another try.

"Meanwhile, Pincer, realizing he was now under direct attack, even as he fell to the beach, knew he had to do something…and fast! Pincer clearly heard the Gull's beak when it snapped shut above his head, just missing one of his wildly flailing legs. Understanding right away that he needed to get back to the safety of a crab hole—before the speedy Gull could get back at him—Pincer spun around to see what would be the fastest and safest way to get home.

"Unfortunately for Pincer, the seaweed clump he had fallen from, while likely saving his life, now blocked the quickest way back to the safety of the crab colony. Pincer instinctively knew that it would not be possible to get back underground, before the Gull would get him. What was he going to do now? For just a second Pincer simply froze in panic, but just as quickly he had a truly amazing idea!

"During his fall through the seaweed to the beach, Pincer noticed the shell from an oyster lying in the sand, a foot or so from where he landed. Oyster shells were not uncommon on the beach. Because they were also very strong, Pincer thought he might be able to use it as a shield from the Gull's snapping beak. Grabbing the shell with his smaller claw, Pincer got ready to move it once he knew where the Gull would be attacking him from. Fortunately, the shell had a small hole near the top that allowed Pincer's smaller claw to grab it more easily. Thus, Pincer could move the shell around like a shield, which was very convenient indeed.

"Of course, even as Pincer was grabbing the oyster shell, Peck was not idle. He immediately returned to the sky to circle around, ready to make another run at his sure-to-be-fleeing target. With some surprise, Peck quickly looked around for the fleeing crab but did not see one scuttling back toward the crab holes, as he expected. That meant his target must still be in the Patch of seaweed, easy prey indeed! Circling and squawking from above, Peck quickly found Pincer still stuck in the middle of the seaweed pile. Figuring he would certainly get the crab this time, Peck dove straight down at Pincer's head.

"Pincer, watching the attacking Gull, brought up his newfound oyster shell at the last possible moment. Whirling it around to face the attacking bird, he brought the shell up over his body, directly in front of the Gull, and braced for impact.

"Peck was completely surprised by the crab's odd behavior. Most crabs will run as fast as they can away from Seagulls when under attack. They certainly do not stand and fight. So odd were Pincer's actions, that Peck didn't even realize the crab was holding something in his claw when he flew straight into the oyster shell, hitting it squarely with his beak.

"OUCH! The shell was so strong that Peck's beak was deflected away from his target. The sudden impact of beak on shell caused a sharp shiver of pain to run throughout Peck's body; he was even a bit woozy after this unexpected impact.

"As shocked as Peck was by the sudden turn of events, Pincer was even more surprised. The shell had not been damaged by the impact, and while the Gull's hit had shaken him up slightly, it did not do Pincer any real harm. Most importantly, he was still alive, ready to handle the next attack, which Peck knew was sure to come soon. This was better than anything he had hoped for. Pincer now had a real defense against Birds!

"But Peck too was just shaken up, not seriously hurt. Now he was very mad at this most irritating little crab, who had survived two passes at him…something unheard of by either the crabs or the Gulls living on the beach. Swinging back into the air, Peck was intent on making sure his third attack was successful so he could still have a nice delicious crab breakfast after this longer than expected workout.

"Pincer was very aware that the Gull was going to try again. As he thought about how to most effectively use his new shield, the little crab realized that if he stood on all of his legs, except his pincers, he could hold the shield with just his smaller claw. This position would free up his larger claw to maybe, just maybe, be an effective weapon for Pincer to use against his larger attacker.

"With a crazy confidence coming from his recent success, the little crab moved away from the seaweed clump, out onto the open sandy beach. Pincer turned to face the circling Gull (something else that had never happened in the history of crabs) moving toward the attacking bird, not running away. With his shell at the ready, Pincer thought he was prepared for the next attack."

By now everyone in the large chamber listening to Crex was totally consumed by the ancient tale. Not a sound was to be heard—even from Devin—except for Crex's rolling, almost-mesmerizing voice as it matched in speed and volume the excitement of the story.

"Quickly now, Peck's third attack came. This time, instead of just dropping right on top of the crab as he had tried twice before, the

Gull dove down toward the sand, a little farther away from his future breakfast. Turning his body to skim lightly over the beach, Peck was going to simply pluck his enemy from the sand as he flew by. Once in Peck's mouth, it would be a simple matter to drop the crab on some nearby rocks, at his leisure.

"Seeing his foe's new plan, Pincer turned on his legs, squatting down so that his shield shell was directly between him and the attacking bird once more. The Gull was now coming straight at him, with no way to change course. Just before the Gull's open beak reached him, Pincer surged up and forward, bringing his large claw around the shield, aiming it right at the head of his attacker.

"Peck convinced himself that the result of the last pass—his hurt beak—had to be just an unlucky accident. There was no way that this crab would ever be able to use a shell in that way again. Was he ever wrong! Not only did Pincer meet Peck's attack with his oyster shield, once more sending a stunning jolt of pain throughout the bird's body, but at the same time the crab's larger claw hit the Gull directly in the head right as the bird was hitting the shell with his beak. In fact, Pincer's claw not only hit Peck's head. It went directly through the Gull's left eye!

"Peck, as his body hit Pincer's oyster shell shield, flipped right over the top of the crab, landing on the beach near the seaweed! After a single somersault, the bird's body stopped moving. Peck was dead.

"Pincer, knocked down by the force of the Gull hitting the oyster shell, was completely surprised at what had just happened. His body was a bit wobbly as he got back up, both from the physical contact of the Gull against his shield, as well as from his surprised realization that the battle had finally ended, amazingly with him as the winner! Taking just a few seconds to catch his breath, while staring at the unmoving body of his opponent, Pincer knew that this event was very, very important; it must be shared with crabs everywhere, as soon as possible.

"Other birds would surely come to the beach soon, so Pincer decided he should get back to the sandcastle to share this new fighting method with all the other crabs he knew. Gathering up his new oyster shell shield, Pincer also grabbed one of Peck's wing feathers as a trophy for his victory. Quickly scuttling to his crab hole, Pincer returned to the crab colony, becoming the first true Gull-fighting hero of all Crabdom."

Now that the story was ending, all the crabs in the audience chamber started to talk among themselves.

Crex turned toward Cracker, saying in a much quieter voice, "So you see, young Cracker, it really was your many-times-over great-grandfather Pincer that started Crabs and Gulls, for that is exactly what it is you play with your friends. In your game, one crab has a shell shield while pretending to fight off the other crab with his claw. The other crab is pretending to be a Gull by holding a shark's tooth as if it were a bird's beak. It's a child's game when played here under the sand, but much, much more when an adult crab is on the beach, and a bird is near."

"Devin," Crex said while turning slowly back toward him, "now to answer your original question, each shell and claw you see on our walls here are those of crabs who have bravely fought birds on the beach since the time of Pincer, the first Gull fighter. We honor their efforts along with their memory." Pausing for a moment while he turned to point at a specific shell, Crex then resumed his explanation. "We also commemorate Pincer. You see, it was he who brought us all together, as more than just a group of crabs, but as a true society…as Pincer was also the first Crex."

"WOW," said Hunter suddenly with a smile on his face as he thought about the story. After a slight pause, he added, "What a great story, Crex. So, what you are saying is that crabs can fight Seagulls and have a realistic chance of winning? I would sure like to see that sometime."

Devin asked, "Have you ever fought a bird, Crex? Will your claw and shield ever be on that wall?"

Crex responded with a little smirk, as if thinking of something only for himself. "Yes, I have, but those stories will have to wait for another day. Besides, Gull fighting has evolved quite a bit since the days of

Peck. The good news is that the Gulls don't bother us here in the sandcastle like they used too. Of course, a stray crab alone on the sand will often be attacked. But as a group we don't fear them as we once did. Now then, you know a little more than you used too about the crabs here in our colony…not to mention a little history about Cracker's family. I hope that helps you while you are spending time with us."

Addressing Cracker, Crex smiled while rumbling, "Go on, have fun with your new friends. I hope they enjoy clamming as much as you do. By the way, make sure they leave the sandcastle before high tide tomorrow. They will need to get home sometime soon, I would think. Now off with all three of you." With that, Crex dismissed all the assembled crabs, leaving the chamber himself through a hole behind his seat.

"What did he mean, leave before high tide tomorrow?" asked Devin.

"Oh that," Cracker responded with a chuckle. "As you know from experience, as long as you go out the same door you came in, you will be returned to your normal size, like what happened to you earlier. The Purple Prism works both ways. Of course, I also think Crex wants to make sure you get home at some reasonable time, so that was part of his message."

Hunter broke into the conversation, thinking about Cracker's comment in a new light. "That's right, won't we be missed? I mean, after a couple hours our parents will be wondering where we are, at least by dinnertime."

"Actually…maybe not Hunter," followed Cracker. "You see, the Prism has a number of interesting effects on those who use it. One of them is that while you are here, only those that know you entered the sandcastle will realize that you have been gone at all. Since no one knows you are here besides us crabs, you will not be really missed by the other Bigs. That's a pretty cool thing, don't you think?"

Pausing to see if Devin or Hunter had anything to add, which they did not, Cracker then cautioned, "But, if the sandcastle door is *not* here when you try to leave, then you will either have to wait until the castle returns, or find another door with a similar jewel. I guess there are probably other ways to get back too. I just don't know anything about them."

"Why would the sandcastle not be here?" questioned Hunter with a slightly nervous look.

"Of course, it will be here, at least until something erases it from the sand," answered Cracker, smiling. "This happens from time to time. One of the ways that can happen is the ocean. See, if the tide is high enough or a big storm pushes in the ocean waters, such on event can temporarily wash away the front of the sandcastle, including the door. When that happens, you would be stuck here, at your current size, until the Purple Prism can restore things. Otherwise, as I said before, you would have to find another Object or Color that could return you back to your normal size so you can get home."

Devin immediately asked, "Are there other ways we can go back to being Bigs, besides using the Purple Prism, I mean?"

"I am sure there are," responded Cracker. "Unfortunately, I don't know what they may be or where to find them. But don't worry about it, a high tide that will get to where we are now isn't very likely. I think Crex just said that so we wouldn't go off and do anything foolish. Adults are like that, you know, trying to keep us from doing things they don't want us to. We have plenty of time to go clamming and have some fun. Besides, what could possibly happen down here?"

So, with a big smile on his face, Cracker led Devin, Hunter, and some of the other curious young crabs straight out a large tunnel to one side of Crex's chamber toward a game that he called 'Clamming.'

CHAPTER 4

CLAMMING

Green Gauntlet of Glory

A very powerful metallic Color created by the Sky-Lords after Putrid's Shredding of the Rainbow. The Gauntlet enables its wearer to lead groups to victory in battle against what might appear to be overwhelming odds. It also warms the hearts of those within its influence so that peace and friendship exist within a large gathering. Most importantly, the Green Gauntlet dispels Gloom and Despair for all who are near. There is a rumor that the Green Gauntlet, when working in combination with the Purple Prism of Peace, provides an almost impregnable defense against unwelcome attack.

LORE OF THE SKY-LORDS

"Hey, Cracker, that was quite the story Crex just told us about your ancestor. It was so cool. Do you ever play Crabs and Gulls?" Devin asked.

Cracker responded happily, "Oh yes, I play all the time, it's a great game."

One of the other crabs, who had just joined the group, suddenly spoke up in a derisive voice. "Cracker plays lots of games, he just doesn't win very often, especially against me."

The speaker was a slightly larger crab than Cracker. He had a brown streak across his body, along with what would pass for a haughty air among crabs. Hunter noticed that this was the same crab that had been watching him earlier, during Crex's story about Pincer, the one that had winked at him for no apparent reason. He also noticed that as the newcomer spoke, Cracker's face seemed to take on a slightly sad look, as Cracker seemed to take a step back from the group while the other crab, with a couple of his friends, pushed forward to talk to the two boys.

Puffing up his chest while pointing his smaller pincer at himself, this new crab announced, "My name is Orion, and I am the best clammer you will ever meet." Changing the direction of his claw to now point at the boys, Orion finished, "I will show you two how to Clam so fast we will leave Cracker in the sand. You can play Crabs and Gulls anytime. Now we should go clamming!"

"Nice to meet you, Orion. My name is Devin," responded Devin directly. "This is my friend Hunter. Why would we want to leave Cracker in the sand? And what is clamming, will someone explain that to me?"

"Ha ha! That's just an expression. It means that we will fly so fast on the clamming hill that Cracker will end up way behind us. Of course, that's assuming you boys can keep up with me," responded Orion. Then in a lower voice only Devin and Hunter could barely hear, he added smugly, "he just isn't very fast, you know." Orion winked once again at Hunter and pointed at a couple crabs off to one side. "These two over here are my pals, Decker and Skitter."

Orion first pointed to a large dark crab that was missing his smaller pincer, then on to a much smaller light-sand-colored crab, who had to be Skitter. The smaller crab never looked up at the boys. Instead he seemed to be looking everywhere else at once, except directly at Devin or Hunter, as if he had some type of nervous tick.

Ignoring Orion's friends, Hunter jumped into the conversation. "What's a clamming hill?" he blurted. "Whatever it is, I want to try it!"

"Is it dangerous?" asked Devin.

Cracker responded, now jumping back into the conversation, "It's not dangerous, Devin, if you follow the rules." Looking toward Orion and his pals, Cracker added while still frowning, "Unlike some of us, who do whatever they want."

Orion just smiled as he pounded his chest with both pincers and exclaimed loudly, "Who needs the rules if you can go as fast as I can go? What's the danger? Nothing can hurt ME on the hill. I am the best clammer in the colony!"

Suddenly, Decker spoke up. Looking directly at Devin, he added in a slow, low, slightly intimidating voice, "And we make sure *no one* gets in the way too. Don't we, Skitter?"

Looking straight down at the ground, Skitter hissed something incoherent and was completely ignored by everyone else.

Hunter and Orion immediately started walking together, discussing clamming in earnest. They pushed forward, followed by Decker and Skitter, while Devin dropped back to walk with Cracker. As they approached the end of the tunnel, Devin noticed that their path started to get wider. Soon the group all exited into a large cavernous area that appeared to Devin—in his shrunken size—to be the single largest cave he had ever seen.

Walking out across a long open ledge, the boys with their new crab friends could easily see over the rocky side, down on what appeared to be a large hill made completely of sand. Even though they knew they were still within the dune itself, to the boys it appeared they had arrived at the top of a huge hill of sand, and that soon they would be going down it in some crazy way.

"What do we do now?" asked Hunter excitedly.

"First, we all go get ourselves a clammer. That's what we call the shells we use to ride on. My favorites are the smaller real clam shells, but any type of shell can do the job. It's up to you," responded Orion.

"Get a clam shell? What for?" questioned Devin.

"Let's show 'em, Cracker," said Orion.

The group of boys and crabs headed on down the ledge. As the little troupe passed around a small curve, they immediately spied another group of young crabs looking over a large number of different types of shells that were laying against the wall. These shells were all different: some were big, wider than they were long, while others were small and circular; some were thin just as others were thick. Even their colors were different, ranging from blackish oyster shells to the bleached white of some types of clamshells. Each crab eventually grabbed their shell of choice, headed farther down to a spot where the ledge was quite a bit wider, then, hopping into their clammer, they took off down the hill.

After giving the boys a little time to watch the other crabs, Cracker began to explain to Devin and Hunter what they were about to do: "Look, guys, this sand hill is so big that we crabs just love to ride shells down it. We call this 'clamming.'" Pointing at the pile of shells nearby, Cracker continued, "What you do is go grab yourself a clammer—one of the shells we use to clam with—that looks fun to you. Here's the thing, smaller shells will go a bit slower than the bigger ones, but you can do more tricks with the little ones, making those shells the more popular, especially with us younger crabs. Once you have your clammer, you hop inside, hold on tight, then just sail down the hill as fast as you want. It is so much fun to fly over the sand, hit the bumps, catch some air, and do all kinds of fun tricks."

"So why is it called 'clamming'?" questioned Devin. "I see lots of types of shells here."

While Orion's friends were still busy picking their favorite shells—Orion already had one—Cracker answered Devin, with more and more cheer returning to his voice, "Because the real clam shells are usually the best to go down the hill with. Since most of us choose to use clamshells, I would guess that is how clamming got its name. Of course, maybe clam shells were the first to be used to do this, which could also explain why it's called clamming."

Walking over to one of the nearest shells, Cracker picked it up to show the boys "You see this shell here?"

Both Hunter and Devin looked more closely at the inside of the shell Cracker was now holding. It was very white, with a slightly oval shape. Interestingly, they both noticed that one of the longer sides of the oval was straighter and flatter than the other, as Cracker was just explaining.

"With a clam shell like this one, I try to keep the flat part to the rear, but that is up to you. Everyone clams a bit differently." Cracker flipped it over to continue his explanation. "See these shell ridges? They run all the way along the underside of a typical clamshell. Since they all go the same direction, when you are going down the hill you can use them to control your speed. To go fast, you spin the shell so the shell ridges are aimed down the hill. To slow down, you spin the shell so that the ridges go across the hill. Only the true clam shells have these types of ridges on them, plus they also happen to weigh less than others. Most of us think these are the very best shells to clam with."

"That sounds so cool," said Hunter anxiously, not wanting to talk anymore. "Let's go do it!"

Orion, bored with Cracker's explanation of things and ready to go, came up to the others, encouraging them to move on. "C'mon, grab yourselves a clammer. Let's get going, or are you going to talk about it all day?"

Hunter was looking over the nearest clammers as Cracker finished explaining things. Seeing a medium-sized shell with a sandy image that looked like a flame on the outside, which he really thought was cool, and hearing Orion's challenge, Hunter went over to immediately grab it.

Meanwhile, Devin saw a smaller white shell sitting off to one side, that seemed to call out to him. Thinking this would make for the perfect clammer, Devin walked over and grabbed it. "Ok, Cracker, what do we do now?" he asked.

Before Cracker could utter a single syllable, they all heard, "Watch me, slowpokes!" Orion was shouting with obvious joy. "Here I go!"

Orion, having moved off the edge of the rock onto the sand, immediately jumped completely inside his clammer. As he did so, Orion was able to grab hold of each side of the flat edge with one claw, while hooking his legs around the curves so that he was now completely facing forward—yet balanced—inside his shell. The ridges of his clammer were now going across the sand, keeping the shell in place. Rocking forward a bit, Orion then rotated the clamshell counter-clockwise slightly, so that the ridges were pointing at an angle down the left side of the hill. Almost immediately, Orion started sliding to the left, down the hill. When he hit the first steeper drop, he began to pick up speed, very quickly. Within seconds he was gone. All the group could hear was a trailing "Wahooooo!"

"I'm ready, Devin. Are you?" questioned Hunter, with a big smile growing on his face. "This is going to be awesome!"

"I think so Hunter," answered Devin. Turning to Cracker, he asked one more time, "You're sure it's not too dangerous, right?"

"As long as you stay on the hill, you will be fine. Just relax and have some fun. Look, this hill is really just a big pile of sand after all, so if you fall out of your shell, it won't hurt…at least not too much," replied Cracker with a big grin. "OK, time to go. You guys are up first. I will follow you down, just in case. After the first couple runs, we can show you some of our tricks!"

Getting out on the sand first, not waiting to hear any more advice, Hunter hopped into his shell, just as he had seen Orion do. Deciding at the last second to cross his legs under his body, Hunter was then able to hold on to the front edge, which happened to be the flat side, with both hands. Even though his clammer was reversed—the flat side was forward—it worked out perfectly, given the way Hunter decided to ride down the hill.

Leaning toward the shell's front, Hunter imitated Orion by twisting his body slightly so the shell's ridges were now at an angle heading down the hill. Almost imperceptibly at first, his shell slowly started inching forward, then suddenly off he went. As Hunter started down the slope, he turned his head back toward his friends, grinning from ear to ear. "See you at the bottom! COWABUNGAA!" he exclaimed with a joyous yell, then he too was gone.

Flying over the first ridge, with his right side aiming forward, brought Hunter his first full view of the clamming area. It was truly very large, with many types of terrain for the crabs to go over. The middle was fairly flat, with only a few bumps in the sand, likely made by previous clammers going down, while the sides appeared to have more bumps and grooves cut into them. Deciding to practice a little before going over the next ridge, Hunter turned his clammer so the ridges once more ran across the sand, which immediately slowed Hunter down, just as Cracker and Orion had both said it would. Turning it the other way, with his left side leading, caused the shell to speed back up.

Really taking off, as the clammer resumed heading down the hill, Hunter's cropped hair stood on end, even as his exhilaration grew, approaching the next set of bumps. Hunter suddenly realized he was approaching the next ridge going faster than he was ready for. Without any time to slow down, Hunter hit the ridge at full speed. Moving so quickly, the clamshell completely lost contact with the sand for a few seconds. Hunter unexpectedly found himself flying through the air, shouting, "YAHOOO!" at the top of his lungs.

Feeling like the king of the hill, Hunter, who was always a bit of a daredevil, came crashing back into the sand after being airborne for what seemed like forever, sending a huge spray up into the air, even as his clammer kept on flying straight down the hill. He tried to slow down his careening shell by straightening the ridges once again, but the next big drop-off on the hill was already upon him. This time Hunter hit it just as he was trying to turn the shell, with a very similar result—he ended up going airborne once more. There was one big difference this time. Due to his trying to spin when he hit the ridge, the clammer kept turning as he flew off the sand. Hunter unexpectedly found himself going down the hill backward, completely unable to see a thing.

His heart pounding crazily, Hunter held on for dear life. As he suddenly returned to the sand, his clammer hit once, bounced back up into the air, then landed again with even more speed. Hunter almost let go of his shell but managed to barely hang on.

As he twisted hard to his right, the clammer spun around again, only instead of stopping when his body was aiming downhill, it kept on spinning. Thinking he now needed to lean the other way, Hunter's move only increased his rotation, hitting the last of the three ridges in a completely uncontrolled spinner!

Hunter was, at the same time, totally thrilled as well as just a tiny bit scared. His heart felt as if it was in his throat, while he was screaming as loud as he could—and not caring about it one bit. This time when he landed, the shell slowed down, as the steepness of the hill lessened after the last bump. Regaining control, Hunter was finally able to once again spin the shell as he wanted to, slowing it down, eventually bringing it to a stop.

Finished with his first clamming run, Hunter simply rolled out of his clammer, falling onto his back, his head now looking straight up the hill so that he could see the entire slope he had just come flying down. The first thought that came to Hunter's mind was simply, *What a ride!* The smile on his face grew. *I need to go again, that was fantastic!*

There was one other advantage to his new position. Lying flat on the sand, able to look back up the hill, Hunter could easily watch as Devin started his first run. Seeing his best friend's shell now hitting the first of the ridges, Hunter smiled as Devin…

When Devin climbed into his clammer, he also decided to hold on to the front with both hands. However, instead of sitting up in the shell as Hunter had chosen, Devin decided to lie down, with his feet hanging out over the backside. Listening to Cracker's advice, Devin set the shell up with the flat side toward the back, so his feat could easily hang off, while his hands were on the curved front, making steering easier—he hoped. This way, Devin thought, he could drag his feet if necessary to slow down, and to better control the shell on his first run down the clamming hill.

As he started down over the first ridge, Devin was able to see the whole hill below him. He was not moving as fast as Hunter had been, but that was OK by Devin. He was just as excited as he began to pick up speed himself. Quickly realizing he could drag one foot in the sand at a time to control the clammer's direction, Devin was able turn the shell toward the foot that was dragging in the sand. But he had to also lean his body if he wanted to make the clammer go completely sideways across the hill. Dragging the opposite foot would turn the shell back, allowing him to once more head straight down the hill.

Gaining in confidence, practicing his turns as he headed down the easy part of the hill, Devin soon picked both feet up off the sand to gain speed. Hitting the first of the three ridges in the next section of the hill, his shell took to the air very similarly to how Hunter's had only moments before. Holding on to the front of the clammer with both hands, Devin flew into the air, completely separating from contact with the clamshell.

When he landed back on the sand, Devin's body came down on the left side of the shell. The clammer immediately began to turn as most of Devin's weight was now on the left side, no longer balanced. By the time he hit the second ridge, Devin was completely turned around. Not thinking about putting his feet down to slow himself, he hit the second ridge with almost the same speed Hunter had just moments before. Devin was also positioned very similarly, looking backward and not being able to see a thing in front of him.

Flying right off the ridge, Devin could be heard screaming loudly, "Ahhhhhh," until his shell landed once again on the sand with a hard bump that shocked him into silence. Not sure of what he was doing, Devin continued to grip the clammer with both hands, while finally remembering to use his feet to slow his descent. Trying to regain some control, Devin dropped his right foot to the ground, so he could twist his body and look over his right shoulder, in an unsuccessful attempt to see where he was going.

This move also had a similar effect to what Hunter had recently experienced. Watching from below, Hunter could clearly see Devin over-rotating his body, causing him to spin around as he hit the third ridge. Devin flew through the air once more, with just his hands holding on to the clamshell, in what he liked to call a death grip. Devin loved the feel of his body flying, without the support of the clamshell. That was until gravity pulled him back down, and he hit the sand again.

Devin's clammer hit hard, while his body flopped back into the shell, landing way too far to one side. The entire shell was so out of control that instead of sliding to a finish, it actually flipped over on the sandy slope at least a couple of times. Devin ended up lying on his back, still gripping the shell tightly as he stopped rolling on the soft sand. As the spray from the wild tumble settled back down, Devin realized he had come to a final stop, surprisingly, just a few feet away from Hunter.

When Devin opened his eyes, he saw Hunter lying there just looking at him. They both started laughing and talking at the same time.

"Did you see that, Hunter?" asked Devin breathlessly.

At the same time Hunter said, "Devin, you did exactly what I did. Wasn't that fun?"

"What?" asked Devin.

"What?" echoed Hunter.

Again, the boys laughed as they lay there comfortably on the nice soft sand. Finally, they both looked up seeing that Cracker was now gliding to a stop just in front of them. As Cracker's shell slowed to a stop it made a funny crunching sound in the sand. *Crrrckkt.*

With a giant smile, Devin laughed. "What was that, Cracker? Did you just toot?"

"No, I didn't!" responded Cracker, slightly embarrassed.

Hunter stuck his right hand under his arm and made a similar sound. *Bbbppptttt.*

Devin laughed. "HUNTER, that's funny, do it again!"

Soon both boys were laughing and making funny tooting noises, while Cracker on his shell also joined in. They did this for another minute or two until they all simply fell down in the sand, unable to laugh anymore.

Finally, Cracker got up and asked, "Well, you two both had an interesting first ride down this hill. Are you ready to go and finish it?"

Both Devin and Hunter quickly jumped up, responding, "You bet we are!" even as their legs were still a bit weak at the knees, after their first downhill clamming run and laughing attack.

As they all got ready to finish the sand hill, Orion surprisingly pulled up next to them, stopping with a hard spray of sand that hit Cracker across his entire body.

"Oops, sorry about that, Cracker. Didn't stop as quickly as I wanted to," Orion said, not bothering to even look at Cracker as he said it, and certainly not sounding as if he meant it.

Devin changed the subject. "How did you get back here so fast, Orion? We saw you take off before us, there is no way you could walk back up the hill. It's a lot longer going up than down I would bet."

Orion smiled while responding, "That is a bet you would lose, Devin. Normally, I would take your bet, but since neither you nor Hunter have been to the bottom yet, you can't possibly know how we get back to the top, can you?"

Devin and Hunter looked at each other and then back at Orion.

Devin responded, "You're right, Orion, we don't know how you do it. Is it fun, is it hard? Where do all the crabs go to get back up to the top?"

Cracker spoke then, having finished brushing the sand off himself. "Let's finish this run, then you will see that jetting back up the hill is almost as much fun as clamming is coming down."

Everyone agreed with that, and both the boys and the crabs got back on their clamming shells, heading down the hill to finish the clamming run. Each of the boys stayed with their initial positions on the shell, Devin lying down while Hunter crossed his legs sitting up, so that they could get more practice as they finished the hill.

No one fell out of their shell going down, even though Orion cut in and out of the path of the others many times, almost causing an accident or two by cutting too close in front of another clammer (something you are not supposed to do) as he passed by them. Orion would speed up to cruise by an unsuspecting crab, then just cut in front while spinning his shell around and shouting, "Wahoo!" After a couple spins, he would keep on going down the hill, while waving goodbye.

Both Hunter and Devin stayed in the middle of the open hill so they could practice speeding up and slowing down by learning how to control the turns they were making. Hunter seemed to really be getting the hang of clamming very quickly; he was even doing his own simple tricks as he finished his first run.

Eventually, the hill bottomed out, opening up to a wide area of softer sand at the finish of the run, helping to slow down the often fast-moving clammers. Looking to either side, the boys could now see the back of the big cavern they were in, while at the bottom there were tunnels heading out, away from the clamming hill in both directions. There was a large adult crab sitting in front of the tunnel to the right, blocking it completely. Obviously, he was there to keep the younger crabs from going that way.

As all the other clamming crabs came cruising down the course, they immediately headed to the large tunnel on the left once they finished—except for one group. Looking back for a moment up the hill, Cracker, Hunter, and Devin watched with some surprise as another group of youngsters were recklessly ending their run. This group finished with an unfortunate accident, tumbling to the sand as a very careless crab clumsily crashed.

Cracker, keeping cool, cried, "Crabs, crabs, keep calm!" Untangling the mess of crabs and shells, he quickly made sure no one was hurt before moving back to his friends.

Devin, very impressed with Cracker's handling of the situation, was still focusing most of his attention on the adult crab guarding the tunnel. Watching the big crab start to move toward the younger crabs, then settling back down when he realized Cracker had things under control, Devin asked, "Why is that big crab sitting over there, Cracker? Why?"

"Because, we younger crabs are not supposed to go down that tunnel Devin," answered Cracker with both a little urgency and excitement in his voice. "It leads to places that the elders consider dangerous. Places we can't easily get back from, so we aren't allowed to go that way. In fact, I have never been down there. It's supposedly a pretty scary place." In a hushed voice, he said, with a smile on his face, "But it might also be very interesting to explore. I mean how dangerous can it be?"

Both Hunter and Devin could hear from the tone of his voice that Cracker really wanted to explore that tunnel. Hunter thought secretly to himself, *I would like to go down that tunnel sometime too, see what's over there, and if I somehow get the chance, I will!*

Orion and a couple of his pals pulled up next to the little group with Orion boasting, "You know, I've been down there before." Smiling, he directed his gaze only at Hunter. "It's a little darker and scarier than this place, so I'm pretty sure you boys couldn't handle it." Orion then laughed as his little group headed the other way, following a large group of crabs that had just come down the hill.

"Really?" asked Hunter with a little awe in his voice and already accepting Orion's challenge in his head. "Cracker, do you think he has really gone over there?"

Cracker answered, "Who knows, Hunter? I wouldn't put it past him, but I think he also brags a lot too, just to be irritating."

With that, Cracker pointed with his pincer toward the path to the left. The boys went with him in that direction, while Hunter looked back for a moment to watch the big crab guarding the other trail.

Entering the new tunnel, everyone soon noticed the sound of rushing water, which seemingly was coming from the direction they were now heading. The sound was like water spraying for a bit, then it would stop. After a short amount of time, the rushing water sound would return, only to then stop once more.

"Do you hear that, Devin?" asked Hunter.

Devin answered, "I hear it, but what is it?" while looking at Cracker for his answer.

"As we were just talking about, you are about to see exactly how we crabs get back up to the top of the clamming hill so quickly. You boys are both about to go jetting!" answered Cracker.

"What's jetting?" questioned both boys in unison, with big smiles on their faces. This sounded really cool, maybe even better than clamming.

Cracker replied with a simple, "Let's go find out."

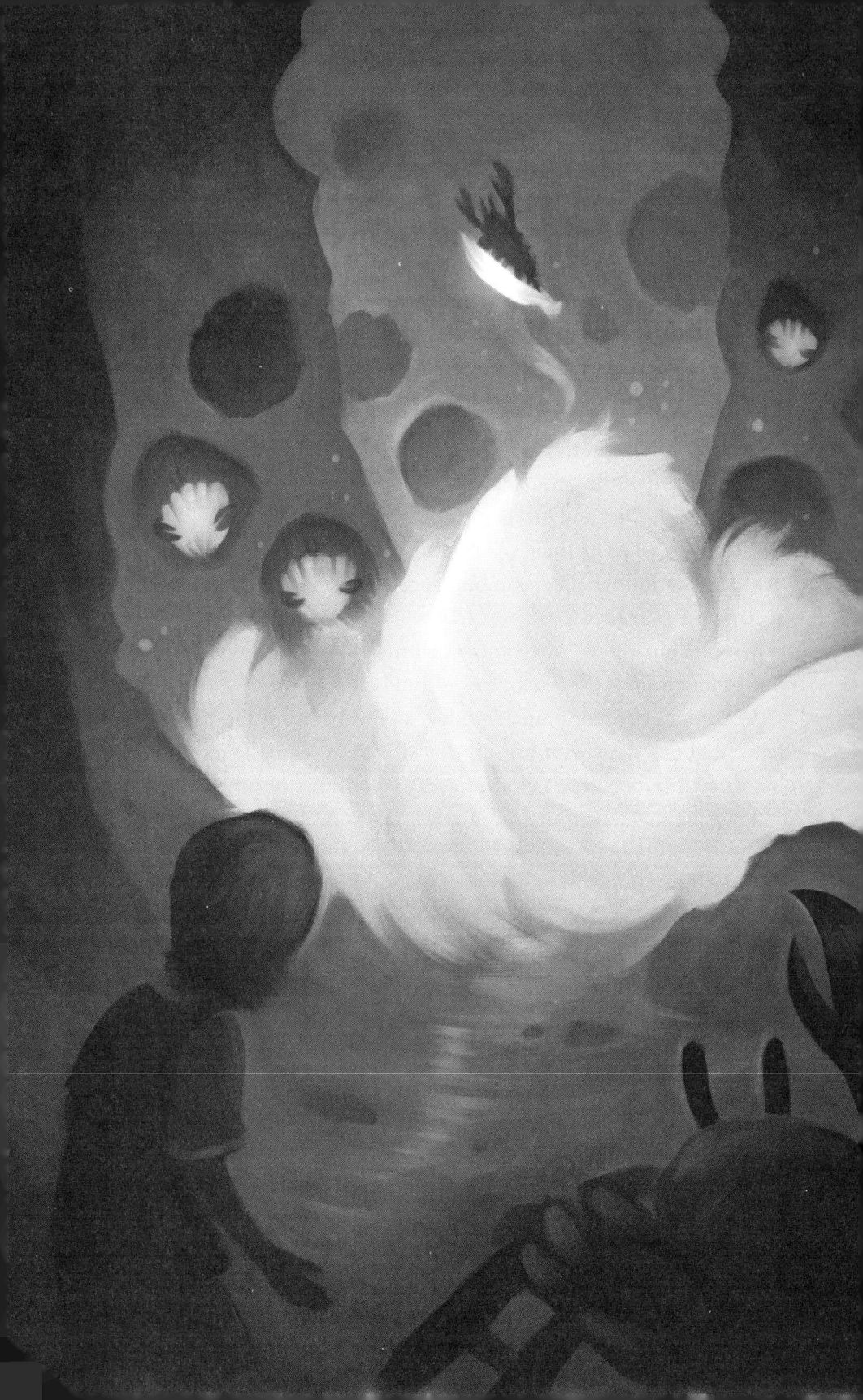

CHAPTER 5

BLAST OFF

> **Jetting**
>
> *A jet of water that results when the incoming sea hits a tunnel within the Pirates Beach Sandcastle. The crabs of Pirates Beach use such jets to move from one place to another, especially when having to move long distances quickly. Jetting was discovered by the famous crab Clipper when he got stuck in a jetting shaft by accident.*
>
> CRAB CHRONICLES

As the group of clammers approached the end of the tunnel, they came to an opening that was obviously the entrance to another rather large chamber. Emerging onto a flat landing area, they arrived just in time to see a blast of seawater come rushing out of a cave opening on their right. The water came very fast, hitting the opposite wall of the chamber with impressive force.

Just as quickly as the water rushed in, after it hit the opposite wall, the water rushed right back out again. The entire area almost looked as if the waters had never been there in the first place. Looking at the wall where the water had slammed into the side of the cavern, the boys noticed many holes or tunnels. Each hole appeared to not just go into the wall, but also to tilt upward, away from the cavern floor.

Cracker spoke up while pointing toward the other crabs. "You two, watch, see what Orion and his pals do to get ready for the next wave to come in."

Fascinated, the boys watched as Orion, his friends, along with the few other crabs who had joined them after their clamming runs, scampered quickly into the holes in the side of the wall. Each one climbed into a different hole. Once in, they pulled their clamming shells behind them so that to the boys it appeared that the holes were now completely covered by the back of the shells with the crabs on the inside, now invisible to those watching from the chamber's entrance.

After a few moments of quiet, the boys could once again hear approaching water returning to the cave. Watching with fascination as the sea charged out of the tunnel and into their cavern, the boys could see the wave of water slam up against the side of the cave where the crabs had crawled into the holes with their shells. The wave broke apart as it hit, with white foam splashing high up onto the air. As the water pulled back after hitting the wall, the holes were completely empty. The crabs with their clammers could no longer be seen at all.

"Where did they go?" questioned Devin quickly.

"What happened to Orion?" asked Hunter almost simultaneously.

Both looked at Cracker, who, with a grin on his face, explained what they had just witnessed. "This is how we get back up to the top of the clamming hill." Cracker pointed toward the wall where the crabs had just disappeared from. "Those openings are not just holes, they are actually the entrances to long tunnels that widen slightly as they go up. All of them expand as they go higher, opening completely as they emerge back on top of the clamming hill. By going up through these chutes, we can get almost back to the top of the clamming runs, then quickly take off again. It makes clamming a whole lot more fun. Otherwise you would have to walk back up the hill after every run, not something I—or anyone else—would do too often."

Neither Devin nor Hunter seemed to understand how this worked at first. As they were waiting for Cracker to continue his explanation in greater detail, the boys were able to watch another set of crabs scamper out to the holes, climb in with their clamshells wedged behind them, then wait for the approaching wave, just like the group with Orion before them.

Another wave of sea water came crashing into the side of the cavern while they were watching; those crabs who had been in the holes were gone now too!

Able to continue as the sound of the rushing water receded, Cracker said, his voice gaining in excitement as he pointed at the cave wall, "The clamming shells are stuck into those holes with the crabs sitting on them on the inside. When the water hits the back of the clammers with all that force, the crabs along with their shells are shot up those tunnels really, really fast. It feels just like you are flying!"

"Wow, that sounds AWESOME!" said Hunter with an excited look on his face. "Can we do it too? How about now? I'm ready!"

Devin added with a little more caution, "Is it very dangerous, Cracker?"

"Yes, we can Hunter," answered Cracker with a grin. "Let's watch one more wave hit, then we will go out to do it ourselves. While we are waiting, I can explain the right way to 'jet' to you. By the way, it's not really all that dangerous Devin, as long as you are sitting on your shell when the water hits. Just make sure you hold on tight during the initial shot up the launcher. It's almost impossible to turn over or to fall off until you come out at the top and land on the hill.

"Remember, once seated on your shell after the initial launch, it's a good idea—but not necessary—to try and stay somewhat centered. Since spinning shells send sand streaming sideways as they explode out of the tunnels, keeping in the middle makes your landing softer while not getting as much sand over anyone who happens to be nearby. Exiting the jet will land you on the side of the clamming hill, very near to where we started and—most importantly—almost all the way back up. Once you land, all you have to do is walk the short distance back to the start of the clamming runs. As I said, it's a lot quicker than walking from the bottom down here, all the way back to the top of the hill… not to mention, as you will soon see, a thousand times more fun."

Finishing his little talk, Cracker concluded, "OK, guys, I think that's it. Let's watch one more time, then we will be ready to go! By the way, just so you know, we Crabs officially call this 'jetting.'"

The boys watched as one more wave hit the launching holes. Feeling fairly confident they knew exactly what to do now, Devin and Hunter waited until the water had cleared, then they quickly ran down to the holes and climbed in. Cracker helped each of them get into one of the jets with their shells pulled up behind them. It was easier than either boy expected to get the shells to hold on to the soft, yet surprisingly strong, walls of the chamber they were now in.

Once they were loaded inside the water tubes, there was almost no light at all. The isolation of being alone in the tube, combined with the darkness and the unknown of what was going to happen when the water hit, made both boys anxious, excited, yet also very nervous.

Devin shouted, "Hunter, Hunter, are you there, are you there?"

Suddenly, the sound of the next on-rush of the sea drowned out their chatter. Quicker than anyone could shout another word, the water slammed into the wall. When the wave receded, the holes were empty. The boys, with their crab friends, were gone!

"Wahoooo!" shouted both boys as each one took a different jetting tube straight up into the air. The pressure from the water's impact pushed the shells up the dark tunnel at very high speed. Spinning around slowly, while accelerating rapidly upward with very little (if any) control, was a completely new and exciting experience for the boys—like a crazy ride at a carnival.

The boys screamed in sheer delight as they suddenly emerged from the much darker jetting shafts, flying out into the well-lit and wide-open cavern on the backside of the clamming hill. Each boy (and crab) was flying through the air while sitting on top of his clamshell. When they landed, the jetters had almost reached the top of the hill, as the shells hit the soft sand with a light crunch.

Laughing out loud in pure joy, Hunter was the first to say, "C'mon, c'mon, that was great. We really have to do that again!"

"C'mon, guys, follow me. This will get us back to the top of the clamming hill so we can do it as many times as we want!" Cracker shouted back to the boys, obviously enjoying himself while waving his pincer toward a path in the sand. "Pretty neat, huh? Jetting saves so much time and is almost as fun as clamming, don't you think?"

Devin and Hunter both ran after Cracker, back up the hill. When they crested the final ridge going up, they ran straight into Orion with a few of his friends—Decker, Skitter, and another crab named Slicer.

"It's about time you got back up," Orion jested. "It seems like we have been waiting forrreeevvver for you to get back here." All of Orion's pals laughed as if this was the funniest joke they had ever heard.

Hunter responded emphatically, while ignoring the laughing of Orion's group, "Well, we're here now, and ready to do some more clamming!"

Orion teased, smiling as if he was glad it was Hunter who he was talking to, "Pretty strong words for someone who has just done his first clamming run. You ready to race yet, Hunter? Or is this hill a little too much for you to handle?"

"You bet I am," answered Hunter, angering quickly. "Let's go. First one to the bottom wins!"

Before Cracker or Devin could say or do anything, Hunter was back on his clammer, racing back down the hill. Orion and his friends following closely behind.

Hunter was a real natural at clamming. He seemed to know instinctively just how to handle his clamshell and how to go over the bumps or around different things on the clamming run. His first time through had given him confidence in his abilities; now, being quite competitive, he just wanted to beat Orion, who obviously thought he was hot stuff on the hill.

Orion had been clamming for a very long time and was one of the fastest young clammers in the crab colony. As fast as Hunter was, Orion—due to his experience—appeared to be just a bit faster. Catching up to Hunter, Orion made a quick left turn around a little hill of sand. Dipping his own shell into the sand during the turn, Orion caused a sandy spray to fly up into Hunter's face. Laughing heartily, Orion sped off as he waved goodbye; Hunter had to slow down to wipe off the sand.

Hunter angrily wiped his face, then quickly regained his speed, almost catching back up to Orion as they got to the bottom, but Orion still won the race.

"Want to go again, Hunter?" asked Orion smugly. "You know, that wasn't a completely lame effort you had back there."

"You bet!" responded Hunter who was both thrilled with his clamming skills, yet more determined than ever to beat Orion in a race. While not enjoying getting sprayed by sand, Hunter was somewhat confused, as he found himself really wanting to continue racing with Orion.

The two immediately headed back toward the jetting area that would return them to the top, so they could race again. As they passed by the crab guarding the entrance to other tunnel, Orion said to Hunter in a somewhat suggestive tone, "You know, the jetting tubes on that side are really a lot more fun than these over here; they blast a lot harder, sending you farther into the air than the ones we are using."

Hunter asked, "Really? What's with that? Why can't we use them? Have you really tried them, or were you just making that up before?"

"The adults are always afraid we younger crabs can't handle it. You know, it's always safety first," Orion answered slyly. "They think young crabs might get hurt, but I know—from experience—I can handle it. I doubt you could though. You haven't done this enough to handle those super jets."

"Super jets!? I can handle anything you can, Orion!" exclaimed Hunter, looking back over his right shoulder toward the other side. Now wanting to try the jets in the other tunnel more than ever as his daredevil nature took over, Hunter was sure those jets would be even more exciting than the jetting he had already done.

"Well then, after we finish this next run, let's go over there and try those." Having seen the young crabs crashing earlier that day gave Orion an idea. "I think I can sneak us by that adult crab with no problem. Whaddya say, Hunter? Wanna do it? Do ya?" questioned Orion eagerly.

"You're on, Orion, let's go!" Hunter exclaimed immediately, so excited he was not even thinking about Devin, or anything else.

Not wasting any time getting into the water jets, Hunter and Orion were soon blasted back to the top of the clamming hill. As before, Hunter experienced a crazy thrill ride as he spun his way up the jetting tube. The ride only made him want to try the other super jets even more. Both boy and crab made perfect landings coming out of the jets, ready to renew their racing as soon as they landed.

Once back on the sand, Orion did not give Hunter any time to gather himself or to think about anything except racing, as he started right down the clamming run immediately. Looking back at Hunter, laughing as he did, Orion shouted, "See you at the bottom, Hunter. Catch me if you can, sucker!"

"Oh no you don't, Orion. I am right behind you! We will see who wins this race!" Hunter shouted back. Flipping his shell quickly to head down the hill, Hunter followed Orion, much closer than Orion had expected. The race was on!

The two young clammers seemed to fly down the sandy hill this time. As they approached the bottom, shells right next to each other, Orion cautioned, "Stay on the right side of the hill, a couple feet from the guarded tunnel, I will distract that big crab. Once he's gone, move down the path quickly, until you're out of sight, then wait for me around the second corner, where no one else can see us."

"Sounds good," answered Hunter excitedly. He was so focused on winning this run, he didn't even notice that Orion allowed him to catch up. When he got to the bottom just ahead of Orion, Hunter was so happy to have won that he stopped on the clamming hill, waiting to see if Orion could really distract the large crab at the entrance to the other path. Hunter didn't think for a second about Devin or Cracker; he was now completely focused on trying out Orion's super jets.

Meanwhile, Cracker and Devin were having fun on the sand too, not going as fast as Hunter and Orion, but doing some tricks of their own on the way down. When they got to the bottom and over to the water jets, they realized that the racers had already gone up for another run, so would soon be back to the bottom. Cracker made a suggestion. "Let's just wait for them down here Devin. Once they finish their run, we can all go back up the jets together. What do you think?"

Devin thought this new idea was perfect, but he had another suggestion. "Cracker, why don't we go back to see them finish, rather than waiting down here by these jets?"

"I like it." Cracker smiled. "Let's go watch."

As the two friends started heading back to the bottom of the clamming run, they saw some strange things occurring.

Orion was already heading their way (having just finished his run) and made an odd motion with his claw to a couple of his pals. He then quickly turned around, retreating back into the other tunnel. One of the crabs started acting ill, lying down on the sand, while the other quickly ran to the large guard, obviously trying to get him to come see what was going on.

Orion went right up to the adult crab still at the entrance, he volunteered to watch the tunnel, making sure no one went down the wrong path. This seemed to satisfy the adult stationed there, and he quickly went off with Orion's pal to help the "sick" crab.

As soon as the large adult moved away, busy with the supposedly sick crab on the ground, Orion motioned to Hunter, who ran quickly down the path, with Orion right next to him. Commenting to Hunter, with a big smirk his face, Orion added, "See, Hunter, I told you we could do it, didn't I? Now it's time for some big boy fun. Let's hit the super jets!"

Devin and Cracker, watching all this, immediately ran after Hunter and Orion, while no one else seemed to notice that anything unusual was happening on that side of the cave at all.

By the time they caught up with Orion and Hunter, Devin and Cracker had come to a tunnel wall that had eight waterjets lined up in a row. The two on the far left were empty, while they saw Orion starting to climb into the fourth one in from the left side. Hunter had obviously gotten into the third tube as it was now blocked with a clamshell—the one next to Orion's—waiting for the next wave to arrive.

"Wait for us!" yelled Devin as they approached the water jets.

Orion turned immediately toward the unexpected, not to mention very unwelcome, new sound. Seeing Devin and Cracker approaching, he quickly improvised on his plan. Responding to Devin, pausing for only a moment or two after the boy's call, Orion pointed a pincer at the wall shouting, "Hey you two, glad you could join us. Hop into those two empty jets right next to Hunter, this will be really fun." Without waiting to see if his words were followed, Orion finished climbing into his own water jet, readying himself for the coming wave.

Devin and Cracker both hurried to the empty shafts on the left side, as there was no time to think about it or to even question Orion's directions before the next wave hit. Quickly climbing in, not stopping for a second to think this might not be such a good idea, they were soon ready to go. If Orion and Hunter could do it, they were not about to miss out on something this exciting. The next wave came rushing in a few seconds later, launching all four of them up into the jetting shafts.

Thirty seconds or so later, Orion landed softy on the sand, near the top of the clamming hill. This spot was on the opposite side of the landing zone from the first set of water jets that had been used originally by the clammers. The only crabs to be seen on that side of the hill were Orion's friends, Decker and Skitter, almost as if they were waiting for Orion to show up there.

After a pause, with no one else appearing, Decker slurred to Orion, "Where is H-hunter? Did you get rid o' him?" Neither he nor Skitter had seen Devin or Cracker follow Orion and Hunter into the other tunnel.

"Oh yes," smirked Orion, "he's now off on a different adventure, somewhere down below, I would guess." Orion added with a mysterious laugh, "Doubt we will ever see him again…or his friends either. Ha!" Then, with a very satisfied grin on his face, he headed back up the hill.

Decker and Skitter just looked at each other with this bit of news. Giving each other a knowing look, they simply turned, shrugged, and followed Orion back toward the top of the hill. Neither Cracker, Devin, nor Hunter got another thought from any of them. They were gone!

CHAPTER 6

WHAT LIES BELOW

Séance Stone

Created before the time of the Sky-lords by powers unknown, a Séance Stone shows its possessor events from the past, When such a story is shown, there is always a connection between the story and possible future events for those involved. However, neither the connection nor the timing is easily understood.

LORE OF THE SKY-LORDS

Exploding through the end of the twisting turning water jets, the three clamshells carrying Devin, Hunter, and Cracker emerged, spinning wildly out of control with their occupants now screaming at the top of their lungs—both in fear and excitement—as their crazy rush through the darkness came suddenly to an end. This jet ride had been completely different from the earlier ones that took the boys straight back up to the top of the clamming hill. Instead of the smooth yet exhilarating ride, mostly heading up, this one had a lot more twists, turns, tangles, tumbles, and terrifying changes in direction. The two Bigs thought they had been thrown onto an out-of-control roller coaster, while to Cracker, it felt like he was being tossed around in the beach surf on a pitch-black night.

Exiting the tunnels at last, each shell approached the final part of the jet, flying fast yet still spinning wildly. It turned out, when the shells came out of the tunnel, they were moving ever so slightly upward as they exited the jetting tubes. The chute's path dipped downward a bit before turning back up just before the final opening, acting as a launching pad to send the jetters up and out. The random changes of direction, combined with the spinning from the wild ride, ensured that none of the riders had any real sense of where they were, or where they were going. Cracker, who happened to emerge from the jets first, was lying flat against his clammer to protect himself from the ride. Once clear of the tunnel, he quickly popped his eyes over the shell's edge to see what was around them.

Fortunately, Cracker was looking forward, as random chance pointed his clamshell that way. Looking in the direction the shell was now flying, the only thing he could see was the jagged edge of the rocky roof of this new cave they had all just entered. Unfortunately, it was now coming right at him. All Cracker had time to do was immediately pull his eyes back down into his shell, while screaming as loud as he could to the others, "DUCK!" Cracker's clammer then hit the cave roof with a horrible scrape, causing the shell, along with the crab inside, to plummet immediately toward the ground.

Emerging from the water jets only a few seconds after Cracker, Devin and Hunter each heard him scream, "DUCK" just as they emerged from their own dark tunnels. Both boys instinctively pulled themselves down as low as they possibly could inside their shells, while still holding on for dear life, even though they desperately wanted to see where they now were.

Cracker's dire warning saved them.

Within seconds of exiting the chute, they too found themselves scraping the roof of the cave, with a similar result—everyone was soon falling toward the unknown ground below.

Each shell fell through the damp cavern air, wobbling a bit—no longer spinning—after hitting the cave roof, as they all rushed toward the bottom. Reaching the ground first, Cracker's shell hit with a hard *splash*, soon followed by two more. *Splash. Splash.* Devin and Hunter also landed in a pool of water that was waiting for them at the bottom of this new cave. The hard impact of landing in the water, while likely saving all of them from serious injury, still shook the trio up. They were momentarily breathless, but otherwise in fine shape.

Drifting along silently in their clammers for a few moments, slowly floating toward the pool's edge while they recovered their breath, Devin, Hunter, and Cracker were all resting easily on their backs, taking in the new surroundings. Looking at the cave's roof, they could now easily see the jagged rocks that made up that part of the cavern. It was very clear to all of them, as they examined more closely the sharp edges their shells had hit, that if any of them had hit the roof with their heads or, for that matter, any other part of their bodies at the speed they emerged from the jets, they would have suffered a serious injury or even gotten killed!

Coming to a sudden stop as they finally washed up against some sand by the water's edge, the three still shaken up adventurers managed with great effort to climb out of their shells, only to immediately plop down on the nice soft sand beneath them. All three were, for the moment, completely exhausted, needing a few moments to allow their beating hearts to slow down and recover from all the excitement of the scary, wild, water-jet trip.

"Cracker, that was just crazy, I mean look at those nasty rocks! You really saved us up there. Thank you." Devin pointed weakly at the cavern roof. He was still looking up toward the top of the cavern they had just arrived in, thinking about what might have happened to them had they actually hit the top. "Do you have any idea where we might be?"

"You are very welcome, both of you," responded Cracker to Devin while looking over at Hunter as well. "I really have no idea where we are. I've never been through such a terribly twisting turning tumultuous tunnel. Truthfully, to try to travel through that jet, and keep my bearings was impossible. Now, and I hate to admit this, I am thoroughly lost, something I rarely find myself." After a slight pause he continued, "We could be anywhere within the sand dunes or maybe even back underneath the beach for all I know."

Lifting up his eyes suddenly, as if jolted with electricity, Cracker exclaimed as he turned to look around in all directions, "Hey, you two, where's Orion?" Looking around again, Cracker continued, "He isn't here. I don't see him anywhere at all, do you?"

The others sat up sharply, now all looking around for Orion too. There was clearly no one else in this cave, not even a hint that someone else might have landed nearby. Looking upward to scan the top of the cavern where they had emerged from one more time, Devin could just barely make out the three holes they had recently flown out of. Counting them a couple times to be sure, he exclaimed, "Guys, look, there are only three water-jet exits up there, not four! I don't see how Orion could have come with us."

"I get it!" exclaimed Cracker, continuing to scan for an additional possible exit. "Orion isn't here because there are only three exits up there. The fourth water-jet that he took doesn't come out here at all, so Orion must have gone somewhere else." Cracker paused. "You know, Hunter, when we caught up to you guys, I wondered why you were in the middle of the jetting tubes, not on the end. Now I understand— Orion knew his tube would take him somewhere else, probably right back to the clamming hill! He put you in the tube next to him, very likely knowing you would end up down here, maybe even badly hurt!"

"Does it really matter, Cracker? You are just guessing about Orion anyway. We are here now, so let's go exploring. Maybe later we can figure out where he went," suggested Hunter somewhat defensively. In truth, he was not all that interested in where Orion might be, but very interested in where they were right now. Hunter was the first to get up off the sand and walk around to see what their new surroundings were like.

Looking in all directions, he noticed that it seemed to be very dark toward both ends of the cavern. In reality, this new cave was so large that he could not see where it might end to either side, making any assessment of their current surroundings impossible. There appeared to be two basic directions the group could go: whether that was north-south, east-west, or some other combination, was unclear to any of them. Picking up their shells, they started to debate what direction they should take, even though there did not appear to be any specific reason to go either way.

"Why don't we just go both directions?" Hunter said. "I mean, I'll go this way"—he pointed to his left toward one end of the cavern—"while Devin, you, or Cracker go the other way. We can walk for fifteen minutes, then turn around and meet back here to compare what we have found? What do you guys think?"

Cracker responded, "Hunter, I don't think we should split up. We don't know where we are or what we will find. Let's stick together. Maybe we should just pick a direction and go that way. If nothing of interest comes up after fifteen minutes or so, we can turn around to go the other way? Devin, any thoughts?"

While Cracker was debating with Hunter, Devin moved away from them just a bit as he thought he heard something new. "Shhhhhh, Hunter, Cracker, listen…do you hear that?" Devin said to Cracker in a hushed tone.

"What is it?" whispered Hunter.

Listening very quietly for a few seconds, Cracker suddenly proclaimed excitedly, "It sounds like running water!"

"Yes, yes, it does, Cracker," cheered Hunter, pointing toward Devin. "Let's all go that way."

Quickly, the group moved toward the noise. Hearing running water gave them all hope that they were going in a direction where the trio would be able to find a way to get out of this cave, maybe even return to the sandcastle itself.

Soon they arrived at what appeared to be a small river or stream running right through that part of the cavern.

"Wow, look at that Hunter," exclaimed Devin, "a river under the ground. This is so cool. Why is it here? Why? Do you know where this might go, Cracker?"

Cracker replied, "I'm not sure, but I have heard about a river that runs underneath all the dunes. Supposedly it's been around for a very long time. In fact, if that's where we are, then the water runs completely under the entire island, connecting the ocean on one side with the bay on the other. So…if that is right, then you know what?" Cracker broke into a big grin. "All we really need to do is simply follow the river downstream. We will eventually come to the sea. Once there I will easily get my bearings, and then we can fairly quickly find our way home. Perfect!"

Hunter wondered aloud, "How long will that take do you think?"

Cracker answered thoughtfully, "No idea, but if this is that river, then it goes for quite a while in both directions. Since I have no idea where we are now, I really can't offer a guess. The good news is, legend has it, the current always runs from the bay out toward the sea." The big smile returned to his face as Cracker explained, "So, you see, if we can hook our clamming shells together in some way, all we have to do is just float down the river, all the way to the ocean…in fact, no work at all."

"Awesome! What a cool thing to do!" Devin exclaimed. "Let's get to it, right now. Come on!" Then he added in a questioning rhetorical voice, "Just to be clear, Cracker, you're saying that all we need to do is find some seaweed or something to tie the shells together with, then float away? This is great!"

Starting their search, the trio quickly found some short pieces of seaweed in the sand, but nothing long enough to tie the three clamshells together. Cracker then moved his efforts into the water, while Hunter headed back toward the nearest wall of the cave. While looking near the edge of that wall, where the sandy ground met the wall's edge, he noticed something that looked like oddly colored seaweed sticking up from the sand. As most curious boys will do, Hunter reached out, grabbed it, and pulled.

Up came what turned out to be some very old fisherman's netting, which was both heavy as well as still quite strong. It continued to get heavier as Hunter tried to pull more of it up. As he did so, more and more sand spilled off to the sides. "Guys, guys, come over here. I think I found something we can use," he cried out, still pulling as hard as he could.

Cracker and Devin ran over, immediately grabbing onto some loose ends, to help Hunter in his efforts. The netting turned out to be much bigger than it first looked, running from under the sand where they were standing, directly into the cave wall itself. It had in fact, over time, become a part of the actual outer layer of the cavern. Pulling on it with all their strength, the entire piece of netting suddenly broke away from its old resting place on the wall. The trio immediately fell backward onto the sand, all landing abruptly on their rear ends, but now they had something they could use like a rope to make a small clamshell boat! While everyone was falling to the ground, the outer edge of the wall, which was just older layers of sand built up over time, came crumbling away as well.

Hunter and Cracker quickly got back up to start examining their new net, trying to figure out the best way to make their boat. Devin stayed seated on the sand for a moment, so that he could look at the area of the cavern wall that had been uncovered as everything was coming down.

"Hey, guys, take a look at this!" Devin shouted, focusing his attention on the wall.

"What is it?" replied Hunter and Cracker together as they looked up at the area of the wall Devin was pointing toward.

Behind the now removed netting and sand layer was the actual cave wall itself. The surface was made of a dark rock, which happened to be smooth enough to write on. Through the bits of sand still clinging to the wall, the boys could see markings of some type—reds, yellows, some earthy greens, and some dirty browns. They quickly cleared off the rest of the loose sand. Once they had cleaned off the surface, a message from the past was now before them, complete with pictures, arrows, and letters that had not been seen by anyone for a very long time.

Hunter, tilting his head for a better look, spoke first. "It looks kind of like directions, don't you think? Look, the yellow arrow pointing down the river has a picture of a key after it. The arrow pointing the other way has a picture of a treasure chest after it. I wonder what that means?"

The picture of the treasure chest was that of a basic brown chest that appeared to be partially open. Inside the chest was the tip of some red object. It was impossible to tell what it was, other than something red, perhaps a rock that was now cut off from view by the bottom part of the chest. Clearly there was more to it sitting inside the chest, but the drawing only showed a tip of red, just a small triangle inside a bigger brown rectangle. Outside the chest, shooting up from the red tip, were three zigzagging red lines, indicating some sort of arcane power was associated with whatever lay inside.

The picture of the Key was quite a bit different. A yellow color was used for the drawing, indicating the Key barrel was likely made of metal, perhaps brass or gold, with two fingers coming out from the very end, the first twice as long as the second—a fairly standard key design for an old treasure chest. The handle, however, was very odd looking, almost hard to focus on. Rather than being the same color as the rest of the Key, the handle was a dark greenish color that seemed to almost blend in with the black rock of the cave. It was difficult to tell what the handle depicted, even though it was clearly a shape of some kind.

Cracker, looking intently at the pictures along with Hunter, added, "I wonder why the treasure chest has those red markings above it? Kind of makes the chest seem to glow. Or, whatever is inside it might be doing the glowing. I wonder…"

Devin was looking at some markings beneath the pictures, rather than the pictures themselves. "Hunter, Cracker, look at this, these initials here, they are exactly the same as those we saw on the log on the beach, J. L. Do you think the same person whose log was on the beach came down here too? Maybe he really was a Pirate. These pictures might be telling us how to find his hidden treasure. My gosh, wouldn't that be just amazing'?!"

Cracker cracked his pincer. "You know, you could be right, the stories about this river occasionally do include Pirates. In fact, did you know that sometimes the jewel that brought you into our sandcastle is called the 'Pirate's Passage'? I don't know why, but these pictures make me think that they really have been here before."

"I know, I know what this means. At least I think I do!" exclaimed

Hunter excitedly. "Look, guys, it's simple, the Key is this way," he said, pointing his finger in the direction that the underground river was flowing. "The treasure chest is that way," he continued. pointing in the opposite direction. "Someone split them up so it would be really hard to find both the Key along with the treasure…unless you know where to look for both. I'll bet we have to get the Key, then the chest, before we can get to the treasure!"

"Why not get the chest and take it to the Key?" interrupted Devin. "Of course, carrying a key to the chest is likely a lot easier than carrying the chest to a key, so I suppose you are right, Hunter, we should get the Key first." Looking at the water, he finished, "Plus it looks like the Key is downstream, so that is the easiest way to go too."

"You both may be right, but look, we don't know where either one is, or if they are even still where this 'J L' Pirate left them. All these things had to be drawn a very long time ago, based on how much sand was covering this wall." Cracker pointed his small pincer at the picture. He then added with clearly more excitement building in his voice, "But it sure is fun to think about, isn't it? We will need to find out more about this mystery, if we can."

Suddenly, as if in anticipation of just such a question, the sand directly in front of the wall drawings began to swirl like a mini whirlpool. Jumping back, the boys watched with amazement as a hole about a foot wide opened up right in front of them. Sitting in the middle of the hole on a rocky platform was a smooth round clear stone that looked as if it might have been made from some sort of glass. The stone itself was about half the size of the hole in diameter, too large for either of the boys to reach completely around with their arms, given their current size.

Looking intently at the stone, the trio could now see inside it, where there were gray and white streaks that appeared to circle and twist throughout its glass body, as if they were alive somehow.

"Devin, Hunter, do you know what this is, do you?" Cracker exclaimed excitedly, pointing at the round stone while cracking his big pincer. Crack, crack.

Devin just stared straight into the glassy orb, not appearing to have heard Cracker at all, mesmerized by the gray and white movement within it. To Devin, the stone appeared to be a giant marble, with a very interesting pattern or perhaps even a secret message inside, waiting to be unlocked.

"No," answered Hunter finally, his eyes also glued to the stone. "I've never seen anything like this before. What is it?"

"It's…it's…a Séance Stone!" Cracker exclaimed, "I've never actually seen a real one myself of course. They are very, very rare, but given the descriptions I've heard from the adults, I don't think I can be wrong about this."

Hunter asked quickly, "What's a Séance Stone? What do they do?"

"From what I have heard, anyone who finds a Séance Stone can touch it. If they do, they will be given a vision from the past, something that will also be important to those who receive the vision in the future." Excited, Cracker continued, "Maybe, just maybe, if we all touch it together, we might all see the same thing. If we are lucky, it will show us a way to get out of here, or even something about the treasure, so we can see if it truly exists!"

Devin finally rejoined the conversation. "Why don't we focus on the treasure when we put our hands on the stone, you know, the red image on the wall? Maybe also concentrate on the initials 'J L' since they seem to be part of all this. Lastly, when we touch the stone, I think we should do it at the same time. Don't you guys agree? Let's see what happens. Maybe we can influence what it shows us. OK, guys?"

Both Cracker and Hunter immediately agreed with Devin's suggestions. All three made a circle, then sat down around the stone, the boys with their legs crossed in front of them, while Cracker sat with all six of his legs crossed, leaving his pincers free.

Cracker made a final suggestion. "You know, maybe we could also link ourselves in some way, to help get the same vision? How about we link with each other while also touching the stone? That way we are all connected."

Adjusting themselves a bit so that they were now all equal distant from the stone, the boys followed Cracker's advice. Hunter put his right hand on Devin's shoulder, Devin put his right hand on Cracker, and Cracker put his right pincer on Hunter's shoulder.

"OK, I think we are ready. Here we go," said Devin. Pausing to take a slow breath, in through his nose then exhaling by blowing out his mouth, he continued, "Close your eyes, boys, try to think only about 'J L' and his treasure chest."

Each one of them touched the stone. Following Devin's lead, they all shut their eyes, focusing only on J L's hidden treasure. At first no one saw or heard anything, just darkness and quiet. As their own excitement died down, their breathing became calmer, more rhythmic. Suddenly the stone came into focus for each of them as if their eyes had reopened, which they had not. Instead, the members of the little triangle, now touching the stone while breathing slowly in the same rhythm, were taken on a journey—like a dream.

With the clear image of the stone sitting directly in front of them, the trio could see that there was more to this sphere than just a simple glassy rock sitting in the sand. Slowly, it appeared as if the orb too was waking up—almost coming to life—as it began pulsing ever so slightly. The solid gray and white streaks existing within the stone softened, taking on a lighter wispier appearance, similar to clouds. The cloud-like streaks then began swirling within the orb, slowly at first but rapidly gaining more speed and purpose.

Suddenly, the gray and white dancing clouds came together in just the right way, forming a solid image that burst into life, appearing to each of them as part of a vision from the past. Devin, Hunter, and Cracker all began to see the same story unfold, just as they had hoped. It was as if a movie had started playing for all of them, within their minds.

The first thing they saw was a fierce one-eyed Pirate with a parrot on his shoulder, pointing with a drawn cutlass in his right hand toward something. He was wearing an odd purple eye-patch and yelling as loud as he could at his men, "RUN, you scalawags, RUN!"

"Run, you scalawags, RUN!" the parrot echoed in a scratchy voice.

"SQUUAAWKK!"

Drowning out the commands of the shouting pirate, a new sound could be heard coming from just offshore—BOOM! Two more explosions—BOOM! BOOM! —followed in rapid succession. With each explosion came a flash of bright light, mostly white but with a tinge of orange flame in the middle, that temporarily lit up the warship firing the cannon.

Off the warship's bow could be seen another ship, burning brightly in the heart of the night's darkness. The flames consuming that ship were now being eaten by the sea, as the large boat slowly sank into the murky waters off the coast. From the light of the flames, the men on the beach, along with those on the warship, could still see the Pirate's flag whipping in the breeze on top of the sinking ship. It was the Jolly Roger, feared symbol of New World Pirates. The flag itself was completely black—a dark background whipping back and forth in the wind, keeping its white message aloft for the time being. The image on the flag was the simple picture of a grinning skull with a single eye socket above two white bones, crisscrossed like an X turned on its side.

As the flames died out, the remaining light from the full moon allowed all to watch the grinning flag slip slowly into the dark water; then it too was gone. The warship had just sunk the most feared of Pirate ships, but the Pirates themselves had already luckily escaped to the island's shore.

"I said, RUN!" repeated the Pirate Captain.

"RUN!" squawked the parrot right after.

The men had just jumped out of their longboat and were now running as fast as they could down the open beach. None of them, except for two that were hauling some sort of chest, were carrying much more than the clothes on their backs along with their weapons. Suddenly, they all felt the effects of the cannon that had fired just moments before. Explosions hit all around! The beach seemed to jump up and down, with sand spraying everywhere.

Some of the fleeing Pirates were knocked to the sand as the cannon balls crashed among them. Two of the Pirates did not get back up.

"We're almost there, mateys," shouted the leader encouragingly. "Another couple hundred yards is all; you can do it, just DON'T LOSE THAT CHEST!"

Another round of BOOMS came washing across the beach, causing the Pirates to turn back to look toward the water. With the light of the moon above them, the fleeing Pirates could just make out a second longboat now rapidly approaching the shore. The leader of that boat was standing at the front, shouting at his hard-rowing men, "KEEP TO THE WEST. GET IN FRONT OF THEM!"

The boat was angling to land in front of the fleeing Pirates, to cut off any possible escape. "DON'T STOP, KEEP MOVING" their leader shouted. Just as he finished, cannon balls began landing once more on the beach, again, very near the Pirates. One of the two Pirates who was carrying the treasure chest collapsed immediately, dropping straight to the ground as the first cannon ball exploded directly behind him. He never moved again.

Since the treasure chest was being carried on two large strong wood poles the size of small logs, when the first Pirate fell, the chest dropped too, tumbling backward onto the sand. As the chest fell, the image focused in on the chest itself, along with the logs being used to carry it. The front piece of wood came into focus, showing the initials "J L" intricately carved right into the middle of the pole. The same initials the boys had found in the wood on the beach. Two more explosions then occurred, with cannon balls landing directly in front of the fleeing Pirates, causing sand and chaos to erupt all around those near the chest.

The Pirate leader, who had also been knocked down by the impact of the cannon balls, got up a bit slowly, sheathing his sword while shaking his head to clear it. Stumbling slightly, as he ran over to check on the treasure chest, the Pirate quickly noticed, with his good eye, a number of related things: one of the two carrying poles was completely destroyed, the second pole had both its handles blown off, finally, that the chest itself was now just lying there, alone in the sand.

Greatly relieved at the sight of the chest, he quickly ordered the nearest still-walking Pirate to grab one side just as he was grabbing the other, so that together they could carry it onward.

No longer able to run or even move quickly given the weight and bulk of the treasure chest, the leader paused for a moment to get his bearings. It was lucky for him that the moon was full this night, so he could see most of the beach they were now on.

"THERE IT IS!" shouted the Pirate.

"There it is, there it is," whistled the parrot, who had somehow managed to stay on his master's shoulder.

"HEAD TOWARD that grassy area!" the Pirate tried to scream. His voice was no longer able to carry over the entire beach, as it was quickly giving out from all the recent shouting. Walking rapidly now, the Pirate once more pointed to an area where the grass on the beach's edge hung over particularly far, seeming to hide whatever was underneath.

It was the parrot that continued on for him, giving his final command to the rest of the Pirates, "Grassy area, grassy area. Give us a kiss, SQUAWK!"

The remaining Pirates all turned to run, barefoot in the sand, to the spot pointed out by their captain. Just as they were all changing direction slightly, toward the indicated spot, the bright moon dimmed dramatically as it was suddenly covered by a solitary passing cloud. The Pirates could no longer see the approaching soldiers in their longboat. Perhaps more importantly, the soldiers could not see the Pirates.

"Captain Lafitte, Captain Lafitte, is this it?" huffed one of the fleeing men as he ran up to an area where the beach met the sand dune. At this spot, the grass from the dune seemed to lie over or even grow down, rather than stand up toward the sun, almost covering completely the edge where the dune met the beach.

"Yes, yes, it is," panted an exhausted Captain Jean Lafitte with obvious relief. "We are safe at last."

"Safe at last, Safe at last," came a whistling echo from the parrot.

One of the Pirates suddenly noticed that Captain Lafitte was missing his odd purple eye patch and asked, "Captain, Captain, are you OK? Looks like you lost your eye patch."

"WHAT!?" roared the Captain. He frantically searched his face, where his right eye would have been, with both hands, seeking the Purple Patch that he always wore there. Realizing the Patch was missing, he responded with desperation in his voice, "I must have lost it in the sand when I fell earlier, I have to go back and get it!" Turning back toward the ocean, Captain Lafitte began a frantic search for the Patch.

After a minute or two of looking through the sand, one of the crew—his first mate, Katerina—grabbed him by the shoulder, while pointing toward the sea. "Jean, Jean, look, we must go, NOW," she screamed at him, making him look at her and away from the sandy beach.

Forcing himself to look up from the spot where he thought he had previously fallen, and out toward the ocean where the soldier's longboat had already landed, Captain Lafitte was able to understand what Katerina meant.

With the pursuing soldiers almost certainly arriving in moments to this section of the beach, where his tired crew was now waiting his orders, Captain Lafitte reluctantly (and only after a fierce inner battle in which he convinced himself that the Patch would still be lying there in the morning) concluded that he would have to come back to get it later, after the soldiers had gone. Thinking to himself that it was highly unlikely the soldiers would find his patch in the night's darkness, he turned away from the search. Sprinting with Katerina and the rest of his crew, Captain Lafitte returned to the edge of the grassy dune.

The longboat from the warship had indeed landed only a few hundred yards past the beach where the Pirates were last seen. Soldiers jumped out of the boat quickly, ready to do battle, and perhaps even capture some of the Pirates if they could. They ran in an orderly soldier's fashion, two wide in a single column, back toward the area of the beach they had last seen their enemies with their captain in the lead, his bayonet held high.

Just then, the moon emerged from its hiding place as the covering cloud passed on, once again illuminating the entire beach. The soldiers arrived moments later at the grassy area where their enemies should have been. Prepared for battle with swords drawn and shouting a charge, they rounded the curved dune, but what did they find? Nothing! Something was very wrong. There were no Pirates to be found—none at all! The entire crew had simply completely vanished!

The three onlookers, watching this scene play out in their minds, saw the soldiers look for the Pirates for a little while longer, until the sun started to come up, in fact. Then the soldiers simply gave up. Leaving the beach in obvious frustration at not having captured any Pirates, they marched back to their longboat much more slowly than when they first landed. With a final look back toward the beach, the soldier's leader ordered them to depart, as there was no reason left for them to stay.

Interestingly, the last image the trio had of the scene on the beach was not of the Pirates, nor of the soldiers, nor even of the treasure chest; rather, it was a curious image of a Pelican who happened to land on the beach just as the soldiers were marching away, very near to where the treasure chest had fallen. Leaning over to examine a strange purple patch lying partially covered by the sand, the pelican somehow used its beak to scoop its new-found prize up onto its head, where the odd Purple Patch—so desperately desired by Captain Lafitte—seemed to easily slide over its right eye, looking very much just like it had on the Pirate captain.

The pelican shook its head a few times until the Patch seemed to be seated properly then flew off into the morning sun.

The vision of the Pirate's seemingly miraculous escape and the Pelican's acquisition of the Purple Patch suddenly came to an end. The image broke up as the gray and white swirl of clouds came back within Devin, Hunter, and Cracker's vision. The glowing of the Séance Stone slowly went out, with all three falling asleep immediately, as the power of the stone's vision passed away.

After all were asleep, the sand around the stone began to swirl once more. The stone sinking back into the ground, with sand covering up any trace that it had ever been there.

Waking up after some much-needed sleep, all three sat up, remembering every detail of the vision from the night before. "Wow, there really is Pirate treasure down here," was the first thing Hunter said as he woke back up. "I mean, that story has to mean that the Pirates brought their treasure down into the sandcastle to escape from the soldiers. They are likely the ones who drew the pictures on this wall and have hidden both the chest along with the Key down here somewhere. Don't you think so, Devin?"

Not paying attention to Hunter, Devin was already using his hands to dig in the sand where the Séance Stone had been before they fell asleep. Not finding the stone or any trace of even the stone platform it had rested on, Devin finally sat back to wonder where it had gone, while also thinking about the vision from the previous day.

Cracker responded to Hunter before Devin rejoined the group conversation, "What do you guys think was in that treasure chest? Do you think it's still down here? What if we area able to find it?" His words came rushing out with obvious enthusiasm.

"I'm sure it's here…somewhere," joined Devin finally. "Did you see the big pieces of wood the Pirates used to carry it? One of them is the log we found on the beach, Hunter. It had the initials 'J L' on it in the vision, same as on the log." Pointing at the wall, he continued, "These are also the same initials on the cave right there. They must be the initials of the pirate captain. What did they call him? Captain Lafitte, I think?"

Hunter said, "That's right. Someone called him Jean, yes, Jean Lafitte. Clearly *J L* must stand for Jean Lafitte! That's who was leading the Pirates." After pausing for a second to enjoy this discovery, Hunter finished, "Let's keep a lookout for the Key, OK? It must be down here somewhere. We can follow the river just like you said." He pointed to Cracker. "Maybe it will lead us straight to the Key. Once we find it, we can figure out how to come back here, then go upriver so we can find the Pirate's chest too!"

Cracker cracked his claw twice, with a loud *crack, crack*. Laughing easily, he added, "I like it, Hunter, and in the meantime, maybe we can also find our way back to my home."

Both boys also laughed. "Oh yeah, that too," they both added as an afterthought.

Cracker then added, almost too quietly to be heard, "I wonder if it's one of the Rainbow Objects?"

"What's that, what did you say Cracker?" asked Devin.

Speaking to both Devin and Hunter, Cracker turned to answer. "Remember when you asked earlier what might be in the treasure chest? Well, do you also remember the Purple Patch, which the Pirate Captain lost on the beach, and that the pelican later scooped onto his head?"

Both boys nodded in agreement.

"That is the same Purple Patch that One-Eye the Pelican now wears. One-Eye almost got you at the door of the sandcastle, Hunter. You see, we crabs have a legend about the magical Rainbow Objects. One of those objects is called the Purple Patch of Power. I think that is what we saw fall off the Pirate, and why that was the last thing we saw from the Séance Stone vision. If that is right, then there very well could be another of the Objects in the treasure chest."

Devin quickly asked, "Why do you think that, Cracker? What are these objects?"

As they sat there in the sand, Cracker retold the story he had heard as a very young Crab about a Sky-Lord, whom everyone called Putrid—but no one could truly recall his actual name—and the Breaking of the Rainbow. He told his friends about each of the Objects, as well as the Colors, that had been created by the Sky-Lords. How Putrid made the evil Objects, while the Colors had been created by the other lords to counter them, from pieces of a destroyed Rainbow. One good and one evil for each color of the Rainbow, except for Yellow, which the Lords had used to color the sun.

When he had finished, both Hunter and Devin just sat there for a moment trying to understand all they had just been told along with the recent vision from the Séance Stone. The idea of the Breaking of the Rainbow, the evil Lord Putrid, Pirate treasure, magical objects, and One-Eye the Pelican was a lot to think about.

Hunter finally broke the silence. "Let me get this right, Cracker, you think the treasure in the chest might be one of these Rainbow Objects, right?" Without letting Cracker answer, Hunter kept talking. "If we find one of them, we will then be able to gain some sort of special power, depending on which one is in the chest. Is that right?"

"Yes, Hunter, that is exactly what I think," responded Cracker, pointing back toward the picture on the cavern wall. "Look, the treasure chest has something red inside it. I'll bet it's the Red Rainbow Object! Crex says it's called the Red Rock of Ruling. Doesn't that picture look like the tip of a red rock? You know it does! But you can't just use these Objects, they are meant to hurt others, including the user. We crabs are sure of this. The Rainbow Colors, now, they can be used by anyone without causing problems, like the Purple Prism that brought you here, but never the Objects."

Devin snapped his fingers. "Of course, of course, that's how we got here. The stone in the door of the sandcastle is one of the Rainbow Colors."

"That's right, Devin." Cracker continued, "It's also why we can talk to each other. Once you go through the Purple Prism, you can talk to anyone else who has also gone through. It helps different creatures communicate."

Hunter, continuing his thinking, said, "Explain again why you can't use the Objects…only the Colors? That doesn't make sense to me, that you can only use half of these things, but not the other half! Have you ever tried to use an Object, or has anyone you know? I mean, what if we really do find the treasure chest? We have to open it at least, don't we? Plus, it may not even have any of these Objects. Maybe it's just Pirate treasure!"

Pivoting to look back at the wall containing the map, Cracker responded, "You have a point, Hunter. I am not completely sure that the treasure chest has any Objects in it, although the vision we all had has me pretty convinced there are. Besides, why the red lightening coming out of the chest? Maybe it really is the Red one. But I must agree with your other point. I don't know anyone who has actually tried to use an Object. I do know that One-Eye, who really does have one, is always attacking the crabs in our colony, but he likely would do that without any magical help, since Pelicans will eat Crabs whenever they can anyway. One thing I am sure of is that Crex and all the adults who tell stories about the Objects are very clear about one thing: The Rainbow Objects are very bad news!"

Hunter chose not to continue the conversation with Cracker about the treasure or any of the Objects. Instead he kept his desires regarding them strictly to himself.

Devin, whose own thoughts on the subject were clearly different from Hunter's, added, "OK, let's see where we are. We know there is a Color in the sandcastle…and an Object with One-Eye, right? We also now have directions to a treasure chest that might have another Object, along with the Key to opening it. Plus, we are very likely the only ones who know about these things. I mean, besides us, who else has seen a Séance Stone that you know?" He pointed back at the wall. "Not to mention, the directions on this wall here, they were hidden behind all that sand for a very long time. Maybe longer than anyone alive I would guess, right, Cracker?"

Cracker answered Devin with a question of his own as he changed the subject. "You are right, Devin, there is a lot I don't understand. Clearly though, we now have information that no one else does, likely very important, too. But all this talking of treasure, thinking about the Rainbow Objects, seeing a real Séance Stone, and sleeping is making me very hungry. What about you?"

Devin and Hunter, suddenly also aware of their own hunger, both responded together, "You bet we are!" Their stomachs growled so loudly that Cracker laughed.

"OK, boys, we can eat some fish or some seaweed. Both are plentiful here in the river. Let's go get some."

The boys grabbed some of the netting, still thinking about the treasure, but now equally focused on food. They could use the net to try to pull some minnows or other very small fish from the river. Cracker took a different approach: he dove straight down to the bottom, coming back quickly with claw-fulls of seaweed.

Not being very successful in their fishing, the treasure hunters, as they fancied themselves now, settled for a meal of seaweed. While it certainly did not taste that good, it was both filling and nutritious. After eating their fill, the group decided that they were now ready to go find the Key to the treasure chest. That had to be the first step to getting the treasure, even if they didn't know what they would do once they had it.

CHAPTER 7

TO THE RESCUE

Sea Turtles

Enemy of the Sea Snakes, Turtles can be found on beaches wherever Rainbow Objects or Colors appear. Turtles live to be very old and can accumulate great wisdom and knowledge of the world. It is said, the wisest of the true Sea Turtles often have unique knowledge of the Rainbow Objects and Colors, along with events going on about them.

CRAB CHRONICLES

"I think it's about time we move on," said Cracker, as they were all slowly finishing off the seaweed meal.

The adventurers quickly agreed. Returning to their clamming shells and using some of the netting they had found, the trio tied the shells together so that the combination now looked very much like a three-leaf clover floating on top of the water.

"I think our clam boat looks ready, time to get in and see how well it works," said Devin. "Let's also keep a sharp lookout for any sign of the Pirate's key. OK?"

Both Hunter and Cracker agreed, especially the part about looking for the key, even giving Devin a mock salute followed by an, "Aye-aye, Captain!" as if they were now Pirates themselves.

The trio were all sitting comfortably in their shells as they pushed off from the river's edge. The makeshift boat spun around a bit as it made its way into the main current, but soon straightened out as it picked up speed, allowing the little group to follow the river's course and head to a place that would hopefully allow them to get home.

Cracker commented as they started out, "Keep your eyes and ears open, both of you. Our legends always seem to have travelers on this river running into some kind of trouble during their journey."

"Trouble, what do you mean by 'trouble,' Cracker?" asked Hunter immediately.

"Why would you say that, Cracker?" followed Devin. "Is there something up ahead we should know about? I have gone canoeing down a lot of rivers with my scout troop. The only problems we ever seem to have is when the river has rocks, creating rapids that are hard to handle. Is that what you mean?"

"Well, different things actually, and I'm not really worried about the river itself," answered Cracker a bit defensively. Continuing on, as if not sure what to say next, he added, "Depends on the story, but look, there are always other creatures inhabiting this river, or so it seems to me. More importantly, not all of them are friendly, either. Since we are now committed to going this way, I thought I would mention it, that's all. Maybe things will work out, and we won't run into anyone… or anything."

Devin asked Cracker with just a touch of worry in his voice, "Do you think this river will really be able to get us back to your home?"

Cracker responded, pulling himself up onto all six of his legs to say with more confidence than he felt, "Oh yes, we crabs can eventually find anything…if we can somehow get out to the beach, or even back to any of the tunnels that are connected to our network in the sand. I will surely be able to get us back. Don't worry about that, Devin."

Meanwhile, as they floated along with the river, the cavern they were now in began to curve to their left as it also sloped slightly down. The amount of sand between the riverbank and the cavern's rocky edge began to shrink noticeably, with the walls appearing to close in on the river. As Cracker and Devin were talking, Hunter was looking ahead, where it appeared to brighten up just a bit. "Devin! Cracker! Look over there!" he shouted, pointing straight ahead.

"Let's pull off the river and take a look, shall we?" suggested Cracker.

The group paddled their makeshift boat to the side of the river that was now little more than a strip of sand a couple of feet from the cavern's edge. What they all quickly realized was that things were now changing.

"Something must be coming soon, I think. Look, guys," Cracker said, pointing forward at the inward sloping cave walls. "This cave is clearly coming to an end. Somewhere not too far ahead would be my guess. Isn't it strange, though, that the river, along with the current, is not slowing down? If anything, we have been picking up a little more speed lately, before we stopped here, when I would think we should be slowing down, and the river should become more like a lake."

Neither Hunter nor Devin had any real opinions on the subject, as this adventure was so new to them that they just took Cracker's comments as the way things were likely to be.

Hopping back into their clamshell boat, the travelers pushed off, resuming their journey down the river once more. Hunter was focused on looking for any sign of the Pirate's key, while Devin and Cracker were thinking about what they would do once this cave came to an end.

As the trio floated along, with the sides of the passage continuing to close in about them, they all watched with a growing nervousness. Soon there was no shore left at all, just the river moving through the walls of the cave. Even worse, they were now able to watch the roof itself get lower and lower too, possibly threatening the trio's ability to stay on their chosen path. If this continued for too long, soon there would be no room left for their little boat at all.

Pointing directly ahead, Cracker suddenly shouted, "Devin, Hunter, look, look, here we are, at the cavern's end. What should we do now? There is nowhere else to go."

As the clamshell boat arrived at the end of the tunnel, the river appeared to continue flowing on, straight into an ominous oval opening in the cavern wall. Looking at this odd ending to the waterway carefully, the three adventurers could see emerging from the river's bottom two pointed rocks, maybe a foot high, one on each side. In addition to the rocks coming up out of the river, the trio could see coming down from the cavern roof, two larger stalactites. Both curved slightly inward, toward the opening. This strange combination of rocks—so close to where the river entered the cave wall—made the group uneasy.

Hunter noted in a very subdued voice to the group, pointing with his right hand toward the cave's end, "Don't those rocks kinda look like fangs?"

"Yes, yes, they do. The whole thing looks like the mouth of a giant sea snake to me," replied Cracker, with more than a bit of hesitation in his voice.

"Creepy, isn't it? Why do you think these rocks look this way?" asked Devin as he too was staring in fascination at the odd formation.

No one replied as the three took their time in examining more closely the odd snakelike place where the river entered the rock. Floating toward the "fangs," they all noticed that the "mouth" almost looked alive from this view. In fact, rather than simply flow into the rock, it now appeared to the adventurers that the "snake's mouth" was somehow swallowing the river, along with everything else heading toward it. Soon, maybe it would swallow the travelers as well.

Unfortunately for the adventurers, there was no longer any way for their little boat to continue its easy journey down the river. The water line came right to the edge of the opening in the rock wall, sometimes rising just above and sometimes just below—but never with enough room for the little clamshell boat with its three passengers to fit through.

Making matters worse, the trio could now see that in addition to the fangs in front of the mouth, lots and lots of jagged rocks lurked just inside of the tunnel's roof. Like shark's teeth, the rocks looked ready and able to chew up anything that tried to follow the river into the tunnel opening. These sharp stalactites grew down from the top of the tunnel, ending in sharp jagged points just above or just below the water's surface, making passing by them unharmed—seemingly impossible.

Maneuvering their shells back away from the opening, the boys decided to look at the situation from a bit farther out, hoping a different point of view would help them decide on how best to proceed.

After a few minutes, as they all thought about their situation, Devin broke the silence. "Cracker, do you think there is another cavern farther on? I mean, maybe there is a bigger cave or some type of tunnel up ahead, right? Maybe this barrier is just temporary. The water has to go somewhere, doesn't it? It's certainly possible that the passageway opens up again farther downstream, don't you think?"

Cracker responded nervously, looking up at the pointy fangs now almost directly above them as they floated back from the cavern's end, "I don't know, I guess I could follow the river underwater for a bit, maybe see where it goes, find out if it opens up again farther along." Continuing on after a slight pause, as he gained confidence in his plan, Cracker added, "Once I know what's up ahead, I can just come back, then we can all figure out what we should do next."

Both Hunter and Devin responded enthusiastically, with renewed confidence for Cracker, "Good idea, Cracker. We will wait here. You check it out, come back, then tell us what you find just as soon as you can."

Without even a goodbye, Cracker slipped over his shell, dropping straight down into the water. Immediately, the underwater current swept him into the dark opening of the cave, disappearing from Hunter and Devin's sight within seconds, as if he had never been there at all. The two boys then sat back in their shells. All they could do now was wait anxiously for Cracker to return.

After trying to follow Cracker's progress, but really just staring into the dark, the boys maneuvered their shell "boat" to come to rest on one of the rocks sticking up out of the river. Hunter asked, "What if Cracker gets lost under there or can't make it back for some reason?

What do we do then, Devin? We have no other way of getting home?"

Frowning, Devin answered, "That would be really bad for us, wouldn't it? I don't know what we would do then. I suppose we could either try to follow him under the water for a bit or go back. Neither of those ideas sounds very good to me. Let's just hope Cracker makes it back safely and has discovered some way for us to get past this wall."

Cheering himself up a bit, Devin continued, "Let's look at the bright side. Both the Pirate's key and the treasure chest are still down here, just waiting to be found, I'm sure of it! Given all the strange things that have happened to us so far, I think we are going to be the ones to find them too, don't you? Since Cracker is part of our team now, I'm quite sure he'll come back soon. Maybe he will even find the Key!"

The thought of the Pirate treasure brought a big grin right back to Hunter's face. "You are right, Devin. I really really, really want to find that treasure." Changing his facial expression to one of focused determination, he continued, almost as if he had forgotten Devin was there, "If I can find that key, then I just know I will be able to find the chest, I just know it!"

As if in response to Hunter's words, Cracker's eyes suddenly popped up out of the river. He had been gone only ten to fifteen minutes and from his expression was obviously pleased with what he had found. Both boys' faces lit up when Cracker climbed back onto his shell to report.

"Guys, you were right, there is indeed another cavern farther on. It is huge, probably much bigger than this one I think," spoke Cracker excitedly as he waved his claw, pointing from one side of the cave to the other. "However, it will not be so easy to get us all safely to the other side."

"Why not?" asked Devin quickly. "How far is the next cavern?"

Hunter was thinking the same thing.

"That is part of the problem," Cracker explained. "The passage between these caverns is longer than I would have hoped. I don't think there is any way either of you can hold your breath long enough to make it to the other side." Turning as he pointed toward the edge of the cavern with his little pincer, he continued, "The good news is that those really sharp stalactites guarding the entrance here, they come to an end, after just a little bit. So, once we get past this area at the entrance, there is little danger from them as the tunnel's roof is just above the surface of the water, but pretty smooth." Pausing for a moment, Cracker finished while pointing at the jagged rocks of the cave, "Now for the bad news. Once we arrive at the other side, sharp rocks—just like the ones here—come back again, right as you get to the exit. We will have to be very careful there, as those rocks are very sharp, very dangerous."

Hunter said, "What should we do? If we can't hold our breath long enough, what's the point, should we go back the other way? Are there any spots where we could come up for air? Sounds like there could be. Devin, what do you think?"

"You know, we can't get the Pirate's key if we go the other way," said Devin, trying to encourage Hunter to stay positive about their situation.

Cracker interjected, "Plus, then we would be going toward the bay. I may not be able to find our way back home very easily from that direction."

Suddenly, Devin had a fantastic idea, "I know, I know, I know! Guys, guys, I think we can take some air, along with some protection from the rocks with us, and get to the other side!"

"How would we do that, what do you mean, Devin?" asked Hunter, suddenly hopeful yet puzzled and curious.

With a smile on his face and a twinkle in his blue eyes, Devin explained his new plan, "Think about it! We can just use our shells! Look, all we have to do is flip them over so that they have a pocket of air inside. That way, as long as we are careful, we can bring some air along with us. All we would need to do then is float on down the river underneath our shells. The tops of the shells will protect us against the sharp rocks from above, plus we will still have them to make a boat again when we get to the other side. It should work, don't you think, don't you think?"

"Wow, that's a fantastic idea, let's try it!" exclaimed both Hunter and Cracker together. "High fives for Devin!" The trio all slapped their hands and pincers high above their heads.

With smiles on their faces, still thinking about how brilliant they were, the team started their project. The group took their little boat apart with Cracker having the job of taking the netting with him since he didn't need any air. He also took his clamshell so he could put the boat back together again once they got to the other side.

While getting ready, Hunter had another thought. "Guys, maybe we should keep the shells linked together somehow as we do this? That way, no one can get lost, stuck, or separated inside the tunnel. What do you think?"

"That's a great idea, Hunter. The current running under the rocks is a bit stronger than here at the surface," said Cracker. "I will lead, you both can stay connected to my shell. The flowing water will easily take us right downstream…into the next cavern. It should be a snap."

With that, followed by a quick *crack, crack* from Cracker's pincers, they flipped the shells over, tied them loosely together with some of the netting, and hopped back into river. Each adventurer, after slipping into the water, went underneath his shell, holding on to the edges to keep the shells flat with the air pocket inside. The group then slowly floated along, until they disappeared into that dark dangerous mouth swallowing all that came its way.

Devin and Hunter both kept their heads tilted back so their hair was in the river while their faces stayed relatively dry as they floated into the darkening tunnel. Sometimes, as the river rose or rocks pushed on the shells, just their noses or mouths were above the water's surface, but always inside the safety of their shell's air. On more than one occasion, they could feel the shells hit or scrape the rough spiky stalactites. Each hit changed their direction, as if they had become a steel ball inside some giant pinball game. Still, the current was flowing in the right direction, so the shell's hitting things did not stop their overall progress toward the next cavern.

What did cause some problems was the sound of those sharp rocks scraping on the shell's tops. It felt worse to the boys than listening to fingernails scraping across a chalkboard. Many of the rocks did not come down low enough to actually knock the shells aside; instead, they grazed roughly across the tops of the shells with agonizing slowness as the trio passed by. The awful scraping scratching, sounded strangely saw-like, seemingly sending sporadic shivers straight down the trio's spines. It seemed to last forever, playing tricks on their minds, as the boys slowly made their way through the dark tunnel, guided and thankfully aided by the current.

A couple times, the upside-down shells even broke off one of the pieces of rock as they hit them. These jagged shards would simply drop into the river, making a loud crack as they broke, then sinking, almost without another sound, heading to their resting place on the river's bottom. Devin watched one of the rocks sink right in front of him, as after hearing the *crack* of it breaking, he heard it then rolling off the top of his shell to fall into the water. This particular rock came so close to him that it almost hit his dangling feet, causing Devin to think to himself, *The edge of that rock looks just as sharp as a good knife.*

After what seemed a few minutes, the bumping into rocks and the awful scraping finally ended. Both boys began to relax just a bit. The shells were now easily drifting along with the current when suddenly, to Devin's great surprise, Cracker popped his head inside Devin's shell.

"Shhhhh, Devin," whispered Cracker immediately, even before Devin could ask why. "Listen, don't talk. There is an eel sleeping up ahead, I hope, in his hole at the bottom of the riverbed, just a few feet in front of us. I didn't see him the first time I came through, as it is so dark in here. If we disturb him, it could be big, big trouble. Eels are usually very nasty creatures, so we really don't want him to come after us. Don't make any noise at all. If we are lucky, the current will let us just simply float on by. Hopefully, he will never even know we were here."

Before Devin could answer or say anything in response, Cracker quickly slipped back into the water, heading to Hunter's shell to whisper the same dire warning.

From that moment on, none of the three travelers moved or barely even breathed. As hoped, the river's current carried them slowly, but safely, past the slumbering eel. Fortune smiled on them as no motion was necessary to proceed toward their destination, due to the current's carrying them silently onward. Equally fortunate was the fact that their shells were no longer hitting or scraping the roof of the tunnel as the trio coasted along. Thus, the group was able to travel safely in complete silence.

Passing slowly over the slumbering snake's home—a dark blot on the river's bottom—both Devin and Hunter thought they could just barely make out the eel's head lying in the sand. With closed eyelids covering two large round eyes and the line of its mouth buried in the sand, nothing more than an outline of the sea snake could be seen. The eel's black body disappeared behind its head, seeming to become one with the hole's inky blackness, indistinguishable, as it surely stretched back into the blank emptiness of its' lair.

As they passed above the eel, a new unwelcome feeling wrapped itself around the trio, which could only be described as gloom. It was as if the water started getting colder, thicker, while the underwater passage got even darker—if that was possible. Each member of the little group froze their muscles, even trying to stop breathing for as long as they could, while they drifted by the snake. Cracker kept both eyes forward, trying unsuccessfully to ignore the eel's presence. Thinking the water could explode at any second with frightful activity, Hunter and Devin both looked down into the water, watching with dread as the eel's head slowly slipped past them.

After what seemed to take forever, but was maybe only a minute or two, they had completely passed beyond the peril on the riverbed. Instead of getting time to relax, the travelers were now arriving at the end of the underwater passage. The shells they were in began once more to scrape, even hit, the sharp rocks that had begun to return, growing down from the top of the cavern.

Devin and Hunter quickly recognized that this must be the end of the passage, since Cracker had told them earlier that the sharp rocks would return as they exited the tunnel. Interestingly, the feeling of gloom had not left any of them after passing successfully by the eel. If anything, the resumption of the harsh scraping of the rocks on the shells above them brought about an even darker feeling among the group.

After a few minutes of hitting rocks, moving side to side, and enduring the awful scratching noises, the trio emerged, still linked together, into a new cave. Cracker immediately popped inside both Hunter and Devin's shells to tell them all was now safe. Coming out from under their shells, just as they passed by two isolated rocks growing up out of the water like fangs, the group kept their gaze looking straight ahead. There was an unspoken agreement between the travelers that it might be bad luck to look back in the direction of the eel. Everyone was thinking, if they could just ignore the danger behind them long enough, the sleeping snake might be prevented, in some way, from coming after them.

No one said anything, as that feeling of cold dread could just not be shaken. It was not until the trio could see a tiny strip of sand by the side of the river that they felt any real relief. They had made it safely to this new unexplored region. Floating along for a few more minutes until they all agreed that the eel was no longer a danger, the group decided to take a quick break before resuming their journey.

Pulling themselves out of the river onto the sand, the trio sat down by the water's edge, finally daring to look back where the river emerged from the tunnel of rock. What they saw surprised all of them.

"Wow, look at that! Isn't it odd?" Hunter pointed back toward the cave's entrance where they had all just come from. "I mean, from back here, those rocks look exactly the same as the ones on the other side—just like a serpent's mouth! The only difference I can see is that from this side it almost looks like the serpent is spitting the river out while on the other side it was swallowing it. I wonder what all this means?"

Devin answered, "Yes, I see it too, and just as creepy as before. It's almost like two heads from a giant snake, one guarding each side of the passage. Do you guys think it just a coincidence that these rock formations looking like fangs also have a live sea snake living underneath them, do you?

"It's just a coincidence, Devin. I mean, eels are not uncommon in these waters," answered Cracker a little too quickly. He was not sounding entirely sure of himself, especially since snakes were often connected with the evil Rainbow Objects of legend.

The little group continued to discuss the odd rock structure as they took a short break from their journey. After a bit, the conversation turned to how they all had gotten here, along with the subject of Orion and his possible role in these events.

Hunter spoke first on the subject. "You know, guys, I think that Orion was really upset when I beat him in our last clamming race. He's not that used to losing. I bet he thought that he could get back at me, especially after I beat him at his favorite sport."

Cracker added, "Maybe so Hunter, but I suspect it's more than that. I think he wanted to split us up too, as we are stronger together than we are when separated."

Devin asked, somewhat surprised in the direction Cracker took the conversation, "Why would he think that, Cracker? He doesn't even know us. Why?"

"You are both new to the sandcastle, Devin," answered Cracker. "To us, having Bigs coming here, being chased by One-Eye, having the Questions greet you—none of this is very common. In fact, it's all very strange. Many in the colony are sure to be trying to figure out what all this sudden activity might mean. Given what happened, how quickly Orion isolated Hunter and almost sent him here alone, I think he was trying to get you two split up. Why? I really don't know. Together you guys have each other, but if you are separated, then one or both of you might not be as strong or confident as you are now. Other than myself, you have not had time to really get to know any of the other crabs in the colony. Think about it. Look at what we have now accomplished in just our short time together."

"That's true, Cracker. In fact, Devin and I talked about that while you were looking for this cave. But then why did Orion ask you both to join us in the water jets if he was trying to get us separated? Do you think he really knows about all this down here—the treasure and the Key? How could he?" Hunter questioned.

Cracker answered them both, "Those are all very good questions, and I certainly don't have the answers to any of them. What I do know is that when we followed you, toward the forbidden water jets, I suspect Orion was plenty surprised to see us show up. I mean, there's no possible way he was thinking that we would know you were heading over there. From his view, Devin and I were somewhere else on the clamming hill, maybe coming down again, but certainly not nearby. Truthfully, it was only pure luck that allowed us to see you heading there in the first place. We were just walking back to watch you finish your run, when we saw you and Orion sneaking off.

"When we finally did catch up, you were already loaded into one of the jets, which obviously brought you down here. Orion had to think quickly, so he changed his plans slightly, thinking he could get rid of all of us at the same time. He would then be able to call our going missing an 'accident,' if questioned by Crex or any of the older crabs. Besides, what else could he do once we were there?"

After a slight pause, Cracker continued, "Anyway, as far as I know, this area has not been explored by us crabs for a long time. There are many dangers and unknowns down here, as we have already discovered. Although, now that I think about it for a few minutes, maybe some crabs or their friends have been here more recently…if you know what I mean?"

Devin said, "Well, when we get back to the sandcastle, we can get Orion into a lot of trouble, and he deserves it!"

"I'm not so sure," replied Cracker thoughtfully. "As I already said, Orion will obviously just claim he didn't know where the water jets led to. I bet he will even say he just assumed all the jets went to the same place. How could he possibly know where they all went, as Hunter just asked? He will likely claim it was his first time to try them too or something. Since we did not come out with him, he naturally assumed we went elsewhere, but that is not his fault. He might even pretend it was our idea to try those jets. For all we know, Orion might be getting folks to go look for us, claiming he has no idea what happened. I think, once we get back, we need to keep our suspicions to ourselves… maybe watch what happens very carefully going forward."

Hunter added, without looking convinced by Cracker's line of thinking, "Or, as I said before, maybe he really didn't know where they all led, how could he?"

Cracker answered with a quick snap of his claw, with just a bit of anger, "He certainly knew where *he* was going, and that there was only one water jet that went there—his, I am sure of it!" Pausing for a moment to calm down, as if unsure he should say what he was thinking about, Cracker finally spoke again. "Look, guys, Orion is really just a big bully. Since you haven't been here very long, I didn't think this was something to bring up, but you should know. He only cares about what he wants and doesn't really mind if others get hurt to achieve it."

Hunter responded, "Why do you say that? He seemed pretty OK to me."

"He may seem 'OK,' maybe even fun sometimes, but I guarantee you, it's all about him. If you have something he wants, he will take it, or find a way for you to not have it," responded Cracker. "You haven't lived around him for all these years. He's mean to the youngsters in our colony, using his size and strength to take things from them, or make them do what he wants, especially when there are no adults around." Cracker paused. "The fact that he got you in a jet that led you here while he ended up elsewhere should make you suspicious. I'm just saying we should be extra careful. There appears to be more going on right now than I understand."

"You will need to be very careful then, Cracker," said Devin, hearing more in Cracker's short message about Orion than perhaps Cracker intended. "Hunter and I will need to get home at some point, I would think. Once we find our way back to the sandcastle, we will most likely have to leave pretty soon, right, Hunter?"

Hunter just smiled, choosing not to reply directly; he was already thinking to himself once more about the wondrous treasure chest. In his mind's eye, he could see himself opening it up, using the Key he was so confident they would soon find to discover the fabulous treasure inside. Maybe even to keep some of it for himself.

Having rested for a bit while finishing their talk, Devin, Hunter, and Cracker then quickly rebuilt their boat, linking the shells back together in the cloverleaf shape, to resume their journey. Once again, they found themselves floating down the river, looking for a way back to the sandcastle, as well as—maybe even more importantly by now—seeking any hint of the Key to Lafitte's Chest.

After an hour or so of floating along, without much conversation or other activity, the current began to slow noticeably as the river also started to widen a bit, now barely creeping along. The recent encounter with the eel had frightened each of the group more than they would admit out loud, while the discussion about Orion dampened their enthusiasm. Each of the adventurers was resting comfortably in his shell, so lost in his own thoughts, that the trio almost missed noticing they were approaching something unexpected.

Devin, now sitting upright, was yawning with his right arm stretching out away from his body. Looking over his outstretched hand, he focused his eyes a bit, then called out, "Hunter, Cracker, look over that way. What's that, what's that? My eagle eye sees something ahead of us."

"Your what?" asked Cracker.

Hunter responded, laughing so loud (almost giving a little snort) he immediately brought everyone back to good humor, "Devin thinks he has 'eagle eyes,' 'cause he sees things from far away."

"See, I told you, there it is," replied Devin to both of them, continuing to point over the sand.

Quickly beaching their little boat, the crab with the two boys hopped out of their shells, running as fast as they could toward what appeared to be a very, very large shape just lying there in the sand.

Slowing down as they covered the last few feet, they saw what appeared to be an old sea turtle, motionless on the ground. The turtle seemed unable to move, as it was caught tight in some old twisted fishing net. The trio immediately rushed over to the turtle to see if it was still alive.

Cracker was the first to speak in a hushed voice, "Devin, Hunter, this is a great-grandfather turtle, one of the oldest and wisest of all the creatures of the beach. I wonder, how did he end up trapped here?" Turning his full attention to the turtle, Cracker continued reverently, "Mr. Turtle, Mr. Turtle, can you hear me?"

After a few seconds the great big lid of the turtle's right eye slowly opened, while the orb inside turned so that the turtle could see who was now talking to him. In a slow, deep voice the turtle responded, "Well, hello there, young Mr. Crab, what brings you into this dark, desolate, dreary, dank cavern? Hmmm?" Noticing Cracker's human companions, the turtle added with a bit more enthusiasm, "I see you have a couple of Bigs with you as well. This is very curious, very curious indeed."

"My name is Cracker, what's your name?" asked Cracker with a smile.

Devin, before the turtle could answer Cracker, pointed toward Hunter while introducing himself too. "Hi there, Mr. Turtle, my name is Devin. This is my cousin Hunter. What are you doing here?"

Hunter, with his head cocked slightly to his right, smiled shyly while waving his right hand in a quick hello.

The turtle responded in a slow, almost sad voice, "Well now, boys, my name is Sage, and as you can plainly see, I am trapped here in this awful net." Sage paused for a moment, then asked very politely, "I wonder, might there be something you three could do perhaps to help me get out of this predicament?"

Almost immediately all three started asking more questions.

"What happened to you?" inquired Cracker.

"How did you get caught?" asked Devin.

"Do you know where we are?" asked Hunter.

The turtle responded, "Slow down, slow down, boys, one question at a time. Everything you are asking has its own answer, not to mention they are also all related to each other. Tell you what, if you will see what can be done to help me out of this net, I will tell you how I got here. What do you say boys, hmmm?"

Cracker and his two "Big" friends quickly agreed, wanting to hear Sage's story. As they each started looking over the netting more closely, Sage began to tell his tale.

"There was an acquaintance of mine, although I would certainly not say 'friend,' who recently told me of a story he had 'just heard' about a mother turtle whose eggs were in danger from sea snakes. The turtle's nest was, of course, in a 'secret' cavern where the mother had laid her eggs, so that nothing could disturb them while they were waiting to hatch. Unfortunately, the turtle had not known there were sea snakes living nearby, meaning the eggs were likely in grave danger."

At this point, Devin had to ask, "Why were the eggs in danger? Why would snakes bother them?"

"That is an important part of the story, Devin, which I will explain in due time," replied Sage.

"Initially, I had not believed this odd tale about hidden turtle eggs," Sage continued. "I kept asking myself, *How could my acquaintance possibly know about a 'secret' turtle nesting ground? Who would have told him?* Despite my doubts, I found myself returning to the area he indicated on a fairly regular basis, just in case it was possibly true. You see boys, turtles are becoming rarer in these parts, so even though it was not very likely, I needed to be sure.

"One recent afternoon, just around high tide, my acquaintance sought me out with some very disturbing news. He told me that an old and very unfriendly Pelican was sitting on a stump in the water, watching the area where the turtle eggs were supposed to be. Of course, I was still not sure if the whole thing was true or not, but now I would have to make a decision."

At this point Devin interrupted again, "Why exactly did you have to make a decision? Why would the Pelican just watch the place where the eggs were? It doesn't make much sense to me."

"Two most excellent questions, young Devin," answered Sage.

"Let me explain about turtle nests a bit more; I think the answers to both your questions will become clear, once I do. You see, turtles lay their eggs on the shore, burying them in the sand before returning to the water, while the eggs mature and hatch. Since no one is with the eggs, to protect them from predators, they are always hidden in a place where enemies should not be able to find them. This includes sea snakes and Pelicans, both of whom would make a quick meal of them if they could.

"According to the story I was told, this particular turtle nest happened to be in an underground cave, which so happens to be the very cavern we are in right now, in fact. What you might not know is that there are two ways to get into this cave. One entrance comes from the ocean, where this river ends. That side is, of course, covered completely by the sea. The other entrance is from passages underneath the sand dunes, likely the way you three just came from now, I would guess. As almost no one comes here very often from either direction, this should be a terrific spot for a mother turtle; her eggs would be very safe. Once hatched, the young turtles could wade into the water and just swim out to the sea following the current—a perfect nesting place indeed.

"So, you see, boys, when I saw the old Pelican sitting on the stump, intently watching the entrance area, I really had to make a decision… or so I thought. If I believed that there really were turtle eggs in this cave, and they might be in danger, either from the pelican or more likely some of his friends, then I would have to act soon."

Devin asked, "Why would the Pelican want to harm the young turtles, especially if it could not get at them, Mr. Sage?"

"This particular Pelican is no friend to any turtles, Devin. In fact, he would most certainly go out of his way to harm any friend of mine."

Interrupting Sage's story, Hunter now inquired, "But, Mr. Sage, Pelicans can't swim underwater, so how could he hurt the eggs? How could he even get in here?"

"Aren't you both perceptive, my young adventurers," responded Sage, clearly pleased with the questioning. "As I said earlier, it was more likely his friends, the sea snakes, or other creatures that he might send in after the eggs, that I was afraid of. Since he was sitting on the post overlooking the entrance, I suddenly believed the story about the eggs to be true, or at the very least, needed further investigation.

"Once I made that decision, it was time for action. I would need to first find the turtle nest, then, if there were really eggs there, either hide or move them. All that would have to be done before the Pelican's pals could discover what I was doing, as they would surely find and eat the eggs once the pelican gave them the word." The turtle paused. "Of course, that turned out to be the real trick, it seems."

"What do you mean by 'the real trick,' Mr. Sage?" asked Cracker curiously.

Continuing with the tale, Sage answered: "As I had already been told about the turtle eggs, and thinking that the nest might possibly be in danger, all One-Eye had to do to get me to come in here, was to just sit on his post, staring at the cave entrance. In hindsight, it's all too clear now that it really was just a simple trick. Of course, those are usually the best kind, where one's mind does all the work. Unfortunately, I didn't realize it at the time."

Startled, Devin blurted, "Did you just say, 'One-Eye,' Mr. Sage? Why do you call him 'One-Eye'? Is that the pelican with the purple patch over his bad eye? You know, he is the very same Pelican that tried to eat Hunter when we first got to the sandcastle."

Running out of breath, Devin had to pause for a second, giving Sage enough time to respond in his low slow rumble, "Slow down, slow down, young Devin. That is a lot of news for only one breath. Hmmm, One-Eye was after you as well, hmmm. We will have to consider what it might all mean very carefully."

Hunter then asked, trying to return to Sage's much more interesting story, "But he didn't get me, did he, guys? Now, how could you do all that to protect the eggs, Mr. Sage? No disrespect, but turtles are really very slow, aren't they? I mean, how could you possibly move or hide the eggs if they were in real danger, or even defend against snakes?" He was referring to Sage's having to decide if he would move the eggs or not.

"Ahh, Hunter, perhaps you don't know everything there is to know about turtles," replied Sage. "You see, we turtles are truly excellent swimmers. So, while we might be slow and, I grant you, even a bit awkward on land, as I am here now, once we are in the water, turtles are strong, quick, even graceful. The mother turtle would not have buried her eggs too far from the water. Thus, I was very confident that I could swim into the cavern to rescue any eggs that might be hidden here, before the Pelican could alert his friends that there was an active turtle nest to be found in this cave. Besides, with my hard shell and strong jaws, I am more than a match for almost any snake that might show itself. In other words, it was the perfect trap, and I fell for it completely."

"Why was it a trap? What do you mean?" asked a surprised Devin, whose comments were immediately echoed by the other two. By this time, the trio had stopped inspecting the netting holding Sage and were now just listening to his story.

Sage continued on, "You will understand shortly why it was a trap, and how it was so successful, as I finish my tale. But before I do, to answer your last question, might you all be slightly interested in where we are now? Hmmm?" Cracker immediately spoke up. "Yes sir, we are very interested. In fact, I hate to admit it, but I have gotten quite lost down here. We thought it might be possible to find our way back home by following the underground river to the sea. Didn't you say earlier you knew how to get out by following the river to its end?"

Understanding what had likely happened, even as the three adventurers did not, Sage described their location, "Cracker, you are very wise for one so young, and you made a good decision to follow this river downstream. Your elders would be proud. Yes, at the far end of this cavern, directly behind me, opposite from the direction of the dunes, continues the river toward it's underground entrance where the sea enters this place. Looking at it from your point of view, that is where the river ends, emptying into the ocean where you can then find your way home. But first things first, let me finish explaining my own current predicament."

Sage continued, "Faced with the option of potentially saving soon-to-hatch turtle eggs or letting One-Eye's pals eat them, I chose to try to save any eggs that might be in here. Even if there were no eggs to be discovered, as I told you Hunter, I never considered myself to be in any real danger from the creatures that live here.

"Shortly after the last high tide, I swam into the seaside entrance to this cavern and followed the underground river from the ocean into this cave. Swimming against the river's current can be a bit tiring, but as I said, turtles are excellent swimmers. Every so often, I would leave the river to look for some sign of a turtle nest, which of course I did not find, since there was never one to begin with. Not finding any eggs, I came farther and farther up the river until I arrived here, still searching for the turtle nest. Of course, I was becoming a bit frustrated as well as a bit tired, but still determined to complete what I set out to do.

"You have likely not noticed that farther back behind me, away from the river, there is a small opening in the cave wall. It does not appear to be much, just a black splotch from here, but I spotted it as I crawled over the sand thinking to myself, *This would really be a great place for a turtle to hide her eggs.* I also decided that if I didn't find any back there, then I would turn around and leave. It was highly unlikely that a mother turtle would go any farther up river and pass up such a terrific spot like this one."

Pausing to get his breath, Sage let out a great sigh while the boys and crab all looked for the opening Sage was talking about.

Hunter pointed his right hand over Sage's head. "I see it, Mr. Sage, that dark splotch way over there!"

Sage replied, "That's right, Hunter. Do the rest of you see where he is pointing?"

"We do," answered both Cracker and Devin.

"Good," Sage said, "now you can see where I had to crawl to, looking for the eggs. Of course, as I already told you, there were no eggs to be found, but unfortunately there was something else over there."

Devin immediately asked, "What was it? Tell us."

Continuing with his story, Sage rumbled, "As I got closer to the rocky cave, it was so dark that I could not see inside it at all. I just slowly kept moving forward, hoping for some sign that another turtle had been here recently. I barely felt the netting that I was pushing against until I got all the way inside that opening, then the top of the wall seemed to just fall down on me, including the rest of this net."

Cracker spoke up. "What did you do then, did it hurt?"

"No, Cracker," answered Sage, "fortunately, it did not. The sandy covering on the roof was very thin, crumbling back into loose sand as it collapsed. Hitting the back of my shell, it just bounced off me for the most part. Unfortunately, this net that is now on me, also fell with the roof, completely covering me within it. Once all the sand and dust finally settled, I realized that no turtle had been here in a long time, meaning there were also no eggs to be found. But how was I to get rid of this net?"

"So, what then, Sage, what then?" asked Devin, dropping the *Mr.* (from *Mr. Sage*) in his excitement to hear the ending of the story.

"Well, boys, as you can imagine, by this time I was pretty tired of the whole thing, so I just tried to crawl back to the river, figuring that the netting would just fall off along the way, or at the very worst, I could get out of it once back in the water. Of course, by now you have realized that I was not able to return to the river." With a deep breath Sage finished, "This old netting is still fairly strong, plus it is somehow hooked on a rock so that I cannot escape. Now I am stuck here, very tired with no way out, unless you three can help me escape this most unfortunate situation."

Devin spoke up again. "Mr. Sage, why do you think this was meant for you? Who was behind it, do you know?"

"Those are very important questions, Devin, perhaps even more important now that I have met the three of you down here," responded Sage. "I was sure the trap was just for me, although now I think it is also being used on you, just for convenience I would guess, but maybe not."

"Why would you say that?" asked Devin.

"Once I realized that I was likely trapped here for quite a while, and being unable to move about, I have had plenty of time to think about what actually happened. From my point of view, this trap had to involve my acquaintance, although I am not sure he knows he was involved, maybe just passing on bad information. One-Eye the Pelican is likely behind it all, knowing the idea had already been planted in my mind, just waiting for the right day to set things in motion. I suspect he had inside help, though, to make it work, someone else who lives here, near the water. Someone who knew about the cave back there as well as the netting buried in the sand. In other words, someone who has been here before."

Turning an eye toward Cracker, Sage concluded, "It was very likely a crab, a snake, or some other creature of the sands who might have previously travelled along this river, waiting for me (or someone) to come in and spring the trap. This creature was either able to set up the rocks to bring down the net when its prey got to this spot, or at least knew of the netting, as it may have been here for a long time, a trap set long ago for another purpose. While the netting is clearly strong, it also appears very old. It could have been washed ashore during a major storm, sometime long ago."

Focusing directly on all three youngsters, Sage asked them again, "Do you think you can find some way to help me out of this awful trap?"

As Sage's story was now finished, the three adventurers resumed their inspection of the netting, this time very carefully examining the entire net that was pinning Sage to the ground, looking for any flaws to cut or other way to untie it. They each walked all the way around Sage. Cracker even crawled on top of his shell to see how strong the netting was, pulling and testing it on occasion, then finally concluding that it was hopelessly anchored to a large rock coming up from the sand. The trio would need some additional help if they were to free him.

Cracker, finally responding for all of them, said, "Of course we will help you, Mr. Turtle…if we can." Both Hunter and Devin were nodding their heads in agreement. "Do you have any ideas, Hunter, Devin?"

Hunter replied immediately, "We could try to get back to the sandcastle, to bring back some help. The exit from this cave is up ahead according to Mr. Sage. We could get back to your home, then bring back a rescue team. We don't have any real way to cut through this heavy netting that I know of. It appears very tough, and I can't find any weak spots. What do you think, Cracker?"

"I don't know how long that might take us. Besides, Mr. Sage might not survive here for too much longer without food or water. Plus, getting back here with help might not be easy or quick, given what we have gone through ourselves just to get here," answered Cracker as he held on to the netting with his small pincer. "On the other hand, as you say, I don't see how we can cut through this stuff without any additional help either. We don't have anything sharp enough to get through this net. You may be right, Hunter. We may have to go find some help."

Devin finally entered this part of the conversation after a great deal of thinking, Cracker's "sharp enough" comment triggering a new train of thought. "Mr. Sage, if we get you out of the net, will you be able to help us get back to the sandcastle, where Cracker lives?"

"Yes, I will," answered the turtle, "and of course, I will help you all get away from this cavern…back out to the ocean. Not such an easy task as you would soon find out. You see, once the river makes its final approach to the sea, you will have to go underwater for quite a distance before you can get to the sea's surface by the old post. If I'm not mistaken in my guess, I suspect you three were sent here without knowing the danger as well, were you not?"

All the adventurers looked at each other in surprise.

Cracker spoke for all of them. "Why yes, how did you know that? We were talked into taking the water jets that brought us here as part of a dare. I just don't see how us being here would help him, as we might be able to rescue you. That does not make any sense."

Hunter added, "Since we are all talking about Orion, I agree with Cracker. I don't see why he would send us down here if we might then help Sage. He would have known we might be able to help out, especially if he set up the trap for One-Eye. Maybe he just picked the wrong water jet, and we got lucky that we are now here, able to help Mr. Sage out."

"Or perhaps he didn't think any of us would make it this far? Or we might go the other direction, or any number of things, who knows? There are a lot of possibilities," finished Devin.

The turtle answered, "I do not know this Orion, so I cannot guess at what he was thinking, but I would guess you are all down here for a reason. Maybe not right here with me, but certainly under the dunes. It seems to be a pretty big coincidence that two Bigs would end up in these caverns with no way out, while I have a similar problem. My guess is that whoever sent you down here wanted the same thing to happen to you as would happen to me—to take care of all of us at the same time."

Devin asked, "But if you never knew Orion, then how could he know you were here and make the connection? I agree with Hunter, something does not make sense."

"Maybe it was not Orion who planned all this. It is possible he only is playing a part, that there are others involved, others who might be telling him what to do," suggested the turtle. "Either way, we need to escape from this chamber soon, before I am too tired to carry us all to safety."

Cracker looked at his friends. "We have to do something, guys. Do we try to get help for Sage or what?"

As they were all talking, Devin's thoughts suddenly shifted back to the last comments the Questions had made to him, when he first arrived at the sandcastle. *Before you are through, Devin, remember to help others in need, as Cracker has already helped you.*

Focusing intently on the problem at hand, the Questions' words inspiring him with a new clarity and purpose, Devin replied with conviction, "No! We have to help Sage now. Besides I think I know just how we can do it!" With everyone's eyes turned toward him, Devin continued with growing enthusiasm as his idea took shape, "We can't leave Sage here alone, or he could die, plus we may not be able to get through to the sea on our own, right? Working together is the best way to get us all out of this. We help Sage, then he will help us. That's the way it should be. Remember what the Questions told me: *For three will not always be as good as four?* That has to mean we should help Sage, so he can help us. Don't you think?"

Cracker agreed. "What you say makes sense, Devin, but what can we do with just these three shells and some old netting?" Pointing to the rope holding Sage down, he finished, "We still don't have anything we can use to cut something this thick."

Explaining his plan, Devin answered, "Listen, what if we go back up the river to where those sharp stalactites almost hit the water, you know the 'mouth' in the river? Those rocks looked really, really sharp to me. I'm sure if we can just break off a few, then bring them back here, we could use their edges to cut through this netting…at least enough to get Sage out, I would guess. When we were going through the tunnel the first time, one of those rocks broke off and fell right in front of me; I can clearly remember how much it looked like a sharp knife! I think we can use those rocks to cut this net. Well, what do you think of that?"

Cracker looked quickly at Hunter, then with a big smile turned to Devin. "That is a great idea. You are right, those rocks were so sharp they can cut through any net, but how will we break them off?"

"I'm not sure, Cracker. But we will figure it out, I know we will."

"Hey, guys, what about that eel? What if he wakes up while we are doing it?" asked Hunter.

"Eel, what eel? What spiky rocks are you talking about?" inquired Sage, growing ever more curious about this new story he was hearing.

Cracker told Sage about the journey they had just come through to get here. That there was a stretch of the river farther back that tunneled through the wall at the back end of this cave. Both sides, where the river entered and exited the rock, had the appearance of scary "serpent mouths" due to the way the rocks were formed, especially those looking like giant fangs.

In addition to the strange openings, there were a number of rocks coming down from the roof, right at the entrance to the passage, that appeared to be extremely sharp. Everyone agreed the rocks were sharp enough that they could be used to free Sage from the netting he was trapped in. The only potential problem seemed to be the eel, who was sleeping at the river's bottom when they came through the first time. If he was awake now, or if they accidentally woke him trying to get the rocks, that could bring real trouble.

Sage pondered this for a minute, finally saying, "Well, at least I know there really are sea snakes nearby, that part of my acquaintance's tale was true." Pausing for a moment, Sage continued, "It would be very brave of you three to do this for me. I thank you. Some advice about sea snakes—never forget, boys—they can be extremely dangerous, so you will need to be very, very careful.

"I have one other thought regarding the eels that live in these parts that might be of some value to you three. You see, eels always want to collect and guard things, including their homes. It's part of an eel's nature, so beware, as any sea serpent will certainly attack, if he thinks you are after something that belongs to him. On the other hand, the eel could just as easily stay near its lair, if there is no real threat to its hoard. Keep a sharp lookout while you are there. Cracker is right, an upset eel is very dangerous and would likely cause some serious problems for you."

It was quickly agreed then; the trio would follow Devin's plan to get the cutting tools they needed to rescue Sage.

"Good luck! Stay away from that eel if you can!" encouraged Sage, his voice filled with renewed hope as the adventurers headed back up the river, now carrying their shells with them.

Walking along the sandy edge of the river was clearly the fastest way to return to the cave's mouth. Trying to row upstream, against the direction of the river's flow, would take too long as they didn't have any real paddles besides their arms and pincers. As the trio looked back, they could just barely see Sage sitting there, motionless in the netting. Waving their hands and pincers in a quick goodbye as a promise to shortly return, the trio turned back toward their goal and were quickly gone.

CHAPTER 8

THE KEY

Sea Snakes

Natural enemies of the Sea Turtles, Sea Snakes, often called eels, can usually be found whenever events involving the Rainbow Objects are occurring in or near the water. Snakes will often try to attack turtles. However, they are rarely successful unless the turtle is very young, still in its egg, or very old.

CRAB CHRONICLES

Walking briskly, with real determination and purpose, the band of rescuers headed toward the cave opening where they would soon be able to reach the sharp rocks—no longer able to see any sign of the great turtle. Hunter started to ask more detailed questions about their current plan. "Guys, just how will we get those sharp rocks that we need to free Mr. Sage?"

"I don't know, Hunter, we will likely need to see things up close to decide the best way to get at the sharpest rocks," answered Cracker, who then added after a pause, "along with maybe, having a little bit of luck."

"Maybe, just maybe, we can use our shells," Devin suggested in a soft voice, as he continued thinking about the problem.

Hunter quickly followed up with, "What do you mean, Devin?"

Answering both his friends, Devin said, "Look, guys, I've been thinking—I mean, clearly some of those rocks are already breaking away from the roof, maybe even with cracks near their base. A few of the looser ones fell off when our shells ran into them coming through the tunnel the first time, remember? I'm pretty sure we were able to do that because there are natural cracks in those rock formations already. Make sense? My thinking is this: if there is a stalactite close to the opening, where we can see it or grab it, that has a crack near its base—and I would guess at least a few of them have such cracks, right? If that's the case, we might be able to wedge one of our shells into that crack, then use its leverage to help break the rock off. We just have to hope that some of those rocks are likely to be ready to fall off anyway, meaning our job will really be to find the right ones, then get 'em." Snapping his fingers, Devin concluded with a smile, "Should be a snap."

Both Cracker and Hunter thought this was a really good idea—probably the only plan that made sense given the few things they had to work with. Now they all had something positive to think about. This made everyone feel better as they headed back toward the cave's entrance. After a time, as they began to draw nearer to their destination, the cave narrowed back down while also once again getting darker—seemingly feeling colder as well—where the river came out of the stone wall, almost forcing their thoughts back toward the evil looking fangs and teeth at the entrance to the cavern.

As they got closer and closer to the tunnel, those fang-like rocks once more dominating their vision, the trio could not help but think again about the slumbering eel. Devin even thought that he could already see the eel's horrible sickly yellow eyes, suddenly opening up to stare right at him.

"Shhhhh," whispered Cracker to everyone as they got to their destination. "Let's get ready. Try not to wake up or disturb the eel if you don't have to. Hopefully he will just stay near the entrance to his lair."

"Won't he hear us anyway?" asked Hunter in a hushed voice, "especially when we start breaking the stalactites loose? Besides, he was laying farther in, under the tunnel. If Mr. Sage was right, maybe the eel will just hang out by his cave, guarding whatever junk he has down there."

"Yes, it's possible he might think the rocks are falling on their own, as they surely do every so often," replied Cracker. "We might need any extra time…just to get away. Besides, if the eel wakes up, maybe it will be as you say, Hunter. He will worry about his own cave first. Especially if he doesn't see us as a direct threat, he will stay near his lair and not bother us at all."

Both boys nodded their heads in agreement. Everyone tried to make themselves feel better about what they were about to do, wishing away any possible conflicts with the sea snake if they could.

Finishing up their planning in hushed tones, the team decided that the best way to proceed was to first get as close to the cave opening as they possibly could—without actually getting into the water. Once there, Devin, standing on solid ground, would be one anchor for a shell with some netting tied to it. Cracker would go into the water with a second piece of netting to act as another anchor. By pulling the netting in both directions, they would stabilize the floating shell as best they could for Hunter. Cracker would be standing or swimming underwater, so he could also keep watch for the slumbering eel, just to make sure things were OK.

This setup would allow Hunter—who everyone agreed had the best balance on shells after his performance on the clamming hill—to focus his attention on knocking out some of the sharper rocks. Devin and Cracker would focus on providing as much stability as they could to the shell he was standing on, by keeping the ropes as tight as possible while pulling in opposite directions. Cracker, being in the river already, would also be in position to retrieve any of the rocks that fell into the water, once Hunter had knocked them down.

The real work of breaking off the right stalactites was Hunter's job. He would stand up on his clamshell, looking for any rock that he thought they could use as a knife, sword, or cutting tool. Once he found a candidate that looked good, Hunter would try to knock it down by hand or hit it using one of the other shells, as Devin suggested, depending on the situation. Should the rock fall into the water, Cracker could then go retrieve it. If necessary, Hunter could even use one of the other shells as a wedge, assuming there was a crack big enough, to help break loose a rock. Lastly, Hunter was given some extra netting that could be used as rope—in case he thought he could tie it around one of the rocks and simply pull it free.

The little group all believed they had thought through the likeliest possibilities. As long as a rock or two had some natural cracks already, they should be able to retrieve something that would help cut through Sage's netting. It was certainly the best plan the team could come up with in the short time they had, especially without any other tools to use.

As the trio returned to the point where the river emerged from the rock wall, they began to implement their plan. With Devin anchored firmly on a tiny strip of sand, Cracker assumed his position in the river, to see how well they could control the movement of Hunter's shell. Hunter balanced himself on the edge of his clamshell, letting Cracker pull him toward the razor-sharp stalactites. Devin, switching his gaze from Hunter balancing on the shell to the waterline and back again, was carefully watching things from his position on shore. As he switched focal points the third time, he thought for just an instant that he saw a slight glint of sickly yellow, deep under the water. After blinking a few times, trying to tightly focus his gaze below the waterline, he did not see the yellow glint again.

Cracker surfaced one time, whispering to Hunter, "I can just barely make out the eel, back in the passageway below. He seems to be simply lying there, hopefully still sleeping. So, we are good to go. Let's get this over with as fast as we can."

Hunter nodded his understanding to Cracker, then turned to give Devin a thumbs up that he was ready to begin.

They did not have to move Hunter very far, as the stalactites (reminding the trio of hungry teeth even more this time) came right down, almost to the water's edge, where the river exited the wall of rock. Hunter simply stopped his shell next to the nearest of the sharp rocks at the mouth of the water's egress, looking around to see which one he should try to bring down first.

He spied a stalactite just to his left that appeared to be shaped like a Pirate's cutlass. It was curved just slightly, with a nice sharp edge on one side. In addition, there were two notches in the rock, a small one beneath a larger one. It looked possible to Hunter that this rock could be broken off near the larger notch, then he could hold the rock by its smaller notch, just like a Pirate would hold his sword in a fight.

Deciding this was the perfect rock to start with, he easily maneuvered near the rock by pulling on other stalactites, until he got exactly where he wanted to. Taking Devin's shell, Hunter slowly pushed its edge directly into the larger notch, to use the shell as a wedge. To his great delight, the stalactite snapped off almost immediately, without any effort on Hunter's part whatsoever, plunging straight down into the water below—exactly as the group had hoped would happen.

Cracker, under the water already, saw the rock plunge into the river. He quickly grabbed it, immediately taking the piece back to Devin on the shore.

Devin inspected the rock fragment carefully. It looked and fit like a short sword in his hand, as the smaller notch turned out to be very smooth, making holding onto it almost natural. After a moment, he whispered encouragingly to both Cracker and Hunter, "This is perfect, you guys. It will cut that netting, I'm sure it will!"

While not really needing any more rocks, Hunter was having such a good time balancing on the shell (plus, the first one was so easy to get), that he convinced the other two that they each needed something to cut Sage's netting. It would go much faster with more than one sharp rock, he told them.

Cracker agreed somewhat reluctantly, only because it appeared the eel below had not reacted to their first attempt, so either it did not feel threatened or might even be asleep. He slipped back into the water with Hunter's shell in tow. When Cracker got back to the spot they started from the last time, he checked on the eel once again—just to be sure. Cracker saw the eel's dark shape still lying there, seemingly unaware or uncaring of what was going on above him. Going back to the water's surface, he let Hunter know all was well, so they began again.

For a second time, Hunter was able to easily find a suitable rock. It too was curved slightly, like a sword. Just as quickly as before, Hunter brought it down for Cracker to retrieve. Once again, Cracker took the rock over to Devin, noticing while he did that this particular rock broke off in such a way that it fit his small pincer almost perfectly; he could swing it like a real weapon. "This one will work fine for me, Devin," Cracker quietly reported, as he slipped back into the water, one last time.

Collecting the first two rocks—or "swords" as the boys now thought of them—had apparently not brought about any reaction from the eel. This caused the trio's confidence level (perhaps overconfidence) to grow rapidly. Hunter was now feeling so sure of his skill, that for the third and final attempt, he decided to try to get one of the extra-large fangs that guarded the mouth entrance, for himself. As Hunter and Cracker maneuvered Hunter's shell so he could get near the fang, Devin thought, for just a split second, that the glimmer of sickly yellow below them in the water had returned! Again, it quickly disappeared, but not quite as fast as before.

Not wanting to sound scared, but suddenly becoming more than a little nervous, and really wanting to leave, Devin asked, "Guys, can't we leave now? We have two really sharp rocks to cut the nets with, which should be enough to help Sage. Let's get back to him."

Hunter really wanted to get the large fang for his own. *A treasure hunter needs a good sword after all.* "Don't worry, Devin, just let me get this big one here, then each of us can have a tool for cutting the netting. It won't take me but another second."

Still very nervous, Devin didn't answer. He just smiled while moving his attention between the dark water below and Hunter, who was already using his shell to bring down the piece of stalactite he was after. Unfortunately for the little group, this larger fang was not as easy to break off as the first two had been.

Hunter tried a few different ways to break it off. First, he just pushed and pulled, hoping that the rock was ready to fall on its own, as the others had been. When this did not work, Hunter looked for a notch or other weak area that he could wedge his shell into, gain some extra leverage, then snap it off by pushing on the shell. While he was doing this, his friends were becoming more and more anxious.

"C'mon, Hunter, we have what we need. Let's get out of here," whispered Devin again.

Cracker came to the surface too, asking with even more nervousness in his voice, "Hunter, can't we go, please? That eel won't stay calm much longer. I even thought I saw some movement down there just now. We really need to leave."

Swinging his floating shell around to face the other side of the rock, Hunter readied himself for one last attempt to break off the tip. On this side of the stalactite, there was a fairly large notch in the rock that Hunter thought, at first glance, he could wedge a shell into, to give him the extra leverage he needed to break it off. Setting himself up to do exactly that, he spied something odd that made him hesitate before jamming the shell into the rock.

Inside the notch, but clearly not made of rock, appeared to be another object that had somehow been wedged even farther back into the opening, a few inches up from the tip, which appeared to be a couple of feet from the boy's current point of view, as they were still only inches tall themselves.

"Hey, guys," Hunter whispered much too loudly as he was growing more excited, "look, look, there is something else in here, not just this rock. I can't tell exactly what it is. Something metallic, I think. Could be gold or some other metal, but it's definitely not rock. We need to try and get it. Maybe it was left by Pirates!"

"What is it, Hunter?" asked Devin quietly. "Can you tell? Make it quick, OK?"

Examining the area as best he could, given his wobbly stance on the floating shell, Hunter answered, "It looks like something was put here, who knows when, and the rock has maybe grown around it over time. Whatever it is, it appears to be attached to something else, a different kind of rock maybe. It looks different than this brown rock that has grown over it, but I can't tell what it is. We will have to break the tip off to see it." Hunter examined things in more detail for a few seconds. "The only problem is, the rock here seems really hard, so it's going to take some real strength to break it off."

Pausing for a moment to get his breath while looking a bit more closely, Hunter added in a voice growing in excitement, "It's really difficult to see clearly, but I know this is something important, I just feel it! Maybe, just maybe, it's the Key we are looking for!" Calming down a bit, he finished, "Whatever it is, there is a lot of rock that has grown around this thing. I think maybe, just maybe, if we spend a little more time, I can break it out."

Ignoring all risk, as he was now a real "treasure hunter," Hunter took the other shell in both hands while balancing himself just right on his own shell. This allowed Hunter to twist his body in such a way that he could then spin back quickly toward the notch, hammering it with extra force. Without any other thought, Hunter spun, slamming his shell's edge straight into the rock, right below where the mysterious item was wedged. The noise this made exploded immediately throughout the cavern.

Devin yelled, "Hunter, Hunter, stop it! You are making too much noise and will wake up the eel!"

Hunter quickly repeated his efforts two more times, trying to get the stalactite to snap off. To his dismay, the rock would not break after repeatedly being smashed by the shell. Still not budging after the third strike, Hunter finally gave up and stopped to rest.

Cracker, who had been waiting under the water, suddenly shot up, shaking his head while directing a semi-disgusted look right at Hunter. "Guys, I can't see the eel anywhere. That pounding you were doing was so loud that when I looked up to see what was going on, the eel was gone! Given how loud you were, he had to hear it. I don't think he went back into his cave either. We need to leave, and I mean, right now!"

For a few seconds, no one did anything except hold their breath, half expecting the eel to come swimming up from the depths right at them. Cracker bobbing in the water, Hunter just standing motionless on his shell, and Devin watching from his perch on the shore, each one simply waiting— each one having a different vision of the same awful ending— the eel suddenly appearing in the water, its jaws and teeth opening and closing, then snapping shut about them!

After what seemed an eternity, *without* an appearance by the sea snake, Devin let out his breath with an audible "whoo." Cracker, with a huge smile of relief on his face, quickly returned, "Devin, Hunter, it's OK, I think. Besides, we did exactly what we came to do. We did it!" Pointing back at Devin, he added, "See, there are two of the rocks we came for, both very sharp. Now we can go cut Sage's net. Plus, if you notice they are both shaped like swords. So we can be Pirates too! There will be another time to come back to work on the treasure." He shifted his pincer to point at the large rock still attached to the cavern roof.

The word *treasure* brought vivid images of Pirates and their plunder back to Hunter. He did not want to leave, but had no choice as Devin was already pulling hard on the rope to bring him back to shore. Hunter settled back into his shell, letting Devin and Cracker bring him in, so they could head back down the river toward Sage.

Already dreaming about the potential treasure, even of being a Pirate himself, Hunter was still thinking that it would be so cool to go back to Sage with three "swords," one for each of them. It would be even better if they had real Pirate treasure in addition to those swords.

Both Cracker and Devin laughed, seeing Hunter relaxing in his shell, without a care in the world, as he returned to shore, quickly restoring everyone's good cheer. Once back, Cracker grabbed the two rock-swords off the sand, saying, "Here, Devin, you take this 'sword.' I think it fits you better than me." After giving one to Devin, Cracker then gave the second sword to Hunter, who immediately stood up on his shell to practice swinging the sword while Cracker connected the shells back together, remaking their little boat.

Even though there was no apparent activity anywhere, other than the trio getting ready to leave, the cavern suddenly seemed to take on a darker mood. It was as if the unnatural breaking of the rocks with the loud banging that had disturbed the cavern for the first time in many a year, creating an expectation on both the river and in the air. The entire cavern seemed tense, alert, just waiting for something, anything to happen.

Both Devin and Cracker recognized the change taking place, as they both quickly readied themselves to leave. Devin spoke up. "Can we go rescue Sage now, guys? Let's leave this place. I think we have worn out our welcome here."

"I agree," Cracker quickly answered, "it's time to move on."

Hunter was still not concerned, as he was happily swinging his sword, acting like a Pirate and dreaming about hidden treasure. He merely smiled while nodding his head a bit. "Sure, let's get going. Sage is waiting and we have what we came for."

Their boat now put back together, the two boys ready with swords in hand, Cracker asked without expecting an answer, "Ready, Devin, ready Hunter?" Without pausing, Cracker continued quietly, "OK then, let's go." The boys got into their shells, while Cracker pushed off from the shore and hopped into the little boat. As they began to float with the river's current, everyone settled back down into their shells, letting out a silent sigh of relief. As Hunter had just said, they had what they came for.

Relaxing in his shell while dangling both his wrists and feet over the edge, Hunter looked back toward the cave opening where he had just been working. Clearly seeing the entire entrance, he said, "You know, guys, those rocks still look just like a giant snake's mouth, don't you think?" Both Devin and Cracker, now a little more relaxed as they floated away, turned their gazes back to the cave entrance, including toward the fangs marking the front of it.

Focusing his attention on the rock formation, Devin thought that somehow the snakehead looked even more sinister this time. The *snakes teeth* appeared ready to bite down on them, if that was possible. Some water must have splashed back up onto the rocks during Hunter's efforts to break off the largest one. Both were now glistening, water falling slowly back into the river, almost as if snake's venom was dripping off of those fangs.

Impossibly, as they watched, the entire snakehead seemed to be growing darker, angrier—yet also more alive. While Devin stared at it, the head appeared to focus an eyeless gaze on him in some way as if its attention was now firmly on the boys, almost hypnotically. Even the background noise of the river emptying from the mouth seemed to have changed from a flowing stream into a sibilant hissing, like a snake's voice calling out to them. All three of the travelers' attention was now completely consumed by the riveting image of the eerie snakehead. Devin opened his mouth, trying to point out this strangeness to the others, to see if they felt it too. Instead of a boy's questioning voice, all any of them heard was…

"ROOAAAARRR!"

With no warning at all there was suddenly an explosion in the river. But it was in front of them! All three adventurers were caught looking the wrong way—back toward the cave. Immediately flipping around in their shells to see what was now happening in the water, they were just in time to watch the slowly moving river become an exploding geyser. The eel had burst forth from the water with almost its entire body breaking the surface, then crashed back down directly in front of them, creating a huge splash. Pointing its black head at the floating shells, aiming itself like the tip of a flying arrow, the sea snake came rushing directly at them.

Mouth open, razor sharp fangs in front of two rows of clearly showing jagged white teeth, the eel's slimy black body wriggled wildly, working the water while shooting its head straight toward the adventurers. The scariest thing about the eel wasn't its open mouth, rows of extra sharp teeth, or crazily flickering tongue; rather, it was those dreadful beady black utterly lifeless eyes. The eel's eyes also had a sickly yellow glow about them, as if something diseased lived behind those black orbs and could not quite be contained. Each ebony eyeball also had a few streaks of red shooting out from an even blacker blot located right in the center. This blot appeared devoid of life, its center able to suck the spirit away from anything that gazed upon it directly.

Those eyes, along with the rest of the snake, were now aimed directly at the floating shells, as the eel came straight at them, looking to end this most unwelcome intrusion into its territory.

Hitting the middle of the three netting-connected shells head-on, the eel knocked each of the adventurers out of their makeshift boat, straight into the water. The boys and Cracker reacted instantly. They were so surprised, without any time to show fear or hesitation—they just reacted.

Devin and Hunter both immediately grabbed for their shells, to use as protection. Holding them upright, half in half out of the water, they formed a shield wall against the snake's next attack. Placing the shields directly between themselves and the wriggling eel, who was already turning around to come at them again, the boys tried to swim to shore while also keeping their shells held somewhat together. As luck would have it, the boys' shells' edges were still loosely connected to each other by some of the netting that hadn't been ripped apart during the eel's initial assault. Cracker grabbed his own shell, which was also fortunately still linked to Hunter's by a longer strand of netting. Pulling as hard as he could, Cracker began to bring the string of shells, along with the two boys, back toward the nearby shore, attempting an escape.

But, as fast as they reacted, the black eel was even faster. The adventurers were not making shore before the eel would be able to renew its attack. Swimming once again directly at the two upright shells with its open mouth, the eel slammed into the boys' shell-wall head on! Upon impact, the netting holding the shells together broke completely apart, meaning Hunter's and Devin's shell-wall was now split in two. Each boy went with his own shell in different directions. Since their main defense no longer existed, the eel would be able to get at them so much easier. While this was clearly a big problem, the hit by the slimy eel also pushed the entire group back, closer to the shore—much faster than Cracker had been able to pull them—getting everyone nearer to the sand, and hopefully an escape.

Not hesitating for an instant, the eel continued its assault by wriggling its slick body in between the boys' now split-apart shells while simultaneously snapping its open jaws at the boys' kicking legs. The eel just missed biting off Hunter's left foot with its first bite, then immediately turned its mouth the other way, to snap at one of Devin's thrashing legs.

As the sea snake prepared to bite down on its enemy's foot, from out of nowhere came Cracker's big pincer, crashing down hard on the eel's nose. Reacting with anger, surprise, and some real pain, the black eel surged upward, carrying everyone with it in a tangle of torn netting, shells, boys, and crab! Both Hunter and Cracker, on the eel's left side, closest to the sandy beach, were thrown completely out of the water, onto the shoreline of the cavern, onto the relative safety of the sand.

Devin was on the opposite side of the surging eel, closest to middle of the river. Rather than flipping back onto the sand with Hunter and Cracker, Devin shot straight up, completely out of the water, as a result of the eel's angry attack. Anticipating another assault and applying awesomely amazing aerial acrobatics, Devin managed to twist his body in such a way to actually land right back inside of his shell, which was now just bobbing alone in the water, where the eel could easily attack him again. Quickly grabbing some of the loose netting floating in the water, Devin tried to throw it toward Hunter and Cracker, hoping that they could help pull him to shore before the next attack began.

It was not to be of course; the eel was simply too fast. Just as Devin threw the netting, while shouting to his friends for help, the eel made one last rush at the floating shell. Instead of striking at Devin from the surface, the eel dove back down into the water, attacking from below. Coming up directly beneath Devin, the eel hit the shell squarely with its head. The impact was so great, the nasty snake knocked Devin— along with his protective shell—high up out of the water.

To Cracker and Hunter, both watching with eyes wide in horror, time began to crawl, as if they were seeing things in slow motion. Witnessing Devin's flying shell spin sideways, the two companions could do nothing as Devin and his shell slowly separated. Soon there was nothing but empty space between the boy and the snake.

Tumbling over and over in the air, Devin started his return to the water, where the eel was now waiting anxiously, directly underneath him, with its dripping fangs and sharp teeth on full display, glistening with anticipation! Looking down toward the water at the snake's head, Devin could see straight into those evil, blank, lifeless eyes, whose black centers seemed to whisper silently to him, *This is the end*.

"Ahhhhhhh!" Devin's scream cut through the heavy air as he shut both eyelids to avoid watching his own doom. Tucking his body into a cannonball, Devin waited, for what seemed a very long time, to feel the first cuts from those sharp teeth, fearing the eel's awful jaws would surely close around him.

Surprisingly, the next thing Devin felt was not some horrible wound from those vicious fangs, but rather a painful jolt on his rear end as he came crashing back down onto one of the trio's clamshells. The shell naturally then smashed into the eel, hitting the snake's snout just as its jaws were snapping shut, driving the serpent back down into the water once more.

Opening his eyes quickly, Devin saw Hunter leaning as far out over the stream's edge as he could. Hunter was holding his shell (now floating on the water with Devin in it) with his right outstretched hand, while Hunter's left hand was being held on to by Cracker. This way Hunter could help Devin while not falling back into the dangerous river himself. It was pure instinct that allowed Hunter to quickly push his shell between the sea snake and Devin, knocking the snake back into the water as Devin came crashing down on top of him.

Immediately pulling his shell, along with Devin, out of the river, Hunter and Cracker found themselves suddenly and surprisingly safe from the dreadful sea snake. Looking back into the water, all three searched for any sign of the eel; however, it could no longer be seen, as if it simply disappeared.

Devin, still trembling from his battle with the snake, immediately rolled out of the shell he was in, ending face up on the sand next to the river. Meanwhile, Hunter was walking aimlessly around on the sand, too tired from hauling Devin out of the water to move very far from the river's edge. Cracker, understanding that they were all still in serious trouble, was trying to yell that they needed to move away from the river, to get away from the danger, but the others did not pay any immediate attention. They were just too drained and dazed from all the recent action.

Taking matters into his own claws, Cracker went over to both boys, grabbing each of them by an arm with one of his pincers. He had to pinch each of them, causing a slight pain, to bring the boys' attention back to what was going on around them. The press of Cracker's claw brought both Devin and Hunter to attention. Cracker tried once again to get them to move away from the edge of the shore. Smiling, Devin slowly sat up as Hunter leaned over to help him stand when their little world exploded into noise and chaos once more.

Shooting straight up out of the river came the nasty and clearly very angry eel. Spraying water everywhere, the sea snake somehow managed to fly over the top of the boys, landing on the shore behind the trio. With jaws snapping wildly, the eel swung around to look for its enemies. Seeing one of the boys just sitting on the sand, the it aimed its head and fangs right at him. With a huge whip of its tail, the eel surged suddenly straight at a helpless Devin.

For the second time in less than a few minutes, Devin found himself staring at those wicked-looking fangs, thinking that some part of him was about to feel their bite. And for the second time in less than a few minutes, Hunter's clamshell came between him and the attacking sea snake.

With surprising speed, Hunter had instinctively recognized what the eel was about to do. Quickly spinning around while picking up his shell, Hunter was able to stick the shield between Devin and the eel, just in time to absorb the blow. The impact of the eel's head hitting the shell was so hard that Devin and Hunter were both sent rolling backward, almost back into the water. Hunter's shell landed right on top of Devin; the tremendous impact had knocked it completely out of Hunter's grasp. While the powerful force from the contact had hurt the boys, its power was so great that even the snake was temporarily dazed. It would take a couple of seconds for the eel to regain its focus, shake off the impact, then start again toward its prey.

Those few seconds made all the difference in this battle. Cracker, who was holding on to his own shell for some protection, noticed that the torn netting from Hunter's shell had somehow gotten wrapped around the eel during the collision, with a loose end now dangling near the snake's tail. Dropping his own shell, Cracker rushed over to the fight while the snake was still recovering its bearings. He quickly grabbed the netting's loose end, which was lying behind the snake's tail, with both his pincers. Pulling on it as hard as he could, Cracker stopped the eel, dead in its tracks.

Shouting to both Hunter and Devin, Cracker exclaimed, "Pull on the netting, pull on the netting, pull hard! PULL! PULL! PULL!"

Devin reacted first, immediately grabbing the shell lying on top of him and pulling on it to keep the netting tightly wrapped around the snake. Hunter then joined in by grabbing onto the netting as well. Between the three of them, they managed to pull the rope netting tight over the eel's slimy body, preventing it from going after them in either direction.

After a few minutes of desperate struggle, the boys looked like they were part of some odd rodeo event trying to rope or ride the sea snake. The exhausted eel stopped thrashing, allowing the adventurers to relax just a bit. They all took a few minutes to regain their breath, while making sure the snake could no longer move or resume its attack. It was clear to everyone that by keeping the netting held tight about the snake, the trio would be able to prevent it from attacking them again.

They had won this fight.

Devin finally got up to examine their captive in a bit more detail. While looking closely at the sea snake's head, he exclaimed, pointing at the snake's fangs and teeth, "Hunter! Hunter! That was so cool! You saved me from those nasty fangs not once but twice, that was great. I now pronounce you, Hunter the Hero!"

Blushing a little, but smiling too, Hunter answered with obvious pride, "I didn't even know what I was doing. It was all happening so fast, plus Cracker helped too, both times."

Cracker, perking up a bit at the mention of his name, said, "THAT was definitely the craziest, most dangerous thing I've ever done! I can't believe we did it!" Almost as an afterthought he added, "Hey, guys, remember what Sage said about sea snakes, how they collect and guard stuff? I wonder what this one was guarding in that cave down there?"

Both boys looked up at Cracker with surprise. It was not like Cracker to suggest doing really adventurous things, but that was what they all were thinking now—exploring the eel's lair—as they had the eel pinned down and unable to move!

Devin spoke first while pointing again at the now immobile sea snake. "You are right, Cracker, I bet there is something valuable down there. I mean, why is an eel here at all? Why? If Sage is right about these sea snakes, then he has to be guarding something, don't you think? Why don't you go down to his cave and see? Hunter and I can keep Mr. Slimy here from coming back down while you go and check things out."

"Great idea," added Hunter in an excited hopeful voice. "You don't think it has anything to do with the treasure, do you? I mean, wouldn't it be cool if it did? Maybe he even has the Key we are looking for hidden away, just waiting for us to find it? Wouldn't that be crazy?"

No one commented for a moment, as the seemingly ever-growing possibility of Pirate treasure captured all of their immediate attention, and they did not want to jinx the idea. Thinking anew about the possibility of Lafitte's Chest, or even just its Key, served to motivate all three to want to go explore the cave. Caution was no longer a thought for any of them.

"OK!" exclaimed Cracker suddenly. "I'll do it."

With the eel held rigid in the netting, each end anchored tightly,

Hunter on one side, Devin on the other, Cracker immediately slipped back into the river, quickly heading down to explore the snake's lair.

As soon as Cracker was gone, Devin asked Hunter, "Any idea how long he can stay down there? I should have asked him before he left."

Hunter answered, "I have no idea. I never thought to ask either, but as he is a crab, I'm sure it's a pretty long time."

Devin changed topics slightly, wondering out loud while looking at the trapped eel, "You know, Hunter, do you think One-Eye and this eel know each other? I mean, it was One-Eye that sent Sage down here looking for the eggs. I wonder what else is going on that he is involved with. I even wonder why he is so interested in us."

"Wow, Devin, maybe you are onto something. If that's true, then do you also think Orion is involved with slimy here too? What if they are all working on something together?" Hunter nodded his head toward the snake.

Devin, trying to think about all these possibilities, moved his body just a bit so he could be more comfortable while still holding down the eel. "I think we need to talk to Sage about all this to see if there is something bigger happening, which we don't understand. Cracker will have an opinion too, but it just seems more than random chance that all these strange coincidences are happening at the same time. Don't you think?"

"I agree, let's think about this some more," replied Hunter, who went right back to thinking about his "treasure," not the events Devin was talking about. Both boys went silent after that, lost in their own thoughts, waiting for Cracker to come back.

A few more minutes went by without any sign of Cracker returning to the surface. Time seemed to slow down—this time for Hunter and Devin—as it had earlier during the battle with the eel. With each minute passing by in silence, the boy's focus returned to the water where Cracker had disappeared. The only sound to be heard in the cavern was that of the captured snake's occasional light raspy breathing. Keeping their eyes looking forward into the still water, while their ears were focused behind them, listening to the eel, the boy's anxiety grew rapidly

Making matters worse, young boys are not known for their patience, while time's passing was not helping them at all. Becoming more fidgety, each of them would adjust his position holding the snake every minute or two. Sometimes to make sitting on the sand more comfortable, other times to see into the river better, each adjustment slightly reducing the tension on the netting holding down the eel.

"I'm sure he is fine, Devin" said Hunter suddenly, breaking the uncomfortable tension that had fallen around them.

"I know, I sure hope he is too. It seems like Cracker has been exploring for quite a while, doesn't it? Maybe he has found something really cool down there, and will bring it up for us to see soon," replied Devin with only a hint of anxiousness.

Continuing on, if only to fill the air with sounds other than the eel's scratchy breathing, Devin said, "What do you think he will find? Maybe something we can use to get us back to the sandcastle? Maybe some of the treasure from Jean Lafitte? Why do you think it's taking so long? Why?"

Hunter replied, "Cracker is a crab, I'm sure he is fine down there, just checking everything out. In fact, the longer he is gone, the more likely it is that he found something interesting. He would already be back if there was nothing to explore."

Pretending that these thoughts restored their confidence, the boys fell silent once more, eyes returning to the water, eagerly searching for any sign of Cracker's return while mentally imagining all kinds of things that could go wrong. What if there was a second eel down there and Cracker was heading right for it? What if it was a trap? Both boys' minds started to wander from the real task at hand, keeping the eel securely stretched out behind them until Cracker's return.

As their attention drifted away from the main priority, the boys did not notice that the snake's beady eyes had suddenly popped open once again, glowing their horrid pale yellow with red streaks now shooting angrily through them. Also, very unfortunately for the boys, the snake had begun to move just slightly, as the pressure from the netting was no longer quite as tight. The boys had lost focus on holding down the snake, while watching the river for any sign of Cracker.

Waiting patiently—until his two captors were staring intently into the water in front of them—the eel could feel the pressure preventing its movement slowly easing to the point it could begin to flex its body. Deciding the time was now right, the eel suddenly came alive with a wild twisting surge. Thrashing its black body—first by arching its back straight up, then quickly slamming itself back down, so hard that both boys immediately lost their grip on the netting—allowed the eel to slither free, slipping back into the water, away from its jailors.

Rather than turning to renew the battle with Hunter and Devin on land, the slimy sea snake swiftly submerged, sending several strong splashes showering the two boys in seawater. It then headed directly back toward its cave as fast as possible, very angry and knowing that the "awful" crab was at this moment plundering its lair…

***

Exploring the eel's den, Cracker was somewhat surprised at the size of the lair—along with the number of oddities it contained. Fish bones, various types of seashells, and even crab claws lay within the cave. Also, strewn across the sandy bottom were other items not native to the sea, or that Cracker couldn't even recognize. Clearly, this snake, or others like him, had been here for a long time, given the collection of things that were scattered all over the place. But there was nothing that appeared to Cracker to be worth anything to him or his friends or for that matter even worth guarding. Cracker thought this both strange and disappointing, given what Sage had told him about eels and their desire to hoard things of value, but could not figure out at first what it might mean.

Taking his time, as he would likely never have this chance again, Cracker thoroughly searched the entire cave. This eel's lair was basically circular in shape with an oval shaped entrance in the front. The walls were dark, rocky, and rough—very similar to the stalactite rocks above them—meaning the circle was not exact. The first time around did not yield anything particularly interesting. Cracker then made one more much slower pass. This time, when he was at the rear of the cave, he realized that he had missed a much smaller opening in the back wall, about halfway down, the first time he had looked.

As the cave was very, very dark to begin with, especially toward the back, the opening was almost impossible to see if one did not know where to look. It was more of a natural crack in the wall than a real entrance, appearing to blend in with the existing contour of the cave, making discovery difficult, even for someone being as careful as Cracker was.

Creeping carefully into this new crevice, Cracker realized at once that this area was much smaller than the main cavern. Directly in front of him, Cracker found a number of ledges built naturally into the wall of rock. These shelves appeared to be used to store the more valuable items that the eel had obtained over the years. Pleased with his discovery, Cracker thought, *This must be the eel's real lair.*

Cracker, taking his time, searched the various shelves with a bit more care. Compared to the useless things he had found strewn about in the outer chamber, here he found truly interesting, maybe even useful, relics. The first thing Cracker found, on the bottom shelf, was an old rusted pistol, the kind used by Pirates in the nineteenth century. Smiling, Cracker thought with new excitement, Now we are getting close to the Pirate treasure, I know it.

On another shelf was a very large shell, shaped in such a way that one could blow through it, like a horn. Cracker could not see how either the horn or a rusted pistol would be of any use to him or his friends, so he left them alone to search the next shelf up.

This shelf contained stacks of old coins, both silver and gold. Cracker thought this was the first real evidence of Pirate treasure, so he took what was easily carried—three large gold coins—with him, one each for himself and his friends. While each shelf had something of interest on it, what was most important to Cracker, finding a key for a treasure chest, was not meant to be. There were no keys in this cavern.

The last thing Cracker noticed as he prepared to leave, was that on each shelf, carved into the rock, as if in decoration, was the face of a gargoyle. The strange thing about these carvings was their location. On the lowest shelf the gargoyle was on the far right, with each level up the gargoyle was carved farther in toward the left, so that if one drew a line between them, they made a diagonal line across the wall. On the top shelf, where the last gargoyle should have been, was an inverted V that appeared rotated counterclockwise, its point angled at what would have been eleven o'clock on a watch. Cracker, if his directions were correct, thought it odd that this point should aim back toward the exit of the river from the tunnel, almost pointing toward one of the two fangs that guarded the cavern.

Finally, disappointed at not finding any evidence of a key or even hints to where it might be found, Cracker headed back to the cave's mouth, ready to return to his friends and report the bad news—no key. Thinking about what he had found in the sea snake's lair, it became obvious to Cracker that Bigs had to have been down here in the past. All of the items on the shelves were crab sized, which meant they were most likely with humans that had come in through the prism, or some other method to shrink them to their current size.

Glancing upward as he was preparing to leave the eel's den, Cracker saw the one thing he did not expect or want to see: two angry yellow eyes above snapping fanged jaws…and they were coming straight down from the surface, directly toward him!

***

The snake, having just re-entered the water, was heading back to its den, away from those two awful boys who had tied him up. Descending quickly, it was clear to the eel that the crab he fought earlier had indeed invaded his home and was still lurking inside. The snake had only one angry thought—REVENGE!

Devin and Hunter both knew that in the water the larger snake would be too much for Cracker by himself, but how could they help him? All they had were their clamshells, some netting, and the stalactite swords they had just obtained from the cave roof. Not knowing what else to do, the boys grabbed their newly collected swords, looked at each other for a moment, and shouted, "Let's go." Then they jumped into the water, diving in to chase after the snake.

Scrambling back into the cave to hide for as long as possible before the snake's inevitable arrival, Cracker waited as the fear inside him grew. Readying his big pincer for the creature's attack, he thought suddenly of the story Crex had told earlier about his ancestor Pincer, and the surprising victory over the Seagull. Maybe, just maybe, he too could survive a battle against a more powerful foe—this thought helped Cracker get his potentially paralyzing fear under control. It was at just that moment, when he felt the water around him suddenly stir from the eel's arrival.

It was time. Cracker struck!

The diving snake, maddened by the thought of an uninvited creature, especially this horrible little crab, rummaging through its lair (which no one had invaded in a lifetime,) decided that returning home and killing the crab would be its first priority. There would then be plenty of time to return to the surface, and deal with those terrible boys who were also its enemies. Knifing through the water, the sea snake swam quickly and directly back to its foul cave. Approaching from above, the eel caught a brief glimpse of the crab, now retreating back into the dark opening at the bottom of the riverbed.

Becoming even more enraged at the actual sight of the crab, the sea snake swam directly toward the cave entrance. Jaws once again open wide, the snake prepared to attack. Arriving quickly at the bottom of the riverbed, the snake had to bend its body into a slight arc, so it could go straight into the dark hole without slowing down. Turning just a bit, in toward the cave opening, the sea snake entered into the cave's darkness, just in time to meet…

Driving his large pincer directly up, straight into his enemy's open jaws, Cracker was able to hit the soft underside of the snake's mouth with his sharp claw, sending a jolt of pain throughout the eel's body. The eel—shocked by the sudden unexpected pain—stopped advancing. All its effort was now redirected at getting away from that awful claw.

Flipping the direction of its tail so he could escape the pain, the snake knocked Cracker backward, into the cave, then headed back toward the water's surface. Getting back into the open river to calm down a bit, the nasty sea snake instead found itself unexpectedly face-to-face with the two boys and their newly obtained, extremely sharp rock swords.

The boys, following the eel down into the water as fast as they could swim, arrived just in time to see the flailing snake turning back toward them. Immediately launching an attack, the boys stabbed repeatedly at the eel with their swords. Hitting the snake's head over and over, each blow cutting slightly into their foe's oily skin, the boys quickly added to the eel's already considerable injuries and pain.

Becoming disoriented—thinking it might be in real trouble—the sea snake suddenly launched itself straight up toward the surface with all its strength in a wild, desperate attempt to flee the awful swords. Not realizing or caring where it was, now just wanting to escape the awful biting from the sharp rocks the boys were using, the eel swam straight up, out of the water. Bursting through the water's surface, the injured snake slammed itself head first into one of the pieces of rock coming down out of the roof of the cave, right at the edge where the river came out of the wall and into the big cavern. This was the very same rock Hunter had been pounding on to try to get at the object hidden inside.

A shriek of pure agony erupted from the sea snake as the sharp rock hit directly in the middle of its left eye, the awful sound suddenly cut off a moment later. The tremendous force of the impact had two very different effects: First, it knocked the sea snake completely out, which ended its horrible scream in the process. Second, the snake's body, hitting with incredible force, broke off a couple of the tooth like rocks coming down from the outer edge of the cavern wall, including the large fang-like rock with Hunter's unknown object embedded in it. The snake and rocks all fell back into the water, slowly sinking, coming to rest on the soft sandy bottom.

The boys, followed by Cracker, who had recovered quickly after being knocked backward by the snake's tail, were now chasing after the eel as it headed toward the surface. They arrived just in time to hear the awful snake's terrible scream. As its painful cry was dramatically cut off, the trio watched as the eel fell back into the water, slowly heading downward toward the dark river bottom, without a single twitch or even a hint of life.

Arriving at the surface, both gasping now for air, the boys looked up at the spot where the eel slammed into the cavern roof, breaking loose several of the rocks in the process. To their great surprise and delight, one of the broken rocks was the big one Hunter had been working so hard to break off, meaning they could now easily see what was hidden there.

"Hunter! Cracker! Look there!" cried Devin, pointing up. "See what's wedged right into that rock? It's more than a piece of metal. It looks like…some kind of key!"

"Yes! Yes!" shouted Hunter. "It's not just a key, but THE Key to the treasure chest. I know it is, I just know it! Let's get it…right now!"

Equally surprised, yet also just as excited as Hunter, the other two quickly helped him reposition his clamshell directly under the broken rock so that he could stand once more on the shell's edges to reach for the Key. Clearly, the Key had been placed there some time ago, possibly for hiding or for safekeeping. Maybe even both.

Hunter grabbed the Key as best he could with his fingers, trying to pull it out. "Guys, I think part of the Key is still wedged into the rock just a bit. We will all need to pull on it to get it out," he said to the others, even as his best efforts continued to fail.

Looping some of their netting behind the exposed metal of the Key, so the trio could all pull on it, Hunter took a greater look at the rock handle that was attached to the back end. As the handle itself was made of a dark rock, it blended in with the surroundings so well that Hunter had not even realized at first that it was part of the Key. Looking now much more carefully, he noticed the handle was really a single piece of dark-green, almost gray rock in some sort of intricate shape, like an ancient gargoyle.

This time, grasping the gargoyle rather than the metal, Hunter gave the handle a strong pull, just to see if he could get it to somehow pop out. Focusing his intense desire on the Key while squeezing the handle, the gargoyle seemed to respond back. Unnoticed by the others, just as Hunter tightened his hand on the green rock, a slight cloud of green darkness—or gloominess (if color was an emotion)—moved from the gargoyle handle onto Hunter's grasping hand.

Suddenly, Hunter alone was able to clearly see the true shape of the Key's handle, an intricate Green Gargoyle, even though the cave itself seemed to darken. Frowning now and feeling somehow angrier, as if his mood was darkening a bit for no reason, Hunter tried to shake off this strange effect as he flexed the fingers of his hand while getting ready for everyone to pull on the Key.

After tying off a knot he had made with the netting, Hunter wrapped the middle of the rope around another stalactite to give them all a better angle to pull, with more leverage. At this point, the three adventurers climbed up onto their shells to grab the netting. Like a wobbly tug-o-war team, the trio pulled and pulled. After a few hard pulls, everything happened all at once. First, the stalactite they were using for leverage completely snapped off. Second, the Key came popping loose from the stony grip holding it in place. Third, the adventurers all lost their balance, tumbling into the water and making a big splash.

But...the Key was now theirs!

As a bonus, one of the larger pieces of broken rock had been tied to their netting, retrieving it gave the group three "rock swords," one for each of them. The trio all thought having three swords certainly boded well for things to come!

Laughing and splashing in the water, they celebrated both the defeat of the eel and the discovery of the Key to the treasure chest (or so they hoped) for a few minutes—all other thoughts forgotten. Quickly though, they ended their playing and celebrating. As the effects of all the wild activity caught up with them, the little group was getting very tired.

The Key itself was easily and quickly recovered by Devin. It had dropped into the water, almost right next to him when it fell. Bringing it with him to the shore, he swiftly turned a piece of the netting that was used to pull it out into a small necklace so that he could wear the Key around his neck, which was where he immediately put it, right under his shirt. Hunter really wanted the Key for himself, but rather than say anything, he just watched Devin, letting his sudden unexpected jealousy stay hidden, knowing somehow that the Key would be his before too long.

Getting out of the water while looking over the stalactite held in his pincer, Cracker said, "Devin, Hunter, guess what else I found in the eel's cave?"

Both boys quickly looked at Cracker, curious as to what he had found, almost forgetting that Cracker had been down there before the second encounter with the eel. "What is it? What did you find?" Hunter asked first.

Opening his small pincer, Cracker showed them the coins he had taken from the eel's lair. "See these coins? I brought one up for each of us." Pausing for a moment while handing out the coins, Cracker concluded, "Devin, do you mind carrying my coin? It's easier for you since I don't have any pockets."

Handing a coin to Hunter and two to Devin, the boys examined them carefully before putting them safely in their shorts.

"Of course, I will," answered Devin, now holding two of the gold coins. Examining them closely, he added, "Wow, Cracker, these are really cool. Were there any more down there?"

"Yes, there were, but I didn't have time to get them."

"Let's go back down, right now, Cracker!" exclaimed Hunter, pointing to where the eel had sunk not so long ago. "I doubt the eel will bother us, given his current condition, besides I think we earned that—"

Devin cried out, "Hey guys, come on, what about Sage? We already have the Key to the treasure chest, not to mention our swords. The coins can wait. We need to go back to see if we can cut him free with these…right now!" He swung the newest rock shard in his right hand, back and forth, just like a sword. "Come on."

Realizing they had forgotten about Sage in the excitement of defeating the eel, the other two adventurers eventually agreed with Devin. Only Hunter still wanted to go back down to the eel's cave for a short time to get more treasure. However, Sage mattered the most, and eventually Devin and Cracker convinced Hunter of this, so they returned to their shells, heading back toward Sage with swords, coins, and the Key to what they hoped was Jean Lafitte's lost Treasure Chest.

CHAPTER 9

TURTLE TALES

Lafitte's Chest

Legend has it, an ornate case was once created by an ancient being to contain the Power of the Rainbow Objects. The case itself was made of dark wood with five runes in the shape of the objects it contained engraved on the outside. Exactly one rune per side, except the front, where the Keyhole was set. The case never decayed and always contained at least one Rainbow Object, often more. The inside was shaped to hold exactly five Objects—Red, Orange, Blue, Indigo, and Purple. The chest itself was brought to the New World by the infamous Pirate Jean Lafitte in the 1800s.

RUMOR

The three adventurers now leisurely rode their shells downstream, back to the spot where Sage was patiently waiting for them to return. As soon as they got near enough for Sage to see them, the three started waving their newly obtained stalactite swords high in the air.

"Sage, Sage," they all cried out in unison, "we did it, we did it!"

Devin added, "Look, look, we have these swords now—in a few minutes we will have you free of those nets!"

Opening his eyes once more to see his young friends, Sage rumbled, "I knew you could do it—was there any trouble, hmmm?" Pausing for a second he added, "You were gone for a very long time, it seemed."

Looking at each other for just a second, the boys and crab burst out laughing while trying to tell Sage about the wild battle with the eel. As they were talking, they also started to cut the netting away from Sage, so that he could move once again. The stalactite swords were indeed as sharp as Devin had hoped when he suggested this plan. Soon the team was able to cut away all the netting necessary for Sage to slowly inch free.

"YEAH!" everyone cheered, when Sage finally managed to pull his body out of the netting.

"OK Mr. Sage, now that you are free, how are we going to get back to the Sandcastle?" asked Cracker, getting a bit more serious.

The old Sea Turtle spoke then, "As promised Cracker, I will certainly help the three of you. For now, it should be easy enough, you can all simply ride on my back, where the shell curves up slightly, that should make a nice relaxing spot to rest on, as we head out of this cavern."

Devin, trying to speak as fast as he thought, asked three questions in one breath, "What about the water, you said we have to go under water to get out this way, didn't you? How long will we be under the water, do you think? How will we breathe, while you take us out?"

Sage responded in his slow calming voice, "I will be able to get all of us safely through the submerged tunnel up ahead—faster than you can imagine I think—once we enter it. You two," nodding now at Devin and Hunter, "will have to hold your breath for a bit, it won't be easy, but I believe you will be able to do it. Don't you?"

All three answered with a resounding and hopeful, "You bet we can!" to Sage's question.

"OK then, climb up onto the back of my shell, all of you. You can climb on my front leg, then up onto my neck if you like," resumed Sage. "Oh, by the way, one last thing to think about—before we go. There may be enemies waiting for us, once we get out to sea, I think you should be ready—just in case."

"Why?" responded Devin quickly. "Who would want to bother us in the ocean? Who would even know we are going to be there in the first place?"

"Hmmm, well Devin, I can think of at least one bird, a certain dirty old Pelican with only one eye, perhaps, hmmm?" answered Sage. "In fact, I suspect he has arranged to make it very difficult for you to ever return to the Sandcastle. By now, he likely knows or guesses that you are possibly traveling by this underground stream, and will be planning whatever unpleasantness he can, just in case you somehow find your way out."

Hunter asked with obvious interest, "What can he do, Mr. Sage? I mean, he is a bird and we will be coming out into the ocean."

Sage continued, "I would guess that he will try to get his friends and allies to try and stop you. Jellyfish, Pelicans, Seagulls, Sea Snakes, whomever he can get, those are just a few of the creatures he relies on. You see, One-eye can be very persuasive, especially with those who naturally support the Rainbow Objects. He might even come after you himself. Of course, while you are with me in this river or the sea, I can help you quite a bit."

"How can you do that?" questioned Cracker.

"As I told you before, I am a mighty swimmer, which will certainly help when we get to the ocean," answered Sage. "Not only that, but my shell can protect us from any Jellyfish we happen to encounter, or from any diving pelicans or seagulls."

"Diving pelicans, diving seagulls?" all three adventurers exclaimed simultaneously, "what do you mean, Sage?" continued Devin.

"Birds of the sea often 'fish' for their food, Devin," replied Sage. "They usually fly just above the water's surface looking for something to eat. Once they see a fish they will turn up higher into the air for more room, then spin around in the sky, diving straight down with their mouths wide open, straight into the sea to catch their food. Fish or small crabs (Sage was looking at Cracker when he said this) have little hope of escaping a pelican diving into the water like that. On the other hand, a turtle shell is so hard, that a pelican will rarely try to dive at one when in the water." Chuckling to himself as he finished, Sage ended, "Or he will do so only once. Hitting a turtle shell - beak first - is an experience a pelican does not ever forget. So, you see, we should be quite safe - at least until I drop you off on the beach."

Devin then asked a very astute question, "Why is One-eye really after us? Do you know Sage?"

Sage looked carefully at each of his new friends, trying to decide how much he should reveal to them, before finally answering, "Boys, I believe One-eye wants all of the Rainbow Objects of Power for himself, always has. How much do you know about them? I assume you are familiar with them Cracker, as Crex still tells his 'Rainbow' tale every year or two, doesn't he?"

Devin answered for both himself and Hunter, "Yes, we know something about them Sage. Cracker told us the story of the Sky-Lords and the breaking of the Rainbow last night."

Sage continued, "That is good to hear Devin. Since Cracker has shared that story, I won't repeat it. What's important you see, is that One-eye wears an Object even now, the Purple Patch, and under its influence he is seeking more of them. Those who possess Objects will always try to find the others, One-eye seems to be more focused on this of late. For some reason, I am not yet sure exactly why, he appears to believe that you two might interfere with his efforts. One-eye has been looking for the lost Objects for a very long time. I suspect that by now he may even know where some of them are hidden or who might have them. Many, including One-eye, believe some of the Objects are either within the dunes here or elsewhere on this very island."

All three then asked, "Why would he think that, Sage?" Devin added, "Why?"

"I think we can all relax for a few moments, before we need to go. Let me tell you three another story about the Objects—from a long time ago—almost 150 years ago in fact," Sage replied. "This is the story about a mighty European Emperor and a pirate he thought was his friend. More importantly it is also about three of the Rainbow Objects, including why those who have heard the tale believe some of them may be here, on Galveston Island. I tell it to you now, as One-eye certainly knows this particular bit of history, and he believes in it completely.

Devin interrupted for just a moment, "Do you believe it Sage? Do you?"

"I do indeed, young Devin," replied Sage. "In fact, it seems the Objects are once again active in these parts, you three may be becoming an important part of their story, so you should learn all you can about them, the Colors too. This tale may help just a bit, so listen carefully my young friends.

And so, Sage began creating a vivid image in their minds with his wondrous story-telling, almost as clear as the vision they received earlier from the Séance Stone:

"Napoléon Bonaparte, Emperor of Europe, King of France, and friend to Pirates of the new world, was having a bad day. Not just any bad day, but a really, really really bad day. 'Captain Lafitte, Captain Lafitte,' Napoleon shouted, 'attend me at once.' Captain Jean Lafitte, leader of the New World Pirates, entered the Emperor's throne room, quickly striding to the opposite side where Napoleon sat on an oversized throne. With his one good eye, the right one, looking directly at Napoleon—he wore an odd-looking purple patch over his left eye—Lafitte awaited the Emperor's bidding in silence.

"'SSQQuuaakkk, whach you want from us? Sqquuaak, give us a kiss, Sqquuaak!' blared a large green parrot with red tail-feathers who was perched on Captain Lafitte's shoulder.

"'I have no time for that bird now,' Napoleon shot back at the Captain, looking up at him for the first time. 'I have lost something very valuable, and need your help immediately.'

"'What would you like me to do, oh mighty emperor?' asked Captain Lafitte in a quiet controlled voice, with just the slightest smirk on his face.

"Napoleon continued hurriedly, 'I need for you to take this treasure chest far away from here, so that none may find it, Captain. Attend me well, Lafitte. Someone has stolen my Orange Orb of Oblivion! Obviously owning objects of occult origin open opportunities for men of vision, such as myself. However, such things can also make for powerful enemies. I did not think anyone knew the Orb's true value. How wrong I was. Now it must be recovered soon…if my plans to conquer Europe are to have any hope of success! I have placed my other Rainbow Object, the Red Rock of Ruling, within this treasure chest. Make sure that no one other than myself, or someone I direct to you, can access it. I am off to recover the Orb. I think I know who stole it, but if I fail, keep the chest as far from here as you can. It must never fall into my enemy's hands. NEVER, I tell you!'

"'What is so important about keeping the Rock and the Orb apart?' wondered the Captain out loud, looking intently inside the open chest.

"'Each of these Objects has its own unique value, Captain,' answered Napoleon. Staring into the chest at the jagged ruby item sitting inside, he continued, 'The Rock, ahhh the Rock, it is a most ordinary-looking rock…until you look at it closely. The inside of the Rock appears to be beating, as if it had a heart of its own, with the blood from that heart coursing throughout, creating its deep red color. The outside of the rock has small engravings, tiny images of people kneeling down, as if to their king. If you look at it directly for any amount of time, the figures on the rock appear to bow and rise and bow repeatedly. When held in your hand, the Rock gives its holder the strength, confidence, and added desire to rule others, which by itself is no great thing. Lots of people want to be king, but only one person can be, and that person is ME!'

"Pointing now toward the empty half-sphere in the open chest, Napoleon calmed himself a bit before continuing on, 'The Orb's power affects those around its possessor, giving him or her, the power to issue certain types of commands, those that lead to violence, destruction, and doom—in other words, war! This power is not long lasting, as once the person commanded leaves the immediate area of the Orb, the effect slowly wears off. I have used the Orb for years to influence my military commanders when battles are at hand.

"'However, when both the *Red Rock* and the *Orange Orb* are used together, they are most powerful! Together, they allow whoever has them both, to completely rule ALL they come in contact with. Only those with extremely strong will, or a Rainbow Color to help them, can resist. Such control works over much longer distances, allowing the owner to command entire armies, not just individuals, to conquer others. This is a most powerful combination, as it has allowed me to build my mighty empire so quickly!' Napoleon focused now only on the Red Rock in the chest, almost shouted, more at himself than at Captain Lafitte, 'No one else can be allowed to have them. Certainly, not together!'

"Peering into the chest, Captain Lafitte saw there were four other empty shapes in the case, all of different rainbow colors—orange, purple, blue, and indigo—including the purple one that was shaped very similar to his eye patch. The Captain thought it interesting for a moment that Napoleon had never noticed the similarity; however, in the chest, the shape appeared to be a simple purple half-moon, rather than an eye patch. But it was the fifth space that captured his eye. Sitting in a red cushion, the Red Rock appeared to throb as the Captain directed his focus that way. As Napoleon had said, the inside of the Rock appeared to be beating just like a living heart, in response to which, Jean Lafitte's odd eye patch began to pulse on its own.

"Unknown to Napoleon was that Captain Lafitte had his own Object on his left eye. So that when he next spoke these words, 'I will take the treasure chest with me to my castle, Maison Rouge, in America, and wait to hear from you,' Napoleon completely believed that Captain Lafitte would in truth hold the treasure safely for him.

"Smiling now, Napoleon added in a much calmer voice as he pointed to the treasure, 'That would be very good of you, Captain. You will certainly be well paid for this service. Let us hope that I am as successful in my quest, as I know you will be. I will contact you once I have recovered the Orb, so you can bring my treasure back to me here in France.'

"As he said this, Napoleon took the Key to the chest out of his pocket. It was a simple metal key the color of copper, yet the handle was made of a dark green rock, carved into the shape of a gargoyle. It was difficult to focus on clearly, even when looked at directly. As

Napoleon put the Key into the lock, the entire room darkened slightly. 'I will keep the Key with me, Lafitte. This chest is truly impossible to open without it. I don't know why that is, or what magic makes it so, but it is a fact, so don't try to open it by yourself. In fact, I wonder if I should keep everything here with me in Europe, now that I think about it.' Finishing locking the chest, Napoleon put the Key back into his pocket. As he did so, the room grew lighter once more. With new-found clarity Napoleon then dismissed Captain Lafitte. 'No, I think it best to send the Rock away for now, just in case whoever stole the Orange Orb returns to try and get them back together.' Napoleon concluded gravely, 'Good luck to you, Captain. You may now go.'

"So, Captain Lafitte summoned two members of his crew to carry Napoleon's treasure. Each pirate carried a thick log that had the initials 'J L' carved into the middle of them. Bending over, the crewmen slipped the logs under each side of the chest, through curved pieces mounted (it appeared) for just that purpose. This allowed the pirates to carry the treasure off with relative ease, as they immediately stood up with a pole end in each hand, and marched out of the throne room. Walking out the door behind his men, Lafitte never even turned around to say goodbye to the emperor, whom he would never see again. Had he done so, Napoleon might have noticed that the Patch on Captain Lafitte's eye was still pulsing with a soft purple glow, which it had been doing ever since the Captain had first gotten near the Rock.

"Of course, as always, the parrot had the last word. Standing on the Captain's shoulder, looking straight back at Napoleon, it cawed in his scratchy parrot voice, 'Treasure to America, treasure to America, SQQUUAAKK!' With that, the door to the palace room slammed shut. The Pirates, parrot, and treasure chest were gone."

Sage added as an afterthought, "Now as I think back on this, it seems a bit strange to me that Napoleon was so successful in all his wars with only just two Objects under his control. He really was such a small person in so many ways." Sage paused. "But having and keeping are two very different things, right, Hunter? This is something that Captain Lafitte eventually had to find out for himself."

Smiling broadly, Devin stood up. "Guess what, Sage. You know that Key you just described, the one that locked the treasure chest?

"Yes, Devin, what of it?"

"We have it!" Pulling the newfound key out from under his shirt, Devin showed it to Sage. "The eel may have been guarding this for all I know, but once the rock broke off during the battle, we were able to get it."

With a giant smile on his face, Hunter pointed at the Key. "That is the Key Napoleon had when he locked the box. Isn't it, Sage? How do you think it got here?"

Sage, clearly surprised by what Devin was now showing him, while thinking to himself how important this was, responded, "You are right, Hunter, that does indeed appear to be the Key to Lafitte's chest. I think we can now also assume that inside the chest is a Rainbow Object of some type, maybe even the Red Rock from our stories. This is a very important find you three have made. It will also make One-Eye even more dangerous for all of you. I would suggest you be very, very careful, once you get back to the sandcastle." In much more of a hurry, given this surprising new discovery, Sage declared, "Now, if you three are ready, I think it's time we leave here and get you all home."

CHAPTER 10

RIVER'S END

Visions

It is believed that during times of great stress, those involved with Rainbow Objects and very close to death can experience past events that they have not actually lived or future events that have yet to occur. Such visions are very rare, and it is unknown how they impact those who have them. Does seeing a vision of the future make it come true, or would the event happen anyway?

CRAB CHRONICLES

As Sage started to slowly move his great body toward the river's edge, the band of travelers had plenty to think about and to discuss while they prepared for the upcoming ride on the great turtle's back.

Hunter started talking about the treasure in Jean Lafitte's chest. "Now we know what's really in the treasure chest, you guys! This is so awesome! Once we get back to the sandcastle, and let everyone know we are all right, let's come right back down here again, OK? If our luck continues to hold, it will be possible to track down the chest holding that Red Rock, then we will really be heroes when we find it!"

Cracker answered, "I'm not sure things will be that simple, Hunter. Although returning for another adventure would almost certainly be very exciting, it's also a lot more dangerous looking for such treasure, especially the dark Rainbow Objects. Besides, we have not yet gotten back to the sandcastle, so let's get home first, then we can see, OK?"

"Sure, sure Cracker, home first. Sage will get us there with no problem. I know he will, then we can all go treasure hunting for real!" Hunter laughed. "What about you, Devin, don't you want to go find the treasure too?"

Rather than responding to Hunter, Devin turned to ask the turtle a question. "What do you think, Sage? Why after all these years, are these things happening now? Why are we so involved, why?"

"Those are difficult questions, young Devin," returned Sage very slowly, as if still being somewhat careful with his answers. The group was just reaching the river as the old turtle continued, "It seems to me that something may have changed recently. What that is exactly, I'm not sure. Now the Rainbow Objects seem to be alert, even actively exerting their influence—both good and bad—throughout the area." Sage paused at the water's edge. "If I was to guess, I would say that somehow a few of the Rainbow Objects have gotten closer together, and are now awake, actively seeking each other out." He mumbled slowly, almost nervously to himself, "At least that is what I hope." Raising his voice back to its normal slow rumble, Sage concluded, "You three are certainly involved in some way that seems very important, but more than that I cannot yet guess." He looked at them directly. "Now, let's see about getting us safely out of here."

Each of the three riders, with their clamshells, rock swords, and Devin wearing the Key to the treasure chest around his neck, scrambled up Sage's leg, right onto his back, answering, "Aye-aye, Captain!" in almost perfect unison. As the great turtle readied himself for the underwater journey, the travelers quickly settled in behind Sage's large head, giving him a mock salute, from the front edge of his sturdy, slightly slippery, shell.

Smiling, Sage started slowly, slipping silently into the river without saying a word—beginning their journey back to the Sandcastle. After floating downriver for a bit, the wise turtle spoke up. "Here is a nice little question for the three of you," he said in his deep rumbling voice. "Do you think the sandcastle was always where it is today?" Sage paused. "Of course, by the nature of the question, you are already suspicious of the answer, isn't that right?"

All three again said yes, with Devin adding, "But if the sandcastle was not always where it is today, where was it? Why did it move? Why?"

"The answer has to do with time, and as we are discussing, perhaps even with the Rainbow Objects, my friends."

Hunter asked for the group, "What do you mean, Mr. Sage?"

"As you have now correctly guessed, the sandcastle was not always located where it is today. Even as the tides can sometimes erase the door, taking time for the sandcastle to reappear in the dune, so too has the dune itself, in which the sandcastle now appears, moved with the passage of time."

Cracker was surprised at this, asking immediately, "Do you mean that all the stories of my ancestors and our colony did not really occur on Pirates Beach? I'm pretty sure they did!"

With an almost-sad smile the turtle said, "Sometimes stories seem so simple, yet such is not the case here. You see, Cracker, living as long as I have, you see a lot of things, some good, some not so good. Such as the slow retreat of the beach and of the dunes themselves, as they are slowly eaten by the sea. Many of the stories you hear about really did occur on 'your' beach; it's the beach itself that was different then. For one thing, it was much larger than it is today, so the dunes were actually sitting closer to the sea than they are now."

Devin followed up with, "What is the most you have seen the beach move, and what caused it, Mr. Sage?"

"As I said earlier, the beaches here are slowly being consumed by the sea. Strong storms can often do a lot of damage, as the hard pounding waves eat away at the sandy dunes." Shuddering with this thought, Sage went on, "The hurricane, of course, is the strongest storm of all. Such pounding wind, rain, and surf can take many, many feet of beach away in just one or two days. Beach that will take years, decades even, before it might return. I can remember the last hurricane—only ten years ago it was—that took away over twenty feet of beach by itself, with winds and waves so strong that it even knocked down some of the Bigs' houses, as if they had never been there at all before the storm."

"What happened to the Dune and the sandcastle then?" asked Cracker, extremely curious.

"The dunes were almost completely destroyed, while the sandcastle itself, did not reappear for almost a year," replied Sage. "Those were difficult times for all the creatures of the beach, except for the scavengers of course. But as with all things, over time, the dunes were rebuilt, bringing the sandcastle back with them."

"Was that the biggest hurricane ever? Was it?" Devin asked excitedly.

"No, it was not even close, young man. In fact, in my grandfather's time, which was long ago now, over one-hundred years at least, I think, there was a huge hurricane that almost destroyed this entire island, and everything on it."

"You know, I think I read about that once. That was the Great Hurricane of 1900," commented Devin, talking out loud to himself.

Cracker asked, "Was there a sandcastle then, Mr. Sage?"

"Oh yes, you are now on the right track, Cracker," continued the turtle. "That storm destroyed all the dunes, as well as many of the Bigs' buildings. In fact, it is my belief it was that very storm which erased the sandcastle that was here during the time of the story I told you earlier. The one about the Emperor Napoleon and his ally, the Pirate Jean Lafitte. That particular incarnation of the sandcastle had been in the dunes for many hundreds of years. Indeed, I believe it was the very sandcastle that the first Bigs used to enter this world under the sand."

"Mr. Sage, Mr. Sage!" They all started talking at once on hearing this news, with Devin continuing for them, "We all saw Pirates on the beach in a vision we had before we found you. What did you call the stone, Cracker?"

Quickly answering, Cracker said, "Yes, Mr. Sage. It was through a Séance stone that we saw Pirates go into the sandcastle carrying a treasure chest. We think it's the one you told us about, Captain Lafitte's chest, the one he got from Napoleon."

"Yes, that is very likely, Cracker, but remember the beach and dunes are not the same as they are now. The beach back then was almost three hundred feet farther out. So also was the dune, meaning the sandcastle was south of its current location too. After the Pirates had been here, but before the storm, a few houses were built on the beach, all of which were wiped out by the giant hurricane from my grandparent's time. In fact, there is only one remnant left from that storm that can be seen from the beach today. Do any of you know what it might be?"

Neither of the boys nor the crab had any idea, so they just shrugged their shoulders and shook their heads, while Sage continued.

"Remember when I told you about the wood stump that One-Eye was perched on? The one that convinced me I needed to go look for the turtle eggs?"

"Yes," answered Hunter. "I wonder if that is the same wood stump One-Eye was on when he was watching us Devin, before he attacked me on the beach. Remember? I mean, it's weird that he was there when he tricked Mr. Sage, not to mention when he came after me. Don't you think?"

Before Devin could respond, Sage continued, "That wood stump seems to be a favorite spot of One-Eye's. Doesn't it, boys? And for good reason. The dune, back in the days of the Pirates, was only a few yards away. That stump you see, is all that remains from a large pier destroyed in the huge hurricane I have been telling you about. In fact, the original sandcastle itself was to be found in that dune, set back just a little bit from the wooden pier. Of course, it too was destroyed, as just about everything was washed away by that terrible terrible storm."

Breaking into the discussion, Devin asked Sage directly, "Why is One-Eye drawn back to that particular spot, if the sandcastle was truly washed away? Why?"

"Because," replied the turtle, "I don't think it is really One-Eye who is drawn back at all, but rather it's the Purple Patch, which continues to return to a familiar place. One where some—maybe even all—of the other Objects may have been in the past, as well."

"What?" all three asked at once. "What do you mean, all the Objects were together?! How could that be?!"

"I don't know this for a fact, but it is my belief that the great hurricane from my Grandfather's time, was the result of most, if not all, of the Objects being used together. You see, that is the power they give to their user, the power Cracker asked about, to command the Hurricane! The sandcastle was the storm's true target that day. The ruin of the dunes, along with the destruction of many other things on this island, was really just collateral damage from the storm. Now, all that's left from that terrible time is the stump we see in the water, where One-Eye likes to perch."

"Why would someone command a hurricane to destroy the sandcastle? Why, Mr. Sage?" Devin asked.

"I don't know for sure," replied Sage, "but aren't there Rainbow Colors in the sandcastle even now, like the Purple Prism that brought you here, perhaps? Maybe, someday, you will find out the answer to your question."

"Wow, that's a lot to take in Sage. I wonder who all realizes what really happened back then," Cracker commented before changing the subject back to more practical matters. "The good news is, I'm pretty sure we don't have any hurricanes to worry about right now, which means we can focus on getting home. If I understand all that you have said correctly, when we leave here, then we should end up right back where you entered this cave from originally, out by the stump in the ocean?"

"That's exactly right. As you have just said, when we emerge from this river into the sea, we will come out very near the stump which you have seen many times before, which One-Eye likes to perch on, and from which I was tricked into searching for turtle eggs that were never really there. The very stump right in front of your beach…and of course the sandcastle." Sage smiled. "All right then, listen carefully. Let me tell you the five things to expect and to be ready for as we leave here." Sage paused.

"First, I will count to three, then we will dive straight down under the water. You boys must draw as deep a breath as you can when I hit 'two.' That way your air will be topped off when we dive together.

"Second, the current gets much stronger the farther down we go; there will be some unexpected twists and turns as we pass through some rocky areas, meaning the ride will certainly get rougher. Don't be surprised or scared as we will certainly get through. Just be ready, it will likely be pretty bumpy for a bit.

"Third, I will be swimming much faster than any of you are used to, so it's very important that everyone hang on tight, as the water will be pulling hard against you. This is most important, so let me say this again, *hang on tight,* whatever else you do."

Pausing, Sage let the trio think about what he said for a moment before continuing, "Boys, you have all that? Hold your breath. It's going to get rough. And above all, *hang on tight?*"

The others nodded.

"Terrific! Let's finish our checklist. Fourth, it gets really dark about halfway through the passage. The light within these caves goes completely out as we go deeper inside the rock, meaning we won't be able to see much until we are out into the sea, where the natural sunlight can reach us once more. Try not to panic when the light is gone. Remember, if you just hold on, things will be just fine.

"Finally, once we do see light returning above us, that means we are out of this river and back in the ocean. We will head straight up to the surface at that point, so you two can breathe again. Do you have all that? Any questions?" He paused to see if anyone had anything to add. "Remember, boys, deep breath on 'two' and most importantly, *hang on tight!*"

The boys looked at each other, then at Cracker, who looked back at Devin and Hunter in turn. At this point, they just all nodded to each other, each with a serious face for a change. It was time to go.

"OK, are you all set, hmmm?" rumbled Sage.

Waiting until each boy and crab said yes, the turtle then swam over to the side of the pool nearest the end of the cave. Devin and Hunter grabbed the edge of his shell, with both hands holding on as tight as they could, while Cracker was busy anchoring himself to the old turtle as well.

Suddenly, like a roller coaster cresting ever so slowly over the first big hill after the long anticipatory ride to the top, away they went, plunging crazily down the track, straight into the water's depths.

∗∗∗

Devin's Trip

Breathing out a few bubbles as they rode along, Devin quickly became comfortable riding through the water while holding onto Sage's shell. He even closed his eyes as the light disappeared, erasing his view of the passing cavern. Continuously tightening his grip as time went on, while hoping that he would simply be able to make it, Devin blindly rode where Sage took him. For what seemed forever in the dark, his thoughts naturally turned to the events they had just gone through, remembering how his friends saved him not once but twice from the nasty sea snake—at great risk to themselves. Reliving the whole experience in his head, Devin vowed to himself that he would always look after his friends, especially when they were in trouble.

Devin was completely lost in his thoughts when Sage rose unexpectedly, hitting the tunnel's rugged roof hard with the top of his shell. The sudden unexpected jolt knocked Devin's body completely loose from his attachment to Sage. Not being prepared, the jarring impact caused Devin to release his grip, even as the turtle resumed swimming.

Now floating free in the water, surrounded by utter darkness—his inner alarm ringing like crazy—Devin could only flail his hands and arms wildly about. As his left arm circled backwards behind him, Devin's outstretched hand brushed against a piece of rock on the edge of their passageway, the one which Sage must have accidentally hit. Able to feel the scratch of the rock, but unable to see anything, Devin did not know what to do next. He almost went into a full panic at that point–blind, unable to think, disconnected from Sage, and not knowing what was happening around him–all as the need for fresh air in his lungs seemed to pound the inside of his chest. Devin was about to launch himself out into the current–he certainly couldn't stay where he was or he would surely drown–hoping for the best, when his foot hit....

***

Hunter's Trip

Hunter, unlike Devin, tried to watch their underwater voyage just as long as he possibly could. As the river's passage narrowed, Hunter was able to see Sage continue to swim quickly, tipping his left side down to avoid a rock, then suddenly flattening out, turning back to his right only to tilt his left side up, to avoid hitting the wall's edge on the other side. Looking to his left, Hunter could clearly see Devin, clinging tightly to Sage with his eyes pressed shut, hanging on as best he could.

Finally, as darkness made it impossible to see where he was going any longer, Hunter too shut his eyes as he began to realize his air would soon be gone. Feeling his own case of fear and dread building, Hunter's thoughts shifted wildly, jumping from where they had just been, back to when he and Devin first found the sandcastle, then to the recent battle with the eel, finally settling on what Hunter was secretly desiring most of all - the Treasure Chest of Jean Lafitte!

Hunter's lack of air was bringing him closer and closer to panic and drowning. Not able to hold his breath for quite as-long-as Devin, Hunter was in the most immediate danger. Fortunately, even though his thoughts were no longer focused on the trip to the sea's surface, Hunter was able to maintain a strong grip on Sage's shell, even after being shaken quite unexpectedly when the turtle hit the rocks above them.

On very rare occasions, visions of the future appear to those who are perilously near death. It's as if, with the coming of Death, memory is no longer limited to one's past. For a select few people in that position, there is a short time period where they are able to 'remember' the future, as if they had already lived it.

This is what happened to Hunter in those last few seconds under the water. His thoughts suddenly became crystal clear, showing him a 'memory' of an event he had not yet experienced in real life. Becoming so focused on his desire for Lafitte's treasure, Hunter completely lost track of the voyage on Sage's back, as within this strange vision he saw his eyes opening back up, showing him...

Hunter found himself in a strange new scene, looking directly in front of him, from out of the darkness. Clearly, he was no longer riding on Sage's back, as this new location was not even in the water. There was only blackness, as if Hunter had become the center of a blot of ink. Darkness and gloom slowly spread in all directions around him, except for what he was now staring at, directly ahead.

Hunter could see clearly what was in front of him, but could not see himself. Perhaps he was just watching this event unfold, not actually being a part of it? A dark wood table stood a few feet away, so Hunter assumed either he was hiding in the dark, preventing anyone else from noticing him or this was simply a vision of some sort. On the table itself were three items, two small candles, both lit—one at either end—casting faint flickering shadows onto the main item in the room.

There it was, directly in front of him, Hunter's secret desire—Lafitte's chest! Like a magnet attracting a piece of iron, the chest grabbed Hunter's gaze, locking it down so that it was impossible to look at anything else. On the table was a rune covered wooden chest, as big as Hunter's arms if they had both been extended out wide. The box was half as deep as it was long and just as high as it was deep.

The chest's front was directly facing Hunter, allowing him to focus his gaze on the lock. Sticking out, pointed right at him, was the green gargoyle handle, showing Hunter that the key was already in the chest's lock. Only the front was visible from Hunter's point of view. It was obviously still shut, so the Key had likely just been inserted, although by whom it was not clear. Hunter couldn't see anything else, either to the left or right side of the room.

Suddenly, One-eye emerged from the darkness surrounding the table. Coming into view, he settled to Hunter's right, just next to the edge of the table. As One-eye was facing him directly, Hunter could now see the bird's eye patch very clearly, it was glowing a sinister purple, seeming to enjoy the shadows from the candle now dancing across the pelican's face. One-eye slowly turned his attention away from Hunter's direction, towards the front of the chest, looking away from anything else.

"Open it!" commanded One-eye in a harsh yet expectant voice, he clearly was anticipating this moment.

Before anyone could move, a new voice Hunter did not recognize, emerged from the darkness to Hunter's left, adding to One-eye's command with a single powerfully commanding word, "NOW!"

Wondering who else was with One-eye, Hunter strained to see, but couldn't take his own eyes away from the front of the chest. They seemed locked onto the gargoyle, which appeared to now be staring right back at him from the key's handle. Hunter's viewpoint began to slowly change, now it moved closer to the Chest, so that he could see better, anticipating that someone would soon open it.

As if in response to the powerful command to open the treasure box, two arms came slowly into view directly in front of Hunter's gaze, one hand grasping the gargoyle, the other hand the lid to Lafitte's Chest. Surprise! A sudden recognition came over Hunter at that moment. With some shock, Hunter recognized those arms, as he watched them emerge from the darkness to grab the key handle and the lid to Lafitte's chest. They were his own!

What shocked him even more, was the realization that both One-eye, along with the stranger, had for some reason, been talking directly to him the entire time. He was not hidden from them as previously thought; rather he was the focus of this little chest-opening ceremony. One-eye shifted position slightly to make room as Hunter reached for the chest. Watching the vision unfold, Hunter could not be sure who all was in the area, who the strange voice belonged to, or why he was even there. Where were Devin and Cracker, neither could be seen or heard anywhere??

Reaching out with his right hand, Hunter grasped the green gargoyle handle to the key. As his fingers closed on the gargoyle, the area around the table immediately darkened as if the candles had been snuffed out, causing One-eye to focus harder on what lay inside. Listening to the turning of the key, the chest suddenly unlocked with an audible 'click.' Hunter watched the top of the box slowly rise, opening with a loud 'creak,' revealing not the red light he expected, but rather a dull orange glow, coming from within. As the chest's contents revealed themselves, Hunter heard the simultaneous exclamation of victory from One-eye, with a loud scream of "NOOOO!" coming from the other voice.

Hunter's vision faded immediately with that scream, everything quickly becoming a black background. The last thing Hunter thought he saw, was his own hand reaching forward–the one he had used to open the lid–toward the orange glow coming from inside. Desperate to really know what treasure was lying there in Lafitte's chest, Hunter tried to use his last ounce of strength to focus his vision one more time, to finally see what lay inside…

"HUNTER, HUNTER, wake up, wake up, are you there, are you still with us?" was the next thing Hunter heard.

The vision of Lafitte's Chest was now totally gone.

***

Cracker's Trip

Not being affected, as the boys were, by the lack of air, Cracker naturally assumed that this part of the trip would be easy for him. Losing a bit of his focus as Sage began the countdown, Cracker's mind shifted away from the activities of the moment, to what he thought he would need to do during the journey. Cracker assumed his biggest job would be to make sure the boys did not get separated from Sage while under the water; he would also have to keep the shells and swords safe with him, so they did not get lost. Cracker was very confident he could do these things with ease.

Snapping back to what was going on around him, just as he heard Sage call out 'One', Cracker felt a tremendous force as the turtle took them nearly straight down into the water. Not expecting such a strong pull from the dive, as Cracker had never been swimming with a turtle before, he was not nearly as ready as he thought he was. The left half his body (legs and all) came off Sage's shell, but he managed to hold on using two of his legs plus his large right pincer.

From this view—on the right edge of the shell—Cracker could see not only his left legs and pincer flapping in the water, but both Devin and Hunter holding on tightly with both hands, as the rest of their bodies were bumping up and down off the back of Sage's shell.

Recovering a bit from the initial shock at the faster speed they were now traveling, Cracker looked forward to see that the smooth sandy cave walls were quickly changing to rough rocky edges. Contact with the rocks at this speed would be extremely painful and could force him completely off Sage's back, while some of those jagged edges–if they hit his friends–might knock them out, causing them to drown.

Just as Cracker had this critical thought, there was an unexpected change in direction. Sage angled upward, with the top of his shell slamming hard against the rock above them, with the rock's edge barely missing his three passengers. Cracker, barely hanging on to Sage to begin with, found that he now had to let go. Immediately sliding across Sage's shell all the way to the back, Cracker luckily was able to grab onto the shell once again.

Holding on as best he could, onto the back of Sage's shell, with only his larger right pincer and legs, Cracker's smaller pincer was pointed directly above his head. He looked almost like a cowboy, riding a bull in some strange underwater rodeo. To his great surprise, as Sage surged downward again, Cracker's free pincer hit something much softer than the wall, which he instinctively grabbed onto as they plunged away from the rocks.

Soon Cracker felt Sage start upward once more. Within seconds, light reached down to Cracker, allowing his vision to return. Equally important, light meant they had escaped the rocky cave, with a clear path now to the open sea, including the much-needed air from above. Looking back at his pincer—the one he had used to grab something on his way out of the cave—Cracker saw that it was a boy's ankle, now held tightly in his claw. Cracker had managed to grab hold of Devin's flailing foot during the roughest part of their journey. He was now looking at his friend's foot, along with the rest of Devin attached to it, as the group headed straight up to the surface.

CHAPTER 11

CRABS AND GULLS

> ***Dragonflies***
>
> *Dragonflies are mysterious creatures that appear in fields without notice or care. Hovering and darting from place to place, without apparent reason. It has been rumored that while Dragonflies are mostly aloof—avoiding other creatures—under rare but special circumstances, they can take on the battle characteristics their namesakes imply and truly fly like Dragons.*
>
> CRAB CHRONICLES

"GASP!" Devin was finally able to breathe again as Sage escaped from the underground river.

As soon as Sage saw a glimmer of light above him, he headed straight upward, as the light could only be from the sun, meaning that he was now back in the open sea. Breaking the surface as quickly as he could allowed Cracker, still riding on Sage's back, to make sure both boys were up in the fresh air, able to finally breathe once more.

Devin, gently rubbing his slightly sore ankle where Cracker had grabbed hold of it with his pincer, was the first boy to recover his breath. Looking around to see where they were, he realized the group was now just offshore, surprisingly close to the beach he and Hunter had been playing on at the start of this adventure. In fact, they had emerged from the sea almost exactly as Sage predicted. Only a few yards away was the old wooden post—now abandoned—where they had originally seen One-Eye the Pelican perch, before they had gone into the sandcastle the first time.

As Devin looked at the beach, Hunter was lying on the back of Sage's shell, Cracker having dragged him on top once they broke the water's surface. Devin, now focusing on the immediate situation, quickly scrambled over to his friend while shouting, "Hunter, Hunter, wake up, wake up, can you hear me?"

Realizing that Hunter likely swallowed too much water in the wild rush to the surface, Devin put some of his Boy Scout training to work. Not seeing any sign of Hunter's breathing, Devin quickly stretched Hunter straight out on Sage's back. Putting his left hand over his right, Devin pushed down on Hunter's chest with short sharp pulses. Almost immediately, Hunter coughed and out came the seawater from his lungs. Just a few coughs were all it took for Hunter to get his breath back so that he could sit up and thank everyone for rescuing him.

Now awake and able to breathe again, Hunter's first thoughts were of the vision he had of Lafitte's Chest and opening it up. However, rather than tell anyone about the chest, the first thing Hunter did when he opened his eyes was to blurt out, "I'm hungry!"

Devin smiled. "Well, Hungry, I'm Devin, nice to meet you."

"Ha ha, funny, Devin. Very funny and so original," retorted Hunter with a relaxed smile.

Cracker, not quite understanding asked, "What are you talking about?"

"Just a small joke, Cracker, kind of like us now," returned Devin, pointing at himself and Hunter.

"Yes, that is very small, almost not there." Hunter laughed. "Where are we?"

Cracker responded for the group, "You are currently laying on Sage's back, Hunter. We made it to the ocean's surface, just as we planned. In fact, we are now only a few hundred yards from the entrance to the sandcastle. You can almost see it from here!"

"But how?" asked Hunter. "I don't remember anything after things went dark in the tunnel."

At this point, Sage joined the conversation. "You are very lucky to be alive, young man. Just a few moments ago you were not even breathing, and you can thank young Devin for saving you."

"Really?" asked Hunter, looking at Devin, who was now just sitting on Sage's back, smiling right back at him. "How did you do it, Devin?"

"It was easy. I did a little CPR on you, which forced you to spit up all that nasty ocean water that you had swallowed." Devin added with a grin, "And it was really nasty, I might add. Ugh."

Sage interrupted, "Boys, I am sure you can share all that happened on the trip out of the cave, once you are safely back inside the sandcastle. I think we should focus now on getting you there as soon as we can."

Cracker asked the group, "What do you guys think we should do next?"

Sage, while making sure all three adventurers were now firmly on his back, answered Cracker's question immediately, "I think that I should drop you off at the shore, as near the sandcastle as I can. If the three of you are quick enough—I know you are all much faster than I am on the beach—you should be able to get to the entrance, then slip inside the door before anyone can stop you."

Cracker smiled. "Yes, that seems like a good idea, Mr. Sage. I don't see too many birds about right now, so we should be able to make it, no problem. Besides, we still have our clam shells and swords that we can use"—he brandished his mini stalactite like a real sword in mock battle—"just in case a random Seagull or something decides to come after us."

Everyone quickly agreed that this was the best plan of action. They were now so close to the sandcastle that nothing else could possibly go wrong. Strangely, given all the adventures the trio had recently come through, they seemed to forget about the possibility of any danger. Maybe it was seeing the beach so close by, maybe they had survived so many close calls, whatever the reason, the two soaking-wet boys and their crab friend relaxed on Sage's back as the great turtle headed toward the shore.

***

Meanwhile, One-Eye the Pelican had rather different ideas for what was going to happen when the little group reached the beach. He wanted the Key that was hanging around Devin's neck, and he wanted it in the worst way. Naturally, the old Pelican quickly devised a way to get it.

One-Eye had been sitting on the wood stump out in the ocean, looking for any sign of the boys. He knew exactly where the underground river emptied into the sea. All he had to do was perch on his stump, then watch and wait, in case they somehow survived the trip underground. This strategy proved very successful. Late that afternoon there were signs of activity underneath the water's surface, at the cave's entrance. Seeing things stirring and catching just a glint of metal that might be the Key to Laffite's treasure chest, One-Eye immediately took to the air, hoping none of the little group that was emerging would see him. As he launched himself upward, it appeared that his patch was also coming to life, beginning to emit a soft purple glow of its own.

Flying away from the sandcastle, toward the open sea, One-Eye saw a shrimp boat slowly making its way along the coast. Fishing boats that come in from their day's work always attract Seagulls, often too many to count. The Gulls tend to hover or fly around the boats, looking for an easy afternoon seafood snack. This boat was no exception. The fishermen had made a good catch of shrimp that day, meaning that the birds were also plentiful, hoping to get their afternoon meal.

Since it was a number of Gulls that One-Eye was now looking for, he flew directly out toward the boat. Arriving quickly at his destination, the purple patch now glowing with a constant dark purple light, One-Eye found a fair number of Gulls, many of whom he had used in the past to do his dirty work. The influence of One-Eye's glowing patch easily convinced over a dozen Gulls to join him, as he promised them all a nice meaty snack. All they had to do was return to the beach with him to get their reward.

Once assembled, the group of Gulls flew directly in toward the beach, looking to catch Cracker, Devin, and Hunter all alone on the sand. If he was really lucky, One-Eye thought, the turtle would have gone back into the ocean, leaving the trio all alone to cross the sand without any possible help. In addition, One-Eye did not think any of the boys would be able to spot his group of birds until it was too late, as they were now rapidly approaching the shore with the sun setting directly behind, making seeing them very difficult.

With over a dozen Gulls following him, One-Eye didn't really believe there was any way he could be stopped. His group of Seagulls would be more than a match for the two boys and the crab, even if the turtle happened to still be with them. On land, the turtle was just too slow. There was simply no way he could protect them all from so many birds. Preparing to attack, One-Eye flew in with ever-increasing confidence, thinking happily to himself, *Very soon now, the Key will be mine, very soon!*

***

As One-Eye was flying back toward the shore with his group of attack Gulls, Sage arrived close to the water's edge, where he was letting his three friends get off his shell. "Goodbye, Devin, Cracker, and Hunter," Sage rumbled to each in turn. "I am sure we will see each other again, so no reason for long or sad goodbyes." Sage really wanted them to return quickly to the sandcastle but didn't want to show how anxious he was. "Make sure you boys get that key back into the sandcastle, and remember, always keep both eyes open…just in case there are any unfriendly birds around."

The three adventurers barely had time for a quick, "Goodbye, Sage!" before the sea turtle turned around, heading straight back into the ocean. Each watched Sage swim for a couple of moments, until they could no longer see him. Waving anyway, even after Sage completely disappeared, they all turned back toward the sand dune, where the sandcastle was hidden away, waiting for them to return.

It happened to be near low tide when the group arrived back on the beach, which meant there was quite a bit of sand to cross to get back to the sandcastle—almost one hundred yards of sand between the ocean's edge and the door under the dunes. The trio were all smiles now, no birds could be seen on the beach, the Key to the treasure chest had been found, each of them had a new sword to play with, and they would soon be home. What could possibly go wrong?

"What are we going to do with the Key now, Devin?" asked Hunter as he walked onto the beach. "I think we should go right back down to the underground river, then just head in the other direction, toward the chest, as soon as possible, don't you? We can go search for the treasure itself now."

Stopping where he stood, Cracker interjected, "That would really make for another adventure to be sure. We could easily go back down through the water jets now that we know what's down there. Only this time we would head upstream. If the directions we found are correct, that would lead us right to the chest, just like we were led to the Key. Assuming the chest is still there, and I bet it is—right where the Pirates left it—then we could open it up to see what's really inside!"

Still saying nothing about the vision he had of opening the chest himself, Hunter responded, "We will have to be careful though. Some of the other adult crabs may not want us to go back down there. I mean, we tricked the guard once. I doubt it will be that easy to fool him again."

Hunter paused for a moment, then resumed with a new line of thinking. "Speaking of tricking the older Crabs, what about Orion? Do you think he will try to stop us?" With a slight smile, he fondly remembered the excitement of his clamming race with Orion. "Or perhaps, he might even want to join us."

Cracker frowned. "Jeez, how could I forget about him? I had not even been thinking about Orion, but he will surely be around when we get back. I doubt he will be very happy to see us again." Stopping so he could turn to face the boys, Cracker finished, "You are right, Hunter, we will certainly have to be careful if we are to go on a treasure hunt. Maybe we will even need to make a plan."

Devin was just about ready to add his own thinking to the little conversation on the beach when he noticed an odd, pointed, somewhat threatening shadow passing directly over him, moving in from the ocean and heading toward the sand dune. As it was a cloudless day outside, he thought this new shadow a bit odd. Turning his head to look back toward the setting sun, Devin put his right hand above his eyebrows, blocking the bright sunlight just enough so that he could see over the water. Expecting to see a random bird, maybe a kite, or something equally harmless flying well above him, Devin was just about to comment on what he thought they should do with the Key when they got back to the sandcastle.

Instead, all Devin could do was yell at the top of his lungs, "RUN! Quick, get your shells out. Here come the GULLS!" Looking back, Devin saw a line of Gulls flying in from the sea directly at them. While the sun had almost completely hidden the Gull's initial approach, the trio was somewhat lucky that the sun was now sitting so low in the sky, almost directly behind the attacking birds. The position of the sun placed the birds' shadows way out in front of them, meaning that the shadows themselves gave warning to the boys. Those extra few seconds, announcing the bird's presence to Devin, gave the small group a fighting chance.

The trio had clearly made a terrible mistake. Not heading immediately back to the sandcastle as Sage had suggested, left them little if any protection from the birds while they were on the beach. Now, the adventurers would have to pay for it.

Diving straight down onto the sand, all three whipped their clamshell shields over their heads to protect themselves while also readying their swords and pincers to battle the attacking birds. The Seagulls had come over the sea in a flying V formation, with One-Eye at the point of the V and the other birds lining up on either side of him. Swooping down toward the beach, the Gulls flew just over the adventurers' heads, pecking at the shells with their strong beaks as they passed by. After delivering a peck or two, the Gulls would fly back into the sky, wheel around, then attack again.

Cracker shouted nervously from beneath his shell, "We have to get out of here…and fast. There's no way we can fight off this many Gulls!"

"I can see that!" shouted Hunter in a very nervous voice, just as a Gull was pecking directly on top of his shell. "But how can we move at all with these Gulls all around us? As soon as we move, we're done for!"

Devin yelled in response, "I don't know, Cracker, any great ideas?! Now would be a really good time to have one."

Cracker, having noticed something interesting on the beach, about halfway between where they were and the sandcastle entrance, shouted back, "Devin, Hunter, look toward the dunes. Do you guys see those logs over there? I think if we can just get to them, we can hide underneath. Whatever that is, it looks pretty strong. Once there, it might be possible to use our swords to keep away the birds, at least for a little while."

Devin peeked out from under his shell, exclaiming, "Hunter, Hunter, look, that's the fort we were building earlier, you know, the one with the log we found. It just might be strong enough to help us fight off these birds, like Cracker says. At the very least, it will make a great hiding place for us. I say, let's go for it!"

Seeing their "fort," plus having a new plan to escape the birds, gave the boys exactly what they needed most—a flicker of hope. Being very careful to keep their hands and claws on the inside of the shells and away from the Gulls' attacking beaks, while holding their shields directly over their heads, the trio managed to inch ever so slowly toward the logs. It was very tough work, as they had to stay close enough together to keep the birds from isolating any one of them, while combining crawling with scooting to move forward, across the sand.

Fortunately for the boys, their shells were very strong, preventing the attacking birds from getting through too easily. However, the awful sounds from the nearly constant pecking—echoing inside each shell—caused the boys to almost give up before they got to safety.

Every once in a while, one of the trio would lift his shell ever so slightly, just enough to permit swinging a sword or stabbing a pincer at an attacking Gull. Rarely did they make any real contact with the birds; rather, these actions would force the Gulls back—higher into the air for a moment or two—far enough away that the group could then inch slowly forward, toward their goal.

Cracker called out encouragingly to his friends, "Keep going, keep going, we are over halfway there!" He too paused to stab upward with his pincer, barely nicking a Gull's exposed leg and driving the bird away for a few seconds.

Devin, who was the farthest ahead, gulped while responding with a panting voice, "I hear you, Cracker. Come on, Hunter, we just might make it." Stopping for a moment, Devin then swung his rock sword, driving away the pecking Seagull from his shell before inching forward once more.

Hunter was about to respond with his own words of encouragement when one of the larger Gulls began a new attack against him. Hovering above Hunter's shell, as it pecked directly down, right on the top, the Gull's beak hit the exact center of the weakest spot in his shell with a mighty 'peck.' Immediately, an ugly crack appeared, right through the middle of Hunter's clamshell, going both directions, almost to each edge. Completely spooked by this unexpected change in fortune, Hunter swung his sword wildly to drive back the Gull, while simultaneously screaming in true terror to the others, "Devin, Cracker, HELP, I have a big crack in my shell, HELP me Devin! The birds are breaking through!"

Devin shouted encouragingly, "Stay with us, Hunter. We will make it together! It's not completely broken, is it?" while swinging his own sword at a nearby Gull, who easily flitted away.

Hunter did not respond, barely hearing Devin, too worried now about his clamshell to think clearly. He started rotating the shell slowly around as he moved, so he could stick his sword out in different directions, while hoping that turning would make the crack harder to hit, as the birds continued to try to get him.

While Hunter was clearly struggling to keep going, Devin continued to inch his way forward, pausing every few seconds to swing his sword. Unfortunately, he only hit empty air with most of his strokes. On the contrary, one of the attacking birds, hovering directly above his shell got lucky. Bringing its beak down with a mighty peck, the huge blow started an ugly crack in Devin's shell, very much like what had just happened to Hunter only moments ago. Crying out to his friends Devin yelled, "Hunter, Cracker, my shell is damaged too, we really have to get to that log soon!"

Cracker was using his larger claw to try to fight off the attacking birds, just as his ancestor Pincer had done generations ago in the "Crabs and Gulls" story Crex had told them earlier. Unlike Pincer's adventure, this time there were simply way too many birds to deal with. The Gulls would just fly up a bit when his claw got near them, only to drop right back down to peck at his shell when he pulled it back. Clearly, the birds now understood how to crack the trios' protective shells, it would only be a matter of time before their protection was completely gone. Then, the birds would have them.

Still, the little group continued to make slow progress across the beach, toward their goal—the log fort. Fighting fiercely, fleeing from fifteen flying foes, fully fearful for their lives with each step they took, the trio had almost arrived at their 'fort,' cracked shells and all, thinking they just might make it; when suddenly, One-Eye the Pelican dropped down onto the beach, directly in front of them. He was now standing directly between the youngsters and the makeshift fort that was their last hope!

The only thing the boys could do now, with the much larger bird in front of them, was to hunker down while praying for a miracle. One-Eye's sudden landing caused the rest of the Gulls to back away from their attack for a bit, allowing the trio to momentarily peek out from beneath their shells. Seeing the evil Pelican blocking their way, staring straight down at them with his one good eye, blinking only occasionally, watching that eyeball roll around inside its socket—to look at each of trio in turn—was truly horrifying. Worse for the boys, was that below his evil eye, the Pelican's face opened into an awful, toothy grin, constantly opening and closing, ready to chew anything in its path. Such an awful sight dashed what little hope the boys now had.

Grabbing the trio's most immediate attention was actually One-Eye's other eye, or rather what was covering it. The Purple Patch was suddenly ablaze with excitement, giving off waves of purple light as it focused on the trio. One-Eye began advancing ever so slowly toward the little group. One foot dragging awkwardly across the sand followed by the other, his wings extending outward while his mouth opened fully, just waiting to claim the prize he truly desired—the Key to the Treasure Chest of Jean Laffite!

Expecting to be scooped up at any second, by the looming leering One-Eye slowly plodding toward them; his stinky fish-breath made the trio shudder in horrible anticipation, well before One-Eye got there himself. With a last desperate thought, Devin shouted out to his friends, "Guys, on the count of three, split up and make a run for it!" He figured one or two of them might make it to the fort, maybe even eventually back to the safety of the sandcastle.

Just then, as if his voice had been a signal, the Seagulls returned to the attack. One of them, hovering above Devin's shell, delivered a mighty peck directly on top of the big crack already there, splitting what was left of his shield completely in two. Devin was already screaming to his friends, "READY! ONE! TWO!" But before he could yell 'THREE' another sound erupted over the beach, completely changing everything. Emerging from the grassy dunes behind the sandcastle, a loud "HMMMMMMM" swept over the sand, sweeping away all thought and sound coming from the battle. Most importantly, this new unexpected noise immediately halted the bird's attack on the adventurers.

One-Eye also slowed his advance, clearly confused by the unplanned for sounds suddenly coming from behind him. Looking up, he noticed his Seagull friends had completely stopped their attack on the boys' shells. The birds were now simply hovering in midair, focusing their attention back toward the dunes. Shifting his gaze away from the boys, while trying to understand what was happening, One-Eye turned completely around. Seeing what was behind him, he immediately stopped advancing on the trapped trio, even as the glow from his purple patch was snuffed out.

For the boys, it seemed that just as quickly as the birds had attacked, they suddenly stopped. Unable to look straight up into the sky to see what was happening, they were all still partially covered by what remained of their shells. All the boys could only see as they ever so hesitantly peeked out were those awful birds. Rather than flying down to attack, the Seagulls were now simply hanging in the air, just above them. Each bird was looking straight ahead, not down, toward the sand dune, apparently unsure of what to do next. Flapping their wings while looking back toward the sandcastle, the Gulls seemed to simply float on the air, only a few feet above the trio they had been so intent on eating only moments before.

Best of all, there were no longer any horrible sounds or vibrations coming from the dreaded Gulls' pecking. The awful scraping noises on the outside of the broken shells had stopped! Replacing the awful *peck, peck, peck* from the Gull's beaks was a new, but not completely unfamiliar sound, a loud *hummmm*, which seemed strangely to be coming from everywhere all at once. With a surprised squawk, One-Eye flapped his wings, returning immediately to the air instead of continuing his attack on Devin, Hunter, and Cracker. Once One-Eye took off, he was immediately followed higher into the air by all of the hovering Seagulls too. The "Battle of the Beach" seemed to have ended as suddenly as it began.

Standing up, leaving their now useless broken shells lying in the sand, the three friends were quite surprised as they looked around, only to see that the battle had not really ended at all. Rather it was now rapidly changing locations, moving off the beach itself, and into the air above, bringing with it new combatants. Instead of an almost-finished fight on the ground, the air above the beach was suddenly full of confused Gulls (not to mention, one very upset Pelican) trying to get at their smaller, quicker, and very numerous would-be attackers.

Spinning around, trying to quickly understand what all was going on, Devin suddenly found himself staring straight into two very large multifaceted eyes—like some strange alien jewels—covering most of this new creature's head. Hovering barely three arm lengths away, just above the ground, the creature looked straight at Devin while Devin simply stared right back. What Devin saw, behind those brilliant eyes, was a brightly colored green and brown creature with two sets of transparent wings attached to it. When its wings stopped moving, some of the humming faded as it settled easily to the ground on its six legs.

"Hopz onz," called the creature in a strange buzzing voice. "Grabz a seatz inz the Dragonzaddlez. Therz iz a crabz clawz for youz to uze hanginz onz the zide. Nowz let'z goz getz thoze birdz!"

After so many recent crazy adventures, nothing could easily surprise the boys, even a talking Dragonfly. They were too relieved with the sudden turn of events to argue with this strange wondrous creature. Devin hopped up into the saddle on the back of his rescuer. While getting himself properly seated, he noticed that both Hunter and Cracker were doing the same thing nearby, on Dragonflies of their own.

Quickly recovering his gift for talking, Devin said, "Hi there, my name is Devin. Thanks for rescuing us." A short pause. "Who are you?"

"Holdz onz tightz thenz, youngz Devinz, myz namz iz Zipperz," answered the Dragonfly. With that introduction, Zipper's wings started buzzing once more, as he immediately launched them both almost straight up, right back into the middle of the fight.

Devin, holding tightly onto his saddle with one hand, the other keeping a strong grip on his rock sword, rose quickly into the air, as did both his friends. Looking around they could now easily see what can only be described as a miracle. Buzzing around each of the Gulls were at least two or three Dragonflies, occasionally more, each with an adult crab sitting on its back. Every crab held an oyster shell for protection in their smaller claw, while using their larger claw to strike at the flying birds.

It was Crabs and Gulls—now in the air!

The Dragonflies were very, very quick, first darting one way, stopping, then zipping off in another direction, making it extremely difficult for the larger slower Seagulls to get at them with their beaks. The Gulls, seemingly unready for this type of fighting, simply flew around in confusion. Some of the birds continued to hover, trying to peck at the annoying Dragonflies as they passed in front of them, while others tried to fly higher into the air, circle around, then come back to attack with more speed.

Hunter was the first of the three adventurers to enter the battle. His Dragonfly had, upon rising from the beach, darted out, toward the water, where two other Dragonflies with their crab warriors were taking on a lone Seagull. "By the way, what is your name?" asked Hunter as they began flying.

"ZZZargo, at yourz zzervize," responded the Dragonfly politely.

Hunter, smiling at the strange sound of Zargo's voice, returned, "Thanks for saving us from the birds." Using the same formal language of the Dragonfly, he continued, "My name is Hunter, also at your service. Now let's go help our friends."

The Gull they were rapidly approaching was busy flapping its wings, trying to hover in the air so it could use its mouth to hit the nearest attacking Dragonfly. One good shot from the bird's strong beak could easily knock either the Dragonfly or its Crab rider, or both, right out of the air.

The Crabs riding the Dragonflies clearly understood the danger from the Seagull's powerful beak. Fortunately, they had their own strategy for attacking a larger flying foe. First, one of the Dragonflies would dart in, getting close enough to draw the Gull's attention, while the second would wait until the Gull pecked at the first Dragonfly. The idea was clearly for the second Dragonfly to wait for just the right moment to swoop underneath the Gull, allowing the riding Crab to swing its claw at the Gull's exposed wing. If the attacking Crab got really lucky, a strong enough stroke to the wing joint would send the Gull to the ground, ending its ability to fight, as it would no longer be able to fly.

As he got closer to the actual fight, it appeared to Hunter that neither strategy was going to be successful. The Gull and the Crabs on their Dragonflies could only achieve a stalemate, at least until something changed or one side made a mistake. The birds were not quick enough to hit the speedy Dragonflies, while the Crabs were never able to get close enough to damage the Gull's wing.

Once at the battle, Hunter and Zargo never hesitated, going directly to the attack. Hunger, gripping his stalactite sword tightly in his right hand while holding on to the Dragonfly saddle with his left, led Zargo straight above the Seagull.

"Will I fall off if we fly upside down?" Hunter asked.

"Notz ifz youz pullz ze ztrapz onz ze zaddlez overz yourz legz andz zqueezez tightz," Zargo answered.

Hunter quickly explained to Zargo what he had in mind as they flew directly above the hovering Gull. At just the right moment, as one of the other Dragonflies once more drew the Gull's attention, allowing the second one to attack the flapping wings, Hunter and Zargo flipped over in midair, now plummeting straight down toward the Gull from above.

"Yaaahhhh!' screamed Hunter. As they reached the Gull, he jabbed straight down with his very sharp stalactite sword, hitting the Gull's wing right where it connected to the body, delivering a near perfect stroke.

With a shriek of pain, the Gull was suddenly unable to flap its wing normally anymore.

Zargo flipped back over, taking Hunter quickly away from the squawking bird. Both watched as the Gull fell awkwardly to the sandy beach below.

Immediately cheers and buzzes came up from all the Crabs and Dragonflies. Hunter had brought down one of the attacking birds, surely a sign of better things to come for those fighting the Seagulls! Unfortunately, for the boys and their Crab friends, the tide of the battle was indeed about to change, only this time against them.

***

Upon realizing what was happening with the arrival of these new warrior Crabs—all riding on hated Dragonflies—One-Eye quickly returned to the air. Flying back over the beach, calling for more Gulls to help him, One-Eye promised a rich Crab feast to all who would join him in the fight. Using the full power of his patch, he very quickly convinced another twenty or so of the birds to enter the fray. Once assembled, they all rapidly returned in full force to the battle.

Coming in much faster this time, One-Eye with his new group of Gulls didn't use the same tactics as those already fighting above the beach. Rather than use their wings to simply hover, while pecking at the annoying Dragonflies with their beaks, One-Eye and his new crew just flew right at their enemies, trying to knock the much smaller mounted Crabs out of the air with their larger bodies. The other Gulls, still somewhat confused by the initial Dragonfly attack, quickly realized this new method was a much better way to fight the swarming Dragonflies. Soon they all stopped hovering, returning to the sky so they could renew their attack at higher speeds.

The results of this change in tactics were almost immediate. Instead of an isolated Gull or two being knocked to the sand, one after another of the Dragonflies, along with their rider Crabs, started falling to the beach. They simply could not constantly avoid the larger birds.

With the sudden excitement and rush of energy from flying on a Dragonfly for the first time beginning to fade, Devin could think about their situation for a moment. Observing the battle from the air, he was able to instantly understand how the fight was changing. Now that the battle was not going as well for his friends—the Dragonflies were quickly losing the advantage they had with their larger numbers—Devin realized he could end it all very quickly. He just needed to get himself, along with the Key hanging around his neck, back inside the sandcastle. It was suddenly very clear that the only reason for this battle was One-Eye's desire for the Key. If Devin could get it off the beach, the fighting would surely end.

Just as One-Eye had changed the Gull's tactics, Devin would

now change those for his friends. "Zipper, get us to the sandcastle! Quickly!" Devin called out.

Almost immediately Zipper changed direction, heading back toward the sandcastle's entrance at the dune's edge. Hopefully, they could end this fight by themselves.

Rapidly approaching the sandcastle's front door, Devin felt a wave of relief wash over him. The hidden door, with the Purple Prism, was now so close. Devin thought he could even see some purple light coming from behind the overhanging grasses. This battle was just about over— he and his friends would finally all be safe.

Just as Zipper began to drop from the sky, down toward the dune on the beach, Devin heard a loud, scared cry coming from the air— almost directly above him.

"Heeelllpppp!" screamed Cracker. "Ahhhh, I'm falling, help!"

Looking up, Devin saw Cracker plunging down toward him, legs and pincers flailing. During the battle with the birds, a speeding Gull had run directly into Cracker's Dragonfly, completely separating Cracker from his mount. Even worse, One-Eye had also seen the falling Crab. As Devin looked up, One-Eye was now diving down, mouth open wide, ready to swallow Cracker in one gulp.

"Let's go!" shouted Devin to Zipper. The Dragonfly darted up toward Cracker. Unfortunately, they were also now heading away from the sandcastle's entrance, along with the safety the Prism would provide.

Not knowing what else to do, Devin had to try to save the falling Crab from both dangers—crashing into the hard sand below and from One-Eye's open mouth— so he did the only thing he could think of. First, he grabbed the Key hanging from around his neck. Then, after pulling the netting loop with the Key over his head, he stood up in his Dragon-saddle to distract One-Eye from his plummeting friend.

"Hey, One-Eye, see this?" Devin screamed.

One-Eye took his good eye off Cracker for just an instant. Seeing the Key being held out toward him, One-Eye paused for a moment in his downward flight, while his Purple Patch also regained some of its former eerie glow. As Devin was hoping for, One-Eye suddenly turned away from Cracker, now taking direct aim toward him.

Zipper continued to head directly at the Pelican, ready to swerve away on Devin's command.

As Devin and Zipper flew up, Cracker continued his downward plunge, passing by them just a foot away, both claws snapping wildly in the air. Devin could not help but be districted by the sight of his friend falling toward the ground, even with the fast approaching Pelican coming straight at him.

Fortunately for them both, Zipper realized Devin had taken his eyes off One-Eye, who was now almost upon them. Just as the Pelican snapped his mouth shut trying to get Devin, Zipper zagged away to one side.

Startled by the sudden jerky movement, Devin's attention came right back to the fight at hand. Turning his head back toward a now sharply banking One-Eye, Devin held the Key up with his right hand high in the air for One-Eye to clearly see, screaming at the top of his lungs, "You want something to eat?! Do ya? See this, do you see it? Go and get it!" Finishing his yell, Devin threw the Key as far as he could, back toward the ocean.

One-Eye immediately gave up pursuing the boy or his falling friend. Turning sharply, he headed out toward the sea, following his real target—the Key to Jean Lafitte's Treasure Chest! Watching his enemies plunging helplessly down toward the ground as he flew easily over the beach, it was One-Eye's turn to think the battle was almost over. Taking a slow, almost leisurely flight toward the edge of the ocean, One-Eye' s gaze locked onto the spot where the Key had just landed in the soft sand, its Green Gargoyle handle sticking straight up into the air, clearly marking the spot for him.

Cracker, plunging down toward the beach, simply closed both of his eyes, sure that he would soon hit the sand very hard, trying not to think about the likely horrible ending. He had not even noticed how close he had come to being Pelican food, as Devin successfully distracted the bird from trying to eat him. Thinking to himself, how great it had been to have met both Hunter and Devin, along with all the exciting adventures they just had, Cracker watched the last couple of days flash before his eyes. His one regret was that he would not be around after the battle, to go after the treasure chest.

"Cracker! Cracker!"

What was that? Who could be shouting at me now? Thought Cracker as he heard his name being called. Popping open both of his dangling eyes, Cracker's first sight was the onrushing sand, since his eyes were looking straight down when he opened them. Swiveling one of them in the other direction, he saw Devin on Zipper plummeting straight down from above, trying to save him. He somehow knew that they could not possibly get there in time, and would likely hurt themselves too, if they continued to dive toward the sand at their current speed.

With his last strength, Cracker lifted his claw back toward the sky, weakly trying to wave Devin and Zipper away from him. Before he could wave even one time, he was shocked to find that someone else was grabbing onto his extended claw! Sure enough, there was Hunter on his Dragonfly Zargo, now holding tightly on to him.

Finishing their battle with the Gull, Hunter and Zargo were returning to the sandcastle to engage other birds when they heard Cracker's cry. Skimming low across the sand, not yet climbing high enough into the air to engage another Seagull, Hunter was able to clearly see Cracker falling, closely followed by One-Eye, who was intent on eating him. As Devin came out of nowhere to distract One-Eye, it was up to Hunter and Zargo to rescue Cracker before he crashed into the sandy beach. Arriving at the last second, Hunter was able to grasp Cracker's suddenly outstretched claw, pulling him slightly upward—just enough to slow down his descent.

When Cracker hit the sand, he tumbled a couple of times before coming to a stop. Fortunately, the impact was no longer enough to really hurt him—just enough to make a small indention in the sand.

Zargo and Hunter dropped to the ground, right next to Cracker. Everyone was so exhausted that no one said anything for at least a few seconds. They just sat there on the beach, speechless, as the battle continued above them.

Finally, Cracker slowly sat up, cracking his pincer weakly a couple times to make sure he was OK, then breaking the silence. "Hunter, you did it again! Thanks to you…I, I think I made it! Devin was right. You really are Hunter the Hero!"

Perking up a bit, Hunter looked around to see how the rest of the battle was going. It was now just about over. The Gulls were quickly tiring of fighting with the swarming Dragonflies and their Crab riders. Without One-Eye (and his Purple Patch) goading them on, not to mention his promise of an easy Crab dinner appearing less and less likely, the Gulls began to leave the beach. All of this fighting was making the birds terribly hungry. There were certainly easier choices of food to eat than these warrior Crabs on Dragonflies. Maybe some shrimp from the shrimp boat offshore would make a better meal, the Gulls thought as they flew away.

Speaking of One-Eye, where was he? Hunter swiveled around to look for both Devin and the Pelican, neither of whom could be seen in the battle above him.

Devin, who was last seen plunging almost straight down in his attempt to rescue the falling Cracker, could easily see most of the beach from his view on the dropping Dragonfly. Recognizing Hunter flying in low across the sand, it was immediately clear to Devin that Hunter's Dragonfly was much closer than he was to the still-falling Crab. If anyone could rescue Cracker, it would have to be Hunter.

Reaching that conclusion, even as Hunter was stretching out to grab Cracker's weakly waving claw, Devin banked Zipper away, out toward the ocean, where he had—not even a minute ago—thrown the Key. Not pausing for even half a second to see if Hunter had gotten to Cracker, before the Crab hit the sand, Devin went after One-Eye and to retrieve Lafitte's Key.

Devin's flight path had been like an aerial roller coaster. He had come plummeting out of the air, straight down, riding on Zipper. Upon seeing Hunter try to rescue Cracker, he immediately leveled off, flying parallel to the sand. Rising in the air to better see things, Devin turned aiming himself out toward the ocean, where he just moments ago had thrown the Key.

Spying the Key's green handle sticking straight out of the sand near the surf, Devin looked up to see One-Eye now descending toward the Key from higher in the air. One-Eye was himself just realizing that there was competition for the Key once more and was speeding back up so he would reach his prize first!

Hunter finally located both Devin and One-Eye away from the main battle, spying them both heading from different locations toward the same thing, the Key to the treasure chest! With his inner voice, Hunter wondered to himself how the Key had gotten stuck out there in the sand, while watching mesmerized, as One-Eye dropped down from the sky, racing Devin, who was skimming in over the beach. It appeared to Hunter that both would arrive at the Key almost together, but Hunter thought that One-Eye would likely win the race by a hair.

One-Eye, now watching the approaching boy on his Dragonfly, was also convinced they would all reach the Key close to the same time. Being much larger than Devin and Zipper together, One-Eye thought happily to himself that he would very soon get the Key and maybe, just maybe rid himself of a couple enemies at the same time. With that pleasant thought producing a wicked toothy smile, the Pelican brought in his wings to speed up even more while opening his mouth wide, in anticipation of grabbing the Key.

Very much aware of the danger he was in, Devin continued to head directly toward the Key as fast as he could, constantly urging Zipper to beat One-Eye while frantically trying to think of what to do, once they got there.

Just as Hunter had suspected, One-Eye's final burst enabled him to reach the Key only moments before Devin and Zipper. Reducing his descent as well as his speed as he approached the sand, One-Eye angled his body so that he could easily scoop his long sought-after prize straight into his open beak. This he accomplished by allowing the loop of netting still attached to the Key to simply slip over the bottom of his mouth as he flew slowly by.

As One-Eye hoped, the loop slipped perfectly over the bottom of his open maw, which the Pelican shut immediately upon feeling the net pull on his mouth. Flapping his large wings to climb back into the air, while also regaining some of the speed lost in scooping up the Key, One-Eye promptly headed out to sea. His only thought now was to get far away from the Crabs, Dragonflies, Gulls, and everyone else with his hard-fought-for prize—the Key to Lafitte's Chest. He had WON!

Of course, Devin had other ideas.

With the stalactite sword drawn and held high in front of him, Devin, along with Zipper, never slowed down at all as they approached their enemy. Just as the Pelican was grabbing the netting loop, pulling the Key up out of the sand with it, One-Eye's head turned toward the ocean, seeking his escape, while Devin and Zipper were arriving at that very spot. Rather than attacking the Pelican directly, the flying duo came at the larger bird from below as well as behind, aiming themselves beneath One-Eye's just-closed beak. Zipping underneath the Pelican, who was now holding the Key in his mouth by the loop of netting, Devin stood up in his saddle. Rearing back, sword now held tightly with both hands directly above his head, Devin brought the sword straight down onto the loop with all his strength. The sharp stone made a clean cut through the loop of netting with his first swing. As Devin hoped, the Key immediately slid off, falling right back down toward the water below.

Changing directions in midair, as only a Dragonfly can do, Zipper flew back under the rising bird as the Key to Lafitte's Treasure Chest now dropped straight down. Plunging after the Key, Devin switched the sword to his left hand, while gripping the saddle with his legs. Leaning forward with his right arm extended, Devin caught up with the Key just before it hit the surf, even as One-Eye was still heading away from the beach. The Pelican had not realized until too late that he was no longer carrying his recently acquired treasure.

"I've got it!" yelled Devin as he caught the Key in midair. Zipper immediately headed back toward the dune while One-Eye wheeled himself around, squawking furiously that the prized Key was no longer attached to the piece of netting now dangling uselessly from his mouth.

In his head, enraged at the loss and fueled by the now blazing Purple Patch, One-Eye could only think about getting back the Key—nothing else mattered!

Unfortunately for One-Eye, without his goading, every single one of the Gulls helping him earlier had simply lost interest in this battle, already flying off to search for food elsewhere. However, the Purple Patch was still ablaze on his eye, casting its dark power outward as it too sought to reclaim the Key. Clearly, the Patch was no longer focusing on attracting One-Eye's allies. Instead, its wicked light was now covering the area of the beach where the Dragonflies with their riders had landed, with an eerie purple glow.

The mounted warrior Crabs had all settled on the beach for a few minutes, as the main battle appeared over with the departure of the Seagulls. Now they were all just watching the contest between Devin and the Pelican. Bathed in a soft purple light, the Crabs and their mounts appeared perfectly content to watch the action, none of them seemingly wanting to rejoin the battle to help Devin or Zipper.

Hunter, his mind now focused on the Key more than on the actual battle—as he really wanted that key just for himself—was somehow able to shake off his momentary fascination with what he was seeing, even as the others could not. Getting Zargo back up into the air, Hunter shouted to all the other Crabs and Dragonflies, "Come on, let's go!" as he tried to get the group to help Devin.

No one moved—not a single Crab or a Dragonfly! Even with Hunter yelling directly at them, all the Crabs continued to just watch the drama in the air unfold, while the Dragonflies appeared to be waiting for the Crabs to move first. Hunter realized something was very wrong, that he needed to act or One-Eye would soon have his prize, but what should he do? Spying Crex on the ground, Hunter directed Zargo over to him. Jumping off his Dragonfly, he shouted, "Crex, come on, we have to help Devin. Come On!"

Crex, still bathed in the soft purple light, continued to watch One-

Eye and Devin battle, not even looking down at Hunter, who was by now standing directly in front of him. Inspired and desperate as One-Eye kept getting closer and closer with each attack, Hunter grabbed Crex's pincer, the one with the Green Gauntlet, shaking it to try to get the crab leader's attention.

Crex didn't react at all, rather it was the Gauntlet itself that suddenly responded. Emitting a light-green glow of its own, it was as if an invisible hand suddenly shook each of the Crabs on the beach, breaking the purple spell that lay upon them.

Blinking his eyes, then looking down at Hunter, Crex quickly came back to himself. Understanding intuitively what had happened, Crex spoke just two words to Hunter, "Thank you." Looking up, both he and Hunter then launched themselves into the air; they were immediately followed by all of the other Crabs on their Dragonflies, hopefully not too late to help save Devin.

As Hunter, along with his allies, returned to the battle, One-Eye was thinking, *It is time that I end this fight*. Closing on Devin from behind, One-Eye went for the quick finish. Opening his mouth wide enough to eat Zipper, Devin, and the treasure chest key in one bite, he flew right at them.

Zipper—carrying Devin, who was now clutching Lafitte's Key in his left hand, even as he held on to the dragon saddle with his right—suddenly found himself heading back toward the dune with a very angry Pelican in hot pursuit. Using his superior quickness as a Dragonfly, along with the ability to seemingly change directions instantly, Zipper easily avoided One-Eye's first rush past him. Unfortunately, evading One-Eye's attack, while saving them both, had one other consequence—the Pelican was now between Zipper and his goal. He and Devin no longer had a straight shot to the sandcastle, with the much larger Pelican blocking their way.

In addition to having to deal with the attacking Pelican, Zipper was beginning to tire rapidly. While Dragonflies are extremely quick, they cannot move very fast for long periods of time. The battle itself had already taken a lot of Zipper's strength; now he was almost at the end of his endurance. Every time One-Eye made a rush at him, Zipper would have to wait until the last moment, then radically change directions to avoid the Pelican's waiting mouth. Not only were these aerial acrobatics a drain on him, but One-Eye's wings and body were almost as bad. As the Pelican flew by Zipper, the rush of air from the Pelican's passing would hit him as well, tiring Zipper even more.

On the other hand, One-Eye realized that while he could not easily catch the Dragonfly, his bigger size would allow him to prevent his enemies from getting back to the safety of the sandcastle. If something did not change soon, the Dragonfly would either have to land on the beach from exhaustion or make a mistake. Either way, the irritating Dragonfly, along with his rider, would end up on the inside of One-Eye's snapping mouth.

Making things even worse for Devin and Zipper, the Pelican was using his new strategy to force them farther and farther away from the sandcastle as they fought. Both the boy and Dragonfly could tell that even if One-Eye could not catch them in the air, he would eventually tire them out, to the point where they might even be forced to land, by pushing them away from the sandcastle. Most worrisome was the thought that the Pelican might be able to force them out over the water, even having to land in the sea. Once in the water, the advantage would be One-Eye's. He could then take his prize any time he wanted!

Devin, not knowing what to do, shouted to Zipper, "How do we get back to the sandcastle now?"

Zipper replied in choppy fragments while panting, "I'ze don'tz knowz, Devinz. I willz havz toz landz zoon…tooz tiredz…to ztayz…inz ze airz." With those last words, Zipper started to sink lower in the air, readying himself for one more rush from the Pelican.

Seeing One-Eye approaching once more, Devin brought all his focus on the larger bird, as he readied the rock sword for a swing. To his great surprise, instead of hearing screams from the attacking One-Eye, a welcome new sound could be heard filling his ears.

HMMMMMMMM. Every Dragonfly and its Crab rider lifted off from the beach at one time, filling the air over the sand with the sound of rapidly beating wings. Launching themselves toward the sky, the large group of warriors, led by Hunter and Crex, were now heading straight toward the struggling Zipper and Devin, even as One-Eye prepared his final attack.

Hearing the rising Dragonflies, One-Eye looked up to see a horde of his enemies coming straight at him, their pincers and shields at the ready. Even in his anger, One-Eye realized that without his Seagull allies, the battle was turning against him once more. He could no longer get the Key he so desired, at least not yet. With a final blaze of purple light from his patch, along with a last hateful squawk, One-Eye swung away from the fight, heading back out to sea. Just like that, the battle was truly over, almost as quickly as it had begun.

Landing on the beach near the entrance to the sandcastle, Devin dismounted from Zipper, thanking him repeatedly for all his help. They had just won a wild battle that no one had even seen coming. Instead of staying and talking, Zipper quickly gave Devin what might have been a Dragonfly smile, then headed back into the grasslands behind the dunes, as if he had never been there at all.

Looking around, Devin saw the other Crabs, along with Hunter, rapidly approaching him. None of them were with their Dragonflies either, as upon dismounting every single Dragonfly had immediately left the beach—just as with Zipper. Thinking this strange, but with so much else going on, Devin saved his thoughts about the Dragonflies for another time. Best of all, Devin saw that Cracker was coming toward him, along with the others. He had survived the fall. Hunter had gotten to him in time!

Walking right up to Devin, who had a huge ear to ear smile on his face, while focusing his gaze on Devin's neck, Cracker noticed with surprise that the Key was no longer there. Happy to see his friend, but clearly a little worried about the Key, Cracker blurted out, "What happened to the Key, Devin? Where is it?"

Still grinning hugely at the return of his friend, Devin did not immediately say anything; rather, he pulled his right hand up out of his pocket, showing the Key to Cracker it was safe with them once more. Unable to stop smiling, Devin then explained what had happened after Cracker had fallen, that he had used the Key to distract the Pelican during the battle, and to then save Cracker from being eaten by One-Eye!

Meanwhile, the other warrior Crabs were all coming up to see the three adventurers, while congratulating themselves on a hard-fought victory. Crex, who had led the Crabs into the battle, was wearing his still slightly glowing Green Gauntlet. Scuttling up next to Devin, Crex quickly and quietly told the boy to put the Key back in his pocket, not noticing that the Key itself now had a slightly dark-green fog around it, making it difficult to focus on. Crex then led the entire group of victorious Crabs back into the sandcastle.

CHAPTER 12

A BIG FEAST

> ***Conversations***
>
> *A feast comes after a good fight, or does a fight comes after a good feast? Either way, during a feast it is said that stories are told, exaggerations are often made, and conversations occur. One can learn a lot from what is said during those Conversations...if one only listens.*
>
> CRAB CHRONICLES

None of the adventurers said anything about the Key as they proceeded back into the sandcastle. Everyone else was talking about the wild battle with the birds, as if the Key had gone completely unnoticed during the melee. Stories were already coming to life as each Crab described, to anyone and everyone who would listen, their exploits on the field of battle that day. Listening to all the talk, an observer might think that every Crab fighting in the battle had actually defeated a Seagull all by himself. The stories were already becoming legend, as everyone was so happy following such an incredible victory.

Crex, followed by the other warriors, led the now large, and quickly getting larger, group of Crabs back to the main sandcastle chamber. This was the very same large auditorium where the boys had first met him, Crex's audience hall. As the warrior Crabs put up their shields and began to share tales of the battle with friends who had not been out on the beach, including a not so small amount of discussion regarding the extreme bravery they all exhibited, Crex quickly, without being observed, managed to grab both boys along with Cracker, leading them alone into a more private space off to one side, his private audience room.

Once inside this smaller Crab hole, Crex gave each of the adventurers a hug in turn, followed by a sincere congratulations on their successful return to the sandcastle. Hunter was also thanked one more time for helping Crex, along with his fellow warriors, to escape from the influence of the Purple Patch during the battle. That single act likely thwarted One-Eye from gaining the Key for himself, which was the difference between today's great victory, and what might have been a terrible defeat.

Finishing these pleasantries quickly, Crex got right to the real reason he wanted to speak with them alone. He asked the trio to briefly highlight what had really happened to them since they had all gone missing a couple days ago. Crex had already decided that he wanted to hear from the boys as quickly as possible. He needed to know what they had been doing, and why a battle with the birds had been the direct result. Figuring he did not have much time, as they would all soon be missed by the very large group of Crabs gathering for the upcoming feast in the audience hall, Crex tried to quickly get some answers. The rest of the colony would be looking to congratulate the adventurers, so any additional details would have to come later.

Immediately, the triumphant trio took to telling terrific travel tales, taking turns talking to each other, as much as answering Crex, about the strange adventures on the river. Cracker found himself becoming the main storyteller. Devin and Hunter would chime in occasionally, adding important points as they felt necessary. Most of the conversation focused on retrieving the Key to the treasure chest, along with saving Sage the Turtle from the fishing net trap. For some reason though—maybe due to the short time they had to talk or perhaps the direction the conversation naturally took—none of the little group brought up any of the other more interesting events that occurred, especially those dealing with information regarding Lafitte's chest.

While not hiding any of their newfound knowledge about the Rainbow Objects, the adventurers kept to themselves specific details that only they knew. In particular, they avoided anything that might help lead others to the recovery of the treasure chest, before they were able to go search themselves. Certain visions from the Séance Stone, Sage's stories, even Hunter's vision of the future, which he was keeping to himself anyway, were all overlooked in the conversation with the sandcastle's leader. None of them found it necessary to reveal the painted arrow on the cavern wall, which appeared to point the way toward Jean Laffite's Treasure Chest. Only the three travelers knew where to begin any quest for the chest itself. Interestingly, no one brought up Orion's potential role in these events either.

Crex listened intently, keeping his thoughts on what he was hearing very much to himself, bobbing his body up and down as Cracker told the story. Likely understanding more than what was said out loud, Crex asked only a single question during the entire telling of the tale. He knew it was very important to understand what had really happened to the trio, as finding the Key to Lafitte's chest, the recent battle with One-Eye, and Sage the Turtle's involvement in this adventure surely meant changes were likely to be coming, perhaps darker days for the Crabs living here in the sandcastle.

They would need to be ready. However, Crex did not want to alarm the brave young adventurers, nor draw unwanted attention from the rest of the Crabs living in the colony by talking with them for too long. As the boys finished their story, he asked his one question, "Devin, what are you planning to do with the Key, now that you have it?"

Somewhat surprised by the question, as he had thought that the Crabs might just take the Key for themselves, answered carefully, "I'm really not sure, Crex. I think that you and the Crabs living here might have a better idea what to do with it than we do." Devin slowly pulled the Key from his pocket. "This key has been down here a very long time. Given what we have just gone through these last couple days, maybe it would be better off staying here with you in the sandcastle."

Devin continued, "Besides, both Hunter and I will need go back to being Bigs again soon. I'm certain we don't want the Key with us when we do. Not to mention that it's also likely that since Laffite's Key was found down by the river, I would think Lafitte's Chest might very well be down there too." With a little more confidence, Devin added, "Maybe Hunter and I can come back to visit in a few days. It sure would be fun to go searching for the Treasure Chest? What do you think?"

Both Cracker and Hunter were very surprised by Devin's words. Cracker, always thinking ahead, was impressed that Devin was already trying to find a way to potentially gain Crex's agreement for them to go hunting for the treasure, without letting slip the arrow pointing the way. Hunter though, was not of the same thought. *I was the one who found that key. We should keep it and go after the treasure right now, not give it back to the Crabs and go home!* Rather than understanding what Devin might be trying to do with Crex, Hunter's expression immediately changed to an ugly frown, just for an instant, which he kept hidden before he brought back his normal smile, masking his angry feelings.

Cracker, also very excited with his own thoughts about treasure hunting—although with a much different view than Hunter's—asked Crex, "If Devin is going to leave the Key here, will we go looking for the treasure ourselves…or wait for Devin and Hunter to return?"

Crex looked at them all. "I think Devin is right to leave the Key in our care. I also agree that neither of you boys would want to have the Key with you when you go home, for any number of reasons. As for going after the chest, I think we should let some time pass before a search for any treasure is mounted."

Pointing directly at the Key in Devin's hand, Crex continued, "This key is very important, not to just us Crabs, but to all the creatures of the beach, as I suspect you three have figured out by now. Events involving both the Rainbow Objects and Colors are happening more often than usual for some reason. Things like this have not occurred in a long time. It's probably a good idea to slow down any activities related to the Objects for a bit, if we can. I think we all need to consider these recent events very carefully, so good use can be made of the Key now that it is here with us." With a quizzical yet knowing look, Crex added, "Besides, where would we go to begin such a quest for the actual chest?"

Crex focused his gaze now on Cracker, almost as if he was talking directly to him and not the others. "Anyway, since you three have found it, we will keep the Key safe here in the sandcastle, certainly until Devin and Hunter can return. They are clearly part of the Key's tale now, so to answer Devin's question, we will wait for a while, till the boys come back at least, before acting."

Pausing for a moment, Crex then spoke up with added conviction, "Yes, that is exactly what we will do. The Rainbow Objects are active once again. I suspect that maybe more than just the Purple Patch is very close by. I think that we will all have to be extra careful when we are outside the sandcastle…or on any adventures that might involve them."

Changing subjects, Crex concluded, "Well, boys, it's time to head back to the party. Everyone will want to congratulate you and celebrate today's tremendous victory over One-Eye and his Gulls." With a smile, he turned to address Devin. "I bet the entire colony is gathered out there by now, ready to begin the celebration. We have not had a real battle with the birds for quite some time, you know. I think we should show the Key to everyone here in the sandcastle to kick off the feast.

"Such a display will be a reminder to all of today's victory over One-Eye, while also warning our colony of the dangers the Rainbow Objects may bring in the future. As part of the celebration, we will put the Key on display in one of the alcoves in the main audience chamber. I think we can leave it there for a few weeks, then move it somewhere safe, once its newness has worn off and the colony starts to lose interest in it."

Hunter became very focused on the discussion about storing and moving the Key. He asked Crex directly, "Why would you have to move it somewhere safe? I don't understand. Won't it be safe here inside the sandcastle?"

Shifting his gaze to Hunter, Crex answered, "No one in the colony would take it, certainly not after we put the Key on display so it is out in plain sight. Such a Crab would never be allowed back in the colony, ever. With all this renewed attention on Objects and Colors, the Key should be very safe indeed. No, I think it likely the bigger danger will come later, after the current focus, once we show it to everyone, has worn off.

"You see, when something is in front of you every day, after a while it gets taken for granted. That's when the Key will be easier to take, when it is no longer new, and the colony isn't paying as much attention. We will keep the Key public, so everyone can see it for a while, but at some point, will need to store it elsewhere…for safe keeping."

Hunter didn't stop. "Why tell everyone the Key is here at all Crex? Won't showing it off just encourage someone to try to take it? We can just keep this a secret among us."

Crex smiled. "You know, Hunter, it is often easier to keep something you are trying to protect out in the open in front of everyone, rather than trying to be secretive. Those that are looking for such a thing usually know, or quickly find out, where it is anyway. This way, the entire colony will help keep it safe. Besides, One-Eye already knows we have it here, doesn't he? I am very confident he will return to try to claim the Key, so we need to plan on how to stop his next attack."

Still smiling, Crex stood up. "But, fortunately for us, that is tomorrow's problem. We have a little time on our side, as One-Eye can't easily get into the sandcastle, so let's enjoy the feast tonight and show everyone here what this afternoon's fight was all about. Oh, one last thing, Hunter, after the upcoming feast, both you and Devin will surely want to get some rest. You will all sleep in our guest sleeping chamber off the main hall. Cracker can stay there too if he wants." He pointed his smaller pincer (no longer wearing the Green Gauntlet) back out toward the gathering party. "Cracker, can you show it to them quickly?

Make sure they are comfortable. Then you can all join us for the feast."

"Of course, Crex," replied Cracker with a quick snap of his pincer. "C'mon guys, let's check it out. Then we can all go celebrate. It's going to be a lot of fun!"

"Before we go, I have one more question for you Crex," said Devin, changing subjects.

"Yes?" inquired Crex.

"I was just wondering, how were you able to have all the Crabs ready to rescue us when we got back to the beach? I'm even more curious as to where all those Dragonflies came from. I mean, why were they there at all, Crex? Why did they help us? Why did they leave so quickly and not stay to celebrate? Why?"

"That may be the longest single question I have ever heard, young Devin. There were at least five in there, and I would bet I missed one or two more," responded Crex, laughing. "I suspect the rest of you are somewhat curious about these matters too, hmmm?" Looking around at Hunter and Cracker who were both nodding their heads as well, Crex went on, "OK, we should get back to everyone else, but before we do, I will simply tell you that it was not I, nor any of the Crabs here in the sandcastle, that knew you needed our help."

Very surprised, Cracker blurted out in his most surprised voice, "What? How can that be? You were there, you saved us."

"That is technically correct, Cracker. We were there, but as I said, it was not anyone here in the colony that was responsible for your rescue. In truth, it was the Dragonflies who made today's events possible. You see, earlier today, to everyone's great surprise, as we really had no idea something was afoot on the beach, a Dragonfly came to the castle's front door with a warning, telling us we needed to be ready for battle immediately, that a fight with the Birds was already at hand."

Realizing that he would have to explain at least some of this to the boys before returning to the main gathering, Crex sat back on his hind legs, while the others also sat down once more themselves, ready to hear more. After a momentary pause to look at each of the trio in turn, Crex began once again, "Understand, you three, we Crabs do not spend much time with the Dragonflies. No one does here on the beach. They are very mysterious creatures that we know too little about."

Interrupting, Hunter asked until he was out of breath, "Then how did they know to help us, how can they speak to us, and how did they know to come to you? How—"

Crex smiled as he cut Hunter off. "Hunter, with each question this tale will only get longer. And I thought Devin asked long questions. I can only tell you that we believe the Dragonflies must have come through the Purple Prism, or some other similar object, as that is what allows all of us to communicate here in the sandcastle, just as you are able to now. When that might have happened, we Crabs are not sure. No one that I know has any idea, except perhaps Sage the Turtle, but I would guess it was a very, very long time ago indeed, as such a thing had to have happened before our colony was here on the beach. We have no records or knowledge of such a thing ever occurring."

Pausing for a second as if deciding how much more of the story to tell the trio, Crex started talking again. "However and whenever they arrived, the Dragonflies do not spend time with us or any other creatures around here, that we can tell. What we are sure of is that the Dragonflies are not friends with those who use the Rainbow Objects. They are, however, on rare occasions, friendly with those of us who use the Rainbow Colors. Over time, we in this colony have learned that we should work with the Dragonflies when given the chance, as well as to listen very carefully to them when they say something important is happening. The Dragonflies seem to be aware of events before they are happening."

Crex paused again for a second, thinking about what he was saying, then added, "No, on second thought, maybe what I should say is, 'while they are happening,' even if there is no way they should or could know. Zipper himself came to the sandcastle earlier this day, warning that the battle was coming, and that we must be ready. Not knowing exactly what he meant, I, along with all of the warrior Crabs that were nearby, grabbed our shields and went out to the dune. When we got there, we saw a host of Dragonflies waiting for us at the edge of the grass. They seemed to know almost how many Crabs would be coming. There was one Dragonfly waiting for each of us, and as it turned out, there were three extra Dragonflies without Crabs to ride. Now I can see they knew exactly how many Dragonflies were needed, as the three others were meant for you…but I digress.

"Once we emerged out onto the dunes, there was no talking or discussion, as all the Dragonflies were clearly looking intently out onto the sand. Turning around, we could easily see something happening behind us, right in the middle of the beach. What we saw was a large group of Seagulls hovering over a spot in the sand; it was not clear to any of us at the time that it was you three at all. Seeing all the Gulls, along with the obvious interest of the Dragonflies, each of us found our Dragonfly mount, saddled up, then as quickly as possible launched ourselves into the air, ready to attack the birds. You three know the rest of the story. Now we are here. Time to celebrate today's great victory."

"Wow," said Devin, "that is truly amazing, Crex. So the Dragonflies are the ones who were responsible for our rescue. I had just assumed it was the other way around. That somehow, you had gotten them to help us."

"There are a lot of things we don't know about the Dragonflies, Devin. As I said, they seem to be our friends, helping us when needed. But they clearly want to stay away from contact with others as much as they can, which we Crabs have all learned to respect. Anyway, enough talk, there will be plenty of time for more stories later. Everyone has to be hungry, and we should really rejoin the others."

With that, the small group returned to the main assembly chamber, Cracker walking with the boys along the outer edge to another hole on the opposite side of the hall. This was the room Crex had told them about, where they would sleep that night. It was a small room, very simple, with a few sea-grass mats lined up on the floor. One of the walls was lined with smaller shells, each containing fresh water for guests to use or drink, one shell for each mat.

Cracker commented as both boys looked around, "This is where our guests usually stay when they visit. Nothing fancy, but it's very convenient when we have a feast. Come on, let's head back out to the party, nothing exciting to see in here."

Leaving the little sleeping room, the trio returned to the main chamber. Coming back out, they paused for a moment to listen to the mood of the crowd, which by now included just about every single one of the Crabs living near the sandcastle, just as Crex had predicted.

Crex, in the meantime, was easily working his way through the throng of Crabs, congratulating many of them on the day's accomplishments as he went. By the time the boys came back into the great hall, he was almost to the middle of the chamber, next to his audience chair. The boys could see him standing up above the crowd, looking over the entire Crab community, obviously pleased with what he saw. When there was a slight dip in the noise level, he stuck his large claw up into the air for all to see. Snapping it very loudly three times, "SNAP SNAP SNAP," he soon had the attention of everyone there.

In his loudest booming voice, Crex declared, "Fellow Crabs of Pirates Beach, today is a day of…victory!" As he said *victory*, Crex once again stuck his large pincer back into the air, even higher than before, opening it up in the shape of a V. He had to pause for a bit, as all of the Crabs immediately started clacking their own pincers together, acknowledging the day's success against One-Eye and the birds.

After the noise subsided, Crex added, with a voice growing both stronger and firmer, "Tonight we honor all those who recently fought the birds, but also other things as well."

Pointing his smaller pincer toward the adventurers standing off toward the outer edge of the chamber, Crex boomed, "Devin, Hunter, and Cracker, come here, come here, if you please." Sounds of surprise and curiosity filled the ranks of the Crabs while the trio moved through the parting crowd, heading toward Crex. As the trio passed by, one could hear questions and comments from various Crabs, like, "What do you think the Bigs have done? Is that really Cracker up there, he's a little young to be singled out, isn't he? Did you hear the rumor that one of them actually took something from One-Eye?"

Once Devin, Hunter, and Cracker had gotten to Crex's side, the Crab king put his small claw on Devin's back, sticking his large claw back up above his head, snapping it twice. "Fellow Crabs of the sandcastle, today we have not only defeated One-Eye and his Gulls in fierce battle…" He had to pause again as the Crabs' claws renewed clacking made speaking impossible for a moment. As the din subsided once more, Crex was finally able to deliver his real surprise to the colony: "But today, we have also recovered the Long…Lost…Key…to Lafitte's Treasure Chest!"

Rather than cause more applause, this last statement seemed to create some confusion among the Crabs. A wave of quiet seemed to sweep through the great hall, as the Crabs wondered at first to themselves, then to each other, What does this new news foretell? Could it be true? Where is this key? What does it look like? Why today? What does this mean?

Nothing truly new regarding the Rainbow Objects had occurred inside the sandcastle for many generations of sand Crabs. Some of the youngsters did not really believe the stories Crex and the older Crabs told about the Breaking of the Rainbow. One-Eye had always been the Crabs' enemy and the Purple Prism in the sandcastle door was mostly taken for granted. It had always been there. Until today, there had been no real battles involving Objects or Colors to speak of in a very long time.

The full details of today's battle were still known only to a few of the participants, and like most things, many would never know all of it. Crex himself had not been seen using the Gauntlet in combat within the memory of most of the celebrants assembled for the feast. Only a select few of the warriors knew how the Gauntlet had aided them this afternoon. Announcing that Lafitte's Key had been recovered as a result of today's battle would certainly change things for the colony. The Crabs slowly began to talk among themselves about this surprising, even exciting, turn of events.

Following up his revelation, Crex turned his eyes to look directly at Devin, booming, "Devin, will you please…bring forth…the Key?"

Devin slowly reached into his pocket, then grabbing the Key by the metal barrel, pulled it out so that as his hand was thrust up into the air by Crex's smaller claw. After standing there with the Key to Lafitte's Chest held high for a few moments, Devin turned and presented the Key to Crex. Also, grasping it by the barrel as Devin had, Crex then lifted it back up into the air for all to see once more.

Devin, Hunter, and Cracker were all smiling huge smiles while the assembled Crabs clacked their pincers, even louder than ever. Those that were close enough to Crex, and looking directly at the base of the Key, could just see that the green handle was carved to look like a tiny gargoyle. Those farther back saw only green rock, maybe some sort of marble, even when looking straight at the handle.

After another pause while the clacking quieted once more, Crex boomed, "To honor our new friends Devin and Hunter, not to mention our very own adventurer Cracker, for their bravery in recovering this key, let's give them all a fabulous Crab salute!"

Immediately, every Crab in the hall raised its large pincer, snapping it three times in rhythm. *CLACK, CLACK, CLACK* was followed by very loud shouting, "Hip Hip Hooray!" Then three more snaps, *CLACK, CLACK, CLACK*, finished with a short rhyme, "Heroes for today!"

Following the funny cheer, a happy chaos seemed to break loose throughout the chamber as everyone's spirits soared. Suddenly, all the Crabs nearest to the boys were congratulating them with hand and claw shakes, well wishes, along with friendly pats on their backs and heads. The trio, not used to being in the spotlight, soon got to the point where they all began to turn red, partly from delight and partly from embarrassment, given all the attention they were receiving.

As the hubbub finally faded a bit, Crex was able to continue his little speech, exclaiming while still holding up the Key, "As many of you know, the old stories often mention that Jean Laffite's Treasure Chest always contains a Rainbow Object, sometimes more than one!" Waving the Key for added emphasis, he continued, "Only this afternoon, One-Eye the Pelican was surely trying to get this very key, the one I now hold here before you! Yet as you can all clearly see…NOW WE HAVE IT!" Having to pause again as all the Crabs started cracking their pincers in applause, Crex waited patiently so that he could continue.

While the Crabs were applauding, Hunter, who had gotten even more excited about the contents of the Treasure Chest as Crex was talking, turned to Devin and said in a low voice, "See, Devin, there is treasure inside the chest. I just know there is. We should go and look for it now, not wait till after we go home and maybe come back, don't you think? We could even go tonight!"

Before Devin could answer, Crex resumed in his most booming voice, "To honor the recovery of Lafitte's Key, and to remind each of us what it means, we will place this key for the entire colony to see, right here in the Great Hall." Pointing toward a small alcove directly below the hanging claw and shield from Pincer, one of the greatest Crabs of all, Crex moved toward the spot he was pointing to, holding the Key up high in the air.

Once he arrived, Crex gently placed the Key into its appointed spot. The Key could now clearly be seen in its resting place, which was just above the eye level of the Crabs. Crex placed the handle on the bottom with the barrel angled up to the right so the Key itself leaned upright against the side and back walls of the alcove.

Swiftly returning to the center of the great hall, Crex spoke to the assembled Crabs once more. "After today's victorious Battle of the Birds… and the many wondrous things we have all just seen and participated in, I now officially declare…a Crab Feast!" These words brought out the thunderous applause of pincers snapping one more time. Crex had to pause one final time, while the cheers from everyone died down enough for him to be heard. With a final shout to everyone, he concluded, "Now, let the party…BEGIN!"

With that, a tremendous cacophony of cracking claws, cheering, clamoring, talking, boasting, along with every other possible assorted celebratory noise, filled the Crab assembly hall with pure joy. Other Crabs scuttled here, there, seemingly everywhere preparing all sorts of things to feast on. Some began to play music, somehow mixing the ocean's calming sounds with their own unique singing and clacking, while still others broke off into groups to discuss the day's events, enjoy themselves, and have conversations. A few Crabs, friends of Orion's included, went over to look more closely at the Key.

Devin, Hunter, and Cracker were now completely surrounded by many of the younger Crabs, all of them demanding immediate attention, anxious to hear about their recent adventures. Cracker's sister Tracker and her usual group of friends were among the most inquisitive.

Tracker normally paid very little attention to her younger and, in her view, usually irritating brother. Today was a bit different, now that Cracker was suddenly a hero. More importantly to Tracker, he was now hanging out with Bigs, who also were heroes within the colony. She and her friends wanted to find out what those boys had really been up to. How had they discovered then recovered Lafitte's Key, she wondered? It was so unlike Cracker to be adventurous. It simply had to be the Bigs Cracker was with who instigated things. Tracker decided that at tonight's feast, she would make sure to find out!

Meanwhile, the large group of younger crabs was crowding their way right in front of the adventurers, peppering the 'hero's' with all sorts of questions.

"How did you find the key?" asked one.

"Did you really get to ride on a Dragonfly?" asked another.

"Was it dangerous?" questioned a third.

These simple questions were immediately followed by many many more, so all the boys actually heard was, "How did you..?, Did you really..?, Was it..?" and on and on. Smiling, the trio simply nodded their heads up and down, after a bit the flow of questions slowed until they all naturally broke up into smaller groups, making it easier to hear and talk, before the feast was served.

As the entire crab community prepared for the major feast, there were more than a few interesting conversations, including…..

***

Hunter and Trackiana (Cracker's sister Tracker)

Once she had gotten Hunter off by himself Tracker exclaimed, "Everyone is so excited about your adventures Hunter. You must tell me all about them!"

Hunter stood with his back to one of the chamber walls facing Tracker. No one could really see him, as Tracker intentionally blocked the view, so that she could talk to Hunter all by herself.

With a quick clickety-click of a claw she continued with a big smile, "Oh, sorry, I guess I should introduce myself first. My name is Trakiana, but you can call me Tracker, I'm Cracker's sister."

Hunter laughed, "Cracker and Tracker, that's pretty funny, your names rhyme! Plus, you both like to click your claws when you are talking, guess Cracker really is your brother. Just curious, why do they call you Tracker? Is that short for Trakiana?"

Enjoying the laugh along with Hunter, Tracker smiled as she replied with an emphatic, "No!" Then a little softer she said, "Well, OK maybe it has something to do with it, just a little bit, but the real reason they call me Tracker is that I can find anything, anywhere!" With obvious pride in her voice she continued, "I am the best tracker here in the Sandcastle. I bet I could even find that treasure chest everyone is talking about, if I decide to go after it, that is."

Hunter's face immediately perked up at the mention of the Treasure Chest. "Yea, I really wish I could go looking for it, I just don't think I will get the chance too, not very soon anyway. But if I do, maybe you could help. Would you want to?"

"I don't understand, why won't you be able to go looking for it?" asked Tracker.

"As I'm sure you saw, Crex put the Key in the alcove; he does not seem ready to let anyone go searching for the chest right now. Plus, Devin and I will most likely be leaving the sandcastle fairly soon, after the feast is over, or tomorrow morning at the latest. We have to get back to our families sometime, I would think." Almost as an afterthought he mentioned quietly to himself, "Won't Bailey be surprised when I tell her what we have been doing down here?"

Tracker asked, "Who's Bailey, Hunter?"

"Bailey? She's my older sister. Usually she gets to do all the fun and cool stuff, at least most of the time, but not today!' After a pause Hunter refocused on Tracker, continuing with some bravado, "I tell you Tracker, if it was up to me, and I could think of some way to get the Key then slip past everyone, we would go off searching for the Treasure Chest first thing tomorrow—just you and me!!" He smiled at the thought of going after the treasure. "I know we would find it, don't you!"

"Why do you even need the Key to look for the chest?" Tracker was also getting excited, thinking about her own possible adventure with a Big, just like her brother had done. "I mean, if you could actually find it, couldn't you bring the chest back here, or at least find out where it is so Crex would then help? Maybe you are right Hunter. We could find it, if we tried!" Tracker finished with a smile growing on her face as big as Hunter's had been just a moment ago.

Tracker then added with a slight shiver, "You know Hunter, this is pretty exciting for me, meeting a Big, thinking about an actual hunt for Lafitte's Chest, not just listening to the stories, but, if we are really going to do this…" Tracker paused for a moment, clearly thinking about some problem to overcome.

Hunter, looking intently at her, asked, "If we are to do this, then what? Tracker, what?"

"How would we know where to begin? I mean, look, if the Chest was with the Key, you would already have found it, right? So how will we go about finding it? Even I can't just find something if I don't know where to start looking," finished Tracker.

Grinning to himself, and so engrossed by the mere thought of searching for the Chest, Hunter revealed to Tracker what he held back from Crex. Bending forward, insuring his speech was for Tracker alone, Hunter whispered intently, "Let me tell you something Tracker, and you need to keep this just between us, OK? I *do* know where to start looking for the Chest. There is an area underneath the dunes with some directions that I saw earlier. We would start there."

"Are you kidding me, Hunter?" Tracker questioned hopefully as her eyes opened wide with amazement. Not knowing exactly what she was saying at this point since she was so excited, Tracker rushed on, "So its agreed then, tomorrow we go looking for the Chest, you and me? Promise?"

Hunter finished, brimming with confidence, "You bet! Won't everyone be surprised when we find it, too?" Thinking about what he had just said, committing to searching for Lafitte's Chest, Hunter added, "We may want to bring Devin along, and what about Cracker, they both wanted to look for the chest as well?"

"Either one is fine I guess, just as long as they agree to go without telling any of the adults," Tracker grinned. "If they don't, you and I will have to find a way to sneak out anyway! Agreed?"

"Agreed," promised Hunter, giving his new friend a 'high-five' to seal the deal.

Pausing for a moment in their excitement, both Hunter and Tracker let their thoughts wander off, thinking about searching for the lost treasure chest. Still smiling, Tracker broke the silence with another question for Hunter, "You seem very intent on going after the treasure yourself, even after all you did today, why is that?"

"I don't know 'why' exactly, but I feel I just really need to find that chest. It's hard to put into words." Trying to explain his feelings, Hunter paused for a moment before continuing, "Searching for the key made me feel really good inside, I mean really good. I accomplished something important today, something that everyone else thought was cool." Finishing his thoughts while suddenly staring intently into Tracker's eyes, "Don't you see, no one made fun of me or told me what to do. I did it, me! It felt great, now I want to feel like that again!"

A bit confused by Hunter's last remarks, Tracker followed up, "Who makes fun of you? I don't understand. Why is that so important?"

Sighing, Hunter lost the dark intensity of his gaze, as he felt very comfortable talking with Tracker. She certainly didn't know, or would likely ever know, any of his friends at home. He could talk to her about things he didn't talk about with anyone, even Devin.

"You see Tracker, where I live, most of my time is spent in school, with other 'Bigs' my age, it's what we do. Some of them are nice, some are not-so-nice. The 'not-so-nice' ones always seem to be trying to get me to do stuff I don't want to, pushing me around, or making fun of me if I don't do what they want. When I do something *I* want to, they laugh at me, making me feel—I don't know, small or bad inside—even though I should feel good! Finding that key, it made me feel different inside Tracker, especially when I grabbed hold of it. I can't explain the feeling, but I know that I liked it, a lot!" Hunter, who was now pointing at his own chest, finished, "Plus, did you hear everyone here cheering for what I did? I like that, too."

Tracker, feeling for Hunter, followed up with another question, "Hunter, there are not-so-nice creatures everywhere. Here in the Sandcastle, outside in the world of the Bigs, everywhere, that is something we see all the time. I am curious though, why would you hang out with those kind of people, if they make you feel bad?"

"I don't know Tracker, it seems those are the kids that get the most attention, even if it's not always good. They occasionally do cool stuff too, things that seem really fun at the time, especially things that my parents don't want me to do. I really like doing stuff like that you know —stuff they tell me I shouldn't," he finished with a big smile at that last thought.

"Does Devin hang out with those kids?" asked Tracker.

"Devin does not live near me, so he doesn't go to the same school I do. We only get together on weekends or during the summer, so he doesn't know about some of the things I do at school or everyone I hang out with." Finishing his story after a short pause, Hunter concluded, "Tracker, this is between you and me, right?"

"You bet Hunter, just you and me, and we are still going after the Chest tomorrow! Agreed?" Tracker finished, with a huge grin. Her comments about the new quest along with that big smile - made them both feel very good indeed.

***

Orion and One-Eye

Outside of the sandcastle, One-Eye landed on the dune's edge, near Orion's hiding place. Once on the ground, the angry Pelican turned his gaze toward Orion. Still upset—at himself, at Devin, at the Dragonflies, at just about everyone—from missing his chance earlier today at getting the Key, he shouted at Orion, "Where were you when I needed your help?! Where?"

"Calm down, One-Eye. What did you want me to do, let everyone in the colony know we are working together? Maybe I should send them an invitation to join us now?" answered a sarcastic Orion. "Besides, none of the Dragonflies will carry me anyway. So, what could I have done to help in your aerial battle this evening? Nothing! The important thing is, what are we going to do now? How do we get the key away from Crex and the rest of the colony, so we can open up the Chest?"

One-Eye was indeed calming down. Thinking clearly again, he answered in a commanding tone, "You will go grab the key, you must get it tonight, before Crex or the other crabs expect anyone to go after it. He surely expects me to try to steal it away, no doubt about that, but will likely think it safe for the time being, now that it's inside the Sandcastle, where I can't easily go myself. What he won't expect is someone from within the colony to make a quick move to steal it." Focusing directly on Orion, he finished, "Orion, we need to get it out of there, before Crex has time to really think things through. Even tomorrow might be too late."

"OK, I get it, that's fine," responded Orion. "But, while I am risking my claws to get the key, what will you be doing in the meantime?"

"I will be providing a diversion for you, of course, later this evening in fact," answered the Pelican, now actually grinning. "Yes indeed, I have just the thing in mind to get everyone inside the Sandcastle focused on the front door. That way, you can get the Key for us, then easily slip out the back."

Orion, not questioning the plan at this point, complicated schemes like this were something he knew One-Eye was really good at, so he simply asked, "How will I know when it's time to go?"

Laughing now at his own brilliance, One-Eye answered, "Just get the Key Orion. You will know when it's time to go, everyone in the Sandcastle will be very very busy all of a sudden—and I mean everyone!" He paused for a moment before finishing the plan. "Once you get out of there, follow the underground river upstream, back towards the bay. I will meet you at the old decaying mansion, the one on the inlet where the river starts. From there we can get the chest, and see which Objects might currently be hidden inside."

Somewhat surprised by One-eye's comment, Orion asked quickly, "Do you have the chest already? Is it waiting for us at the mansion?"

"No, but I do know where it is, and more importantly, who has it. That's all you need to know for now. We will be expecting you, Orion —and with the Key—don't disappoint us! See you at the mansion." answered One-Eye.

Not saying another word, Orion was nevertheless thinking carefully about what he just heard. One-Eye mentioning 'we' not 'me' and 'us' not 'I', implied there would be more than just One-Eye waiting for him at the mansion. Perhaps he should have some surprises ready too, just in case.

***

Whipper and George (Warrior Crabs)
George smiled at his friend Whipper, they were now relaxing together after the big battle with the birds as George was saying, "Did you see how I took down one of those gulls earlier this afternoon—all by myself?"

Whipper laughing heartily, replying in his own chuckling voice, "You will have to refresh my memory on that one George, as I don't seem to recall seeing too many gulls taken down by a lone crab today." Finishing with a friendly grin Whipper asked, "Did I miss something?"

"Of course, Whipper," George came back in a happy, slightly sarcastic tone, "Be glad to help out your obviously challenged memory. Let me tell you, there I was, sitting on my Dragonfly Zzigger, naturally I was flying right behind Crex, ready to lend my sharp claw and superb shell when we arrived at the battle. Somehow, and let me tell you, I was as surprised as anyone, that on the first pass, I didn't come into contact with a single one of those awful gulls! Zzigger and I actually flew straight through all those crazy birds without hitting any of them! Can you believe that? Didn't hit a single one I tell you! Probably due to my awesome flying skills, can there be any other real explanation? I don't think so."

As George told his story, he held each of his claws up in the air, his smaller pincer waiving and bobbing as if it represented himself flying through the crowded sky, evading his enemies. Continuing on, now focused on the story itself George said, "Anyway, once we had passed through the wave of birds, Zzigger and I found ourselves hovering over the water's edge, with no enemies to be seen, just the open seas. Of course, we immediately wheeled around to attack the gulls from behind, but before we did, do you know what we saw, sitting there, in the water?"

"I have no idea," responded Whipper, wondering where this story could possibly go next.

"Blue crabs!" answered George excitedly, "and in fairly large numbers."

"Really? Blue crabs you say? What would blue crabs be doing here this time of year? That is very strange indeed," commented Whipper, now much more interested in George's words—Blue Crabs were very dangerous and could bring trouble.

George, jumping right back in, exclaimed, "That's Right! They are very unpredictable. But, as big and strong as blue crabs are, they are not really that smart you know—what I mean is, they are always fighting with each other, as much as with anyone else. Yet there they were, underneath us, just looking for food at the surf's edge, while we were battling those gulls right above them."

Pausing for a second, lost in his thoughts for a moment, George then added with hidden meaning, "Yes indeed, they were certainly in the shallows all right–and thank goodness too."

"What was that?" asked Whipper, not sure he heard George clearly–somewhat confused by the comment as well. "Did you just say, 'thank goodness' for the Blue Crabs? Why is that? No one likes blue crabs, I can't believe you do either?"

"Well my friend, with your usual keen insight, you have asked just the right question, so let me explain. While I was sitting out there, wondering to myself about the appearance of blue crabs, one of those nasty gulls had noticed Zzigger and me, just hovering over the top of the water. Now, as you know, those birds were out for blood, this one had managed to get above us somehow, and was diving straight down to attack. Zzigger—thank goodness for my dragonfly–spotted him dropping out of the sky, so we dodged out of the way at the very last second. The gull, thankfully, missed us cleanly, if only barely. But, as we were sitting only a couple feet above the ocean at the time, the diving bird hit the water's surface—before he could pull up. Now, here is what was so interesting, do you know what happened then?"

"No, what happened?" asked Whipper, more and more intrigued by George's story.

"While the gull was flapping its wings as hard as it could, pulling up from his missed attack, surely thinking only about coming after me again, a couple of those crazy blue crabs quickly moved in. Snapping their large pincers, they grabbed hold of the gull's wings and pulled him straight back down, into the water! Those crabs are so strong, not to mention their attack was so surprising, they snagged that gull before he could return to the safety of the air!

It was crazy I tell you, as Zzigger and I simply hovered above–watching the whole horrible thing. The crabs just tore that bird apart, on the spot!! Even though they saved Zzigger and I from a tough fight, it was still a terrible thing to behold. Those blue crabs pulling that bird down into the water, then just killing him, right there in front of me."

Shuddering once, as he remembered the end of the fight, George then drew a deep breath while puffing up his chest and pointing his smaller claw at himself to finish his story, "Now, since that bird was obviously the first of the gulls to go down during our battle, and since he was clearly coming after me, I can say here and now that it was I, George, who defeated the first gull this afternoon! I tell you this though, as brave as I am, I'm pretty sure I would not want to fight those blue crabs. They will go after anything, any time, for almost no reason at all."

Smiling together, both Whipper and George then toasted George's success in the recent battle over the beach.

***

Just as the conversation began to slow, food began appearing as if created from thin air. And what a feast it was! Every kind of seafood seemed to be there: beautiful shells full of fish, clams, mussels, shrimp, various forms of seaweed, not to mention other things that the boys did not recognize either by sight or by smell were soon brought out for all to enjoy. More drinks, including Crab punch, were served, soon everyone was eating and drinking and making merry.

Finding themselves brought back together again to eat, Devin and Hunter were seated next to each other at a place of honor near one end of a very long table. The Crabs had used partly dried palm fronds that were cut perfectly flat, along with small wood stumps that had quickly been pushed into the sand, to create the makeshift table. Many of the other young Crabs that the boys had met during their brief time in the sandcastle, including Cracker and Tracker of course, were seated nearby.

The Crabs would simply squat down on their legs, as this position was just the right height for them to eat from. The boys had to sit either on their knees or cross-legged, in order to fit properly at the table.

Cracker and Tracker, along with other Crabs participating in the feast, immediately started to use their pincers to take various foods from the large shells that had been placed in front of them. They put their choices on smaller shells that were stacked in piles nearby, apparently just for that purpose. Once they both had a shell full of food, they clacked their pincers together, digging in with a vengeance!

Hunter was certainly not very enthusiastic about the food choices, as he was not one to try new things to eat all that often, even more particular than most boys his age. Devin, on the other hand, always tried new things to eat, and he was very curious about what was now sitting on the table in front of them. One thing they both noticed was the delicious smell coming from what looked like meatballs on one of the larger shells, and more importantly, that most of the other Crabs went for these meatballs first, so they must be good.

Hunter looked at Devin, asking in a low, quizzical voice, "I'm really hungry. What do you think we should eat, do you recognize any of this?"

"I don't know," responded Devin, eyeing the food with a big grin while pointing to a shell a few seats down, "but I see some shrimp over there that I'm sure is good, so I will certainly be trying that one. Have you noticed, the meatball looking things have been eaten by both Cracker and Tracker, and petty much everyone else? I think I'm going for some of those too."

"Yeah, that sounds good to me," answered Hunter, with an expectant smile on his face. His hunger quickly overcoming any reluctance to try something new, Hunter started to grab food off the shells, just like the other Crabs had done. "Hey, Devin, look at this, I think its redfish or something," Hunter continued, as he took a slice of a meaty dish as well.

Devin grabbed everything in front of him, especially the shrimp, for his own dinner, including something that looked like it might be a seafood salad. Hunter was a bit choosier, although he tried three or four of the dishes, including shrimp and the meatball-looking dish.

Meanwhile, Cracker took a pause from his initial feeding frenzy. Focusing fully on Devin and Hunter, he noticed that the boys had not even started to eat yet, although they now had shell-fulls of food in front of them. Realizing that his new friends were a little unsure of themselves, Cracker decided to have a little bit of fun with them. "Devin," he called with a laugh while waiving his small pincer in an arc, "Go ahead and eat, it's all good! This party is for us, you know. You should really try some of the great food that we have here."

"Well, to be honest, I'm not exactly sure what some of these 'great foods' are, Cracker," responded Devin, smiling.

"Look at these here, they are really tasty," answered Cracker, grabbing what appeared to be a small, almost perfectly round ball, tossing it into the air with his pincer, catching the ball in his mouth, then swallowing the whole thing in one gulp. Letting out a large burp, he clicked his big pincer, saying with true happiness, "Now that was really good. Why don't you try it?"

Tracker, looking at them both, rolled her eyes around a couple times. "That was disgusting, Cracker. Why don't you grow up?"

Hunter, Devin, and Cracker just laughed, all burping very loudly, followed by more laughter.

Eventually, Devin and Hunter got back to their meal, Hunter sticking with the shrimp for now, but Devin kept eyeing the shell with the balls that Cracker had just enjoyed so much. Curiosity winning out, he eventually decided to give one a try. Picking one up, he too flipped it into the air and caught it in his mouth, biting down hard on the ball. It had a squishy, slippery, slimy feel, almost popping out of his mouth as it tried to move away from his teeth as he bit down. The ball popped open, and to Devin's great surprise, tasted like very good chicken—something he enjoyed very much.

"Theesh are wreat, Whacker. What are 'ey?," he mumbled at Cracker, still chewing with a mouthful of food.

"Those," answered Cracker with a straight face, "are edible eel eyes."

"Grooosss!" exclaimed Hunter, with his next breath adding, "I want one too!" With that he grabbed the biggest one he could find, then stuffed it right into his mouth.

"No way," responded Devin, laughing and finally swallowing his first one. "What are they really, Cracker?"

Tracker joined back into the conversation at this point. "They are really eel eyes. Pretty tasty, eh, boys?" she said, now laughing with the rest of them. The other Crabs at the table were now watching all this and laughing too.

Grabbing one of the balls, Tracker showed how one side was almost all black, while the rest was a bland grayish color. "See this?" she said, pointing to the black part of the ball, "this is the eel's pupil. It gets real big like this when cooked." With that description, she too popped a ball into her mouth.

Cracker added, "Not only do they taste really good, but all the older Crabs say they are really good for you."

Devin and Hunter burst out laughing at that.

Cracker wondered, "What's so funny?"

Devin said, "Cracker, my parents are always trying to get me to eat things that are 'good for me' too. Usually that means they taste terrible, although maybe not in this case. I guess parents are the same everywhere." He then ate another eel eye. "What other tasty treats have you got here?"

Before Cracker could answer, another young Crab walked by. Both Devin and Hunter noticed that his entire mouth was a dark shade of purple, almost black, plus it appeared some of this coloring was on the rest of his face too.

"Look at that, Devin," cried Hunter. "Is he sick or something?"

Hearing this remark, Cracker grabbed at another shell, put something quickly into his mouth, then said to the boys, "Devin, Hunter, look over here. I need to tell you something. Quick!"

Turning to look back at Cracker, both boys saw him open his mouth with the same gross purple-black color now appearing on Cracker's face too. He wobbled a little. "Ugh, I feel really sick all of a sudden. Don't eat the the…" And with that he fell backward onto the sand.

Rushing over to him, they saw Cracker lying flat on his back, legs and pincers in the air, with his mouth slightly open so that a thin black ooze could slowly trickle down one side.

"Cracker, Cracker, are you OK?!" yelled Devin. "Talk to me, Cracker."

Both boys leaned closer, as Cracker whispered, "It's…it's…it's..uhh."

"What? What?" both Devin and Hunter asked almost simultaneously, now leaning over so close to Cracker they could almost feel his breath.

Seeing the dark inky stuff trickling down the side of his face, Devin tried to get up to go get some help, but Cracker pulled him back down with his pincer and repeated, "It's…it's…"

"Tell us, Cracker, tell us!" the boys demanded again, still in a state of shock over what was going on, and even a bit scared. Devin and Hunter were both completely focused only on Cracker. For just that moment the rest of the partygoers didn't exist. They were now bent over him, looking at his almost-closed eyes, waiting for to finish telling them something.

"It's…it's…INK!" Opening his eyes back up, with a huge grin on his face, Cracker started laughing uncontrollably. Black ink sprayed out of his mouth, straight up into the air, only to then fall away into the sand.

"What?" gasped Hunter, getting a bit of ink accidentally sprayed onto his face, and not clearly understanding what was going on. Being a bit closer to Cracker than Devin had been, the ink hit Hunter squarely in his left eye, causing a painful stinging feeling, along with making both eyes water, as he tried to blink it out.

Devin said nothing, he had not gotten any ink in his eyes, just a bit on his cheek, as he just stared at Cracker in silence for a second. Wiping the ink off his face with the back of his right hand, turning it black, Devin took a second to look around at all the other crabs, who were of course watching the scene unfold. He saw that some of the other crabs were laughing, a couple of them were grabbing something off a shell that he couldn't quite identify and putting it into their mouths, after which they too started to dribble out the black ink.

Quickly realizing it was just a joke, he was curious about what those crabs were now eating, Devin looked carefully at what was inside the shell. He saw what appeared to be a bunch of very small cooked squid. Each one was dark purple with the ends almost black. Following the example set by the other crabs, he quickly grabbed one and ate it. Sure enough, there was an immediate explosion of both flavor and something wet, which quickly got past his lips. Rubbing the back of his left hand across his mouth he looked down, seeing that this hand also had turned partly black, but the taste in his mouth was really really good! Now he had the ink on both hands too.

"Hunter, Hunter! This is great!" Devin exclaimed as he munched on the squid, still not realizing that Hunter had been hit in the eye. "Come on, try one, this is so cool!"

Unfortunately, Hunter was no longer listening to Devin. He had turned the other direction after the ink had gotten in his eye. Bending over while blinking repeatedly to clear the tears, he was finally able to look up, even though his eyes were still watering, making his vision unclear, and found himself looking directly at Tracker, who was just laughing at the whole thing. To Hunter, it felt like she was laughing only at him, that somehow, he was the butt of this awful joke, which made him both embarrassed and really mad!

Even as a feeling of uncontrollable anger quickly rose up, Hunter's eye continued to water from the stinging ink, not allowing him to see clearly through blurry tears. Continuing to blink and squint, all Hunter could think about was how foolish he must look to Tracker, with ink all over his face. Not wanting to look bad in front of his new friend, yet sure that he was now turning red as well, Hunter lashed out at Cracker with a very nasty shout, "Jeez Cracker, that was so mean, you scared me to half to death, what were you thinking, you jerk, don't ever do that again!"

Looking around at the rest of the group, still not seeing or even thinking clearly, too mad to understand, Hunter saw Devin laughing. With black ink now pouring out of Devin's mouth too, it appeared to Hunter that everyone was making him the butt of a big joke—even though it was not about Hunter at all. This was what the kids did at school; made fun of him for no reason, with jokes he did not understand. This thought just made Hunter even angrier. Everyone else seemed to be having a good time at his expense. Thinking that even his companions were now against him, he simply got up and left the party, feeling mad and jealous of his friends—not sure what he should do.

Unaware that Hunter was so upset, and with everything else going on, no one paid any serious attention as he left the group. Needing to find some water to rinse out his eye, Hunter decided to go back to the chamber where he and Devin would be sleeping. As expected, he found a large shell with plenty of fresh water, which was quickly used to wash off his face and to finally rinse out his eye. It took a little time to stop the tearing, by the time Hunter had himself ready to return to the feast, his energy, including most of his anger, had all but drained away.

Deciding he would lie down for a minute to rest and gather himself before going back to the party, Hunter stretched out on his mat and immediately started to doze off. Given all the events of the day, he was completely exhausted.

As he fell asleep, almost forgetting his embarrassment at the party, Hunter's thoughts turned away from the feast, back toward finding the Pirate's treasure. The thought of pursuing the treasure, maybe even with Tracker helping him find it, brought a big smile back to Hunter's face. As slumber settled over him, his last thoughts were surprisingly not of the Treasure Chest, but rather how good it felt when he grasped the Green Gargoyle on the end of the Key.

CHAPTER 13

THE HUNT BEGINS

> **The Key**
>
> *It was rumored that Lafitte's Chest always contained Rainbow Objects. For this reason, those desiring the Objects always looked first for the chest, even taking unnecessary risks for a chance to see what's inside it. To open the chest, one must have the Key. The most interesting part of this copper-colored the Key is its handle. Emerald green in color, the handle is shaped like a small carefully carved Green Gargoyle with a hole in the top that one could slip a small rope or string through if desired. The Key is thought to be just as valuable as the Rainbow Objects contained within.*
>
> CRAB CHRONICLES

As the feast finally wound down, the participants left the party, heading to their own Crab holes or down various tunnels to go to sleep. Devin went with Cracker back to their sleeping chamber and saw that Hunter was already down for the evening. After talking about the feast for a couple minutes and trying to stay awake, as with all youngsters, the day's activities soon caught up with them. Cracker and Devin were soon fast asleep, laying comfortably on small beds of sea grass.

All three had interesting dreams that night, but Hunter's were particularly vivid. In his dream Hunter, still very much fixated on Lafitte's treasure, could see himself, not Devin, with the Key hanging from his neck after the battle with the birds. Returning to the sandcastle, Hunter told Crex that he would keep the Key for himself during the feast. It was he who was wearing it proudly for all to see during the festival that had followed.

Rather than enjoying the party with the younger Crabs, Hunter was seated at the head table, as he spent most of the evening telling the Crab elders about the adventures of the day. Everyone at his table was discussing what kind of treasure might be waiting for them, once the chest was opened with the Key. When the eating had finished, it was Hunter, not Crex, who put the Key in the wall alcove, to the delight and cheering of all the Crabs in the sandcastle.

As his dream of the evening ended, Hunter even saw himself lying down to get some rest, with Devin and Cracker already asleep in the same room, snoring away happily. However, instead of going right to sleep, in this dream Hunter stayed wide awake, watching the main hallway and every so often getting up to go look at the Key. He wasn't sure why, but in this dream, he kept looking to see if the Key was still where he had put it—safely in the alcove.

Coming suddenly awake for real, Hunter silently got up and left the sleeping room, to go look once again at the Key to Lafitte's Chest. The feeling from his dream, that he needed to constantly check on it, was still very much driving him. After making sure Devin and Cracker were still asleep, Hunter crossed the seemingly empty audience chamber to the alcove where Crex had put the Key on display. Hunter was surprised to find another Crab silently standing nearby, staring intently at this prize.

It was Orion!

Wondering whether he should go back to wake up Devin or not, since he was still just a little mad at both Devin and Cracker for embarrassing him earlier, Hunter decided to see what Orion was up to first. Besides, it had been really fun to race with Orion on the clamming hill, even if Cracker didn't like him. It was Orion who had slipped them past the older Crabs guarding the jetting tunnel, which is why they were able to have the wild adventures leading up to finding the Key in the first place. Orion was certainly fun to clam with, so there might be even more excitement ahead with him.

Orion, hearing the boy approaching, turned from the alcove to focus his eyes directly on Hunter's face. In a very quiet, yet earnest whisper, Orion asked him, "Hunter, do you want to go after Lafitte's treasure with me?"

Hunter was just a little hesitant, instinctively realizing that Orion was suggesting that they take the Key right now, while everyone else was still sleeping. Even though he really wanted to go treasure hunting, as this was exactly what he had been secretly thinking about, even hoping for, when coming over to see the Key, he whispered back to delay the decision a bit, "I'm not sure we should, Orion. Won't Crex get upset if we just take the Key and go?"

Orion replied smoothly, with just the right words to keep Hunter engaged with him, "I doubt it. Besides, it will be lots of fun to go on another adventure, don't you think? Remember, Hunter, *you* are a hero down here in the sandcastle after today's events, so no one will mind if you choose to go."

"Maybe we should wake Devin and Cracker. They would want to come too, I think," suggested Hunter weakly.

"I don't agree," responded Orion quietly but firmly. "Didn't Devin give the Key to Crex in the first place, rather than try to go look for the treasure with you? Why would he do that? I doubt he would want to go now, and the fewer who hear about this, the better. If we aren't very, very quiet, we will never be able to get away with the Key before others wake up around here. Once that happens, who knows how many might want to go? You and I both know that won't work, don't we? The fewer the better for this kind of trip, don't you think?"

Still a little hesitant, even though he really wanted to go looking for the treasure, something inside Hunter tried one last time to delay by asking, "How will we go after the treasure? Do you have some sort of a plan?"

"Yes, of course I do," responded Orion, smiling confidently. "We can catch the clamming hill, take it on down to the jets...just like before. Remember racing down the hill? Pretty fun, wasn't it? We can do it again, if you want too." Orion continued to say all the right things to convince Hunter to join him. "After we get to the jets, we can go back to the underground river and follow it upstream to the Treasure Chest, just like when you searched for the Key."

At these words, some small alarm went off inside Hunter's head. How did Orion know about the underground river leading to the treasure? Either he had heard some of the stories being told at the feast from others who were there, Hunter hadn't seen Orion the entire time, or—and certainly more disturbing—he might have already known what was at the end of the tunnel when they got into the jets the last time.

Now just a bit worried, Hunter said, "Let me go and wake up Devin. He will want to come with us, I just know it." Not giving Orion a chance to argue with him, Hunter turned to head back across the great hall, to the room where Devin and Cracker were still sleeping.

Getting almost halfway across the chamber, Hunter's curiosity got the better of him and he turned to look back at Orion—just to see what he was doing. What he got was a most unexpected surprise! Instead of waiting for Hunter to simply return, Orion was now looking back at the boy, clearly holding up the Key's metallic barrel in one of his claws for Hunter to see. Orion had taken the Key!

Hunter stopped dead in his tracks, not sure what to do. Should he go wake the others...or turn and go after Orion?

As Hunter considered his options, Orion could be seen heading back toward the chamber's exit, waving his large pincer as if saying, *Come with me, you won't regret it.*

Hunter could no longer resist the desire to go after the treasure. Ignoring the last of those little warnings going off inside his head, Hunter struggled for a moment to convince himself that he needed to go with Orion, so he wouldn't lose the Key and his chance at the treasure. If he went back for Devin, it was clear that Orion would surely be gone before he returned. Plus, it was an opportunity to get back at everyone for making fun of him at the feast. That embarrassment was still slightly bothering Hunter.

But now he would find the treasure without help from any of the others! And he recalled one of the Questions' remarks to him, *When you have a tough choice, follow what you can see.* Right now, Hunter had a very tough choice, and what he could see, he decided to follow—the Key!

With his mind now made up, Hunter turned and ran silently back toward Orion, who was already exiting the chamber. Quickly heading to the clamming runs, Hunter chased Orion down. Keeping quiet on the soft sand, he easily caught up with the Crab in the passageway leading out of the great hall.

Still speaking softly, Orion welcomed Hunter to the new adventure, "C'mon, Hunter, Lafitte's Chest awaits us. This treasure hunt is going to be fun and rewarding, that I can promise you." With that, Orion completely surprised Hunter by handing him the Key, along with a piece of netting that he had brought along. Turning, Orion added quietly but persuasively, "Now you have your prize. Put it around your neck for safe keeping, and let's get out of here!"

Feeling the cool metal barrel now solidly in his hand, Hunter felt a surge of excitement. The Key was finally his!

He quickly tied off the netting, creating a necklace to slip over his head. Doing so caused the green handle to settle right in the middle of his bare chest. The touch of the Green Gargoyle on his skin instantly inflamed Hunter's desire to go searching for the ancient treasure.

This was exactly the reaction Orion was hoping for, when he gave Hunter the Key to hold for them. Having it in Hunter's possession would motivate the Big to help Orion, maybe even make him the Crab's ally. Hunter would focus on hunting for the Treasure Chest, not realizing that Orion and One-Eye had other plans. Besides, Orion believed he could always take the Key back anytime—he was very confident in his own strength. So, what harm could there be in letting Hunter hold on to it for a while?

At that moment, Hunter wasn't thinking about Orion, or anything else that might happen. He had the KEY—it was his! In his own mind, Hunter could see himself slipping the Key into the lock on Lafitte's Chest, ready to reveal the treasure inside. Remembering his dream from earlier that night and how great just touching the Key felt to him, Hunter put his right hand on the Key handle now hanging around his neck, triggering three things. First, Hunter became more decisive about this adventure. He was, as of that moment, completely committed to looking for the treasure. There would be no turning back until he had it! Second, the cavern itself got slightly darker as Hunter's fist closed about the Green Gargoyle, casting a type of darkness, emotional as well as physical, that would stay with him as long as he kept the Key in his possession. Third, grasping the Gargoyle completely silenced the little voice in the back of Hunter's head, the one warning him not to go on without Devin and Cracker.

Responding to Orion's last words after a moment's pause, Hunter just smiled. Now hoping—just a little—that Devin and Cracker would be jealous of what he was doing, he whispered back, "I'm ready, Lafitte's treasure awaits. Let's go find it. Won't the others be so surprised when we do?"

Hunter and Orion headed on toward the clamming hill, both stopping to quickly grab a couple of clammers to race on, as they passed by the preparation area. Thinking about their upcoming adventure while also beginning to plan ahead just a bit, Hunter asked, "Orion, shouldn't we get some supplies? Last time I went down here, we needed netting, and having the rock swords came in really handy too." Without waiting for Orion's response Hunter asked, "When we get to the bottom of the hill, won't there be an adult guarding the passage to the water jets? And even if we get by the guard, what is to prevent the adults, once they find out the Key is gone, from coming quickly after us?"

"Don't worry, Hunter," answered Orion, "I have everything planned out. There are some things waiting for us at the bottom of the clamming run, things we will likely need. Some netting for rope, plus a couple of sharp rocks we can use as knives if we need them. There are even a few torches…just in case it gets dark, along with a few other items for the trip. Anyway, I doubt there is more than one adult at the bottom now, especially after the big feast, but if I'm mistaken and we can't slip by any guards, there is a big surprise coming soon enough which will distract them, leaving us free to go."

Laughing to himself Orion, continued, "In fact, I'd bet that everyone in the sandcastle will be so busy that by the time they realize the Key is missing, we will be long gone. You realize, after such a big celebration last night, I think almost everyone will be sleeping late today. Everything we need is waiting for us down there. No more excuses, let's go."

Satisfied that Orion likely knew what he was doing and anxious to get on with the treasure hunt, Hunter just nodded his OK. Even though Orion's comment not to worry about the adult Crabs following them was a bit odd. It also seemed that Orion knew about some "surprise" that would distract them, which didn't make a whole lot of sense either.

Hunter might have worried about this a bit more, but the Gargoyle hanging from his neck was casting its strange darkness about them, continuing to erase any doubts. Besides, Orion had managed to get them past the guard Crabs the first time they were down here easily enough, so Hunter assumed that his new partner was right this time too. Without any more hesitation, he was ready to go.

Getting on their new shells, the two raced down the slopes, finding Orion's promised items waiting near the bottom. Gathering their supplies, the duo advanced in shadow and silence for a bit, easily disappearing from the colony when they found only a single adult Crab sleeping soundly at the entrance to the more dangerous water jets.

As dawn began to break a couple of hours after Orion and Hunter left the great audience hall, only a few of the Crabs could be found slowly waking up after the fabulous feast. On a normal day, by this time most of the colony's residents would have already gotten up to go out onto the beach, before any Birds or Bigs got there. Orion had been right about that. In this case, the previous day had been so busy, between the wild battle with the birds, then the party afterward, that all the Crabs in the sandcastle were still very tired. Most were still sleeping happily, not worrying about anything at all.

"THE KEY IS MISSING!"

With a sudden start, up jumped both Devin and Cracker, each wondering what loud sound had so rudely woken them up. After a moment to look around, slightly confused, as they shook off their pleasant dreams from the previous night, both heard the same blaring call once more.

"THE KEY IS MISSING!"

Understanding this time exactly what was being said, both youngsters looked around for Hunter, then rushed back out toward the main audience chamber. As they ran, Devin asked Cracker, "Why is Hunter not here, Cracker? Why?"

"I don't know, Devin. Maybe he was already awake, maybe he is talking with others in the audience chamber. We will find out soon enough."

Crossing the main audience hall, the two headed toward the quickly growing group of Crabs near the now empty alcove, where just last night the Key to Lafitte's Treasure Chest had been placed. Crex was entering the hall with a large group of adult Crabs with him.

Cracker whispered to Devin, "Do you think Hunter might have taken the Key?"

"I'm not sure. Hunter is no thief," responded Devin, also in a very low voice. "I can't believe he would just go off without me like that, but he really wanted to go look for the treasure. Something must have happened while we were asleep, is all I can think of. Plus, I doubt he would go searching down there alone."

Thinking out loud, Cracker replied, "Well then, if he didn't go with us, who would he go with?" Still looking around the hallway, Cracker finished, "I still don't see him. Hunter isn't here at all, I don't think."

"Should we let Crex know? Cracker? What do you think?" asked Devin, very confused by this new set of events.

Cracker thought about this for a few seconds, finally answering, "I think we must, Devin. If Hunter has gone to look for the treasure, he will need help and might even be in danger. Whoever he is with may not really be his friend. Maybe Orion is involved somehow too. I think we should tell Crex, then offer to help look for him."

Just as the two arrived at the alcove where the other Crabs were gathering, Crex was already moving into action. "The Key, the Key has been taken!" he shouted. "Check all of the exits out of the sandcastle quickly. Maybe we can prevent the thief from leaving, or at least find out where he is going with it. Go NOW!"

As suddenly as they had all come into the audience hall, every single one of the adult Crabs quickly scuttled out, heading for various entrances and exits to the sandcastle, of which there were many. Within a few seconds only Devin and Cracker were left in front of the empty alcove, not having the opportunity to speak a single word, much less seriously talk to any of the adults about Hunter being missing. Now they had absolutely nothing to do, except wait.

Cracker turned to Devin. "I bet Hunter took the Key, don't you think?"

"Yeah, I guess so. You may be right. He certainly isn't anywhere to be seen around here," Devin replied. "Hunter wanted to go after the Pirate treasure really badly, but how could he get away from the sandcastle without any of the other Crabs seeing him? He doesn't know his way around here that well, so he must have had some help."

Cracker answered, "Well, the one path he certainly does know about would take him right back to the underground river, which would be a good starting point. Since we didn't tell anyone else about the picture on the wall pointing toward the treasure, no one else will be looking down there. But I agree with you, getting from here to there would not be easy for someone who had only done it once or twice. I think he must be with someone else, and can only think of one Crab Hunter knew that would try to do something like this."

Finishing Cracker's thought, Devin said, "If Hunter is with Orion, and they took the Key together, the best way to find them would be to go back to the river and follow it ourselves. So, the real question is, should we go get one of the adults…or just go after them on our own, right now? Will the adults even let us go back to the waterjets, Cracker? What do you think?"

"I don't know, this could be really, really dangerous. A lot of strange things have happened in such a short time. Maybe we should get Crex or another adult to go with us," replied Cracker. "On the other hand, it might take a while to get things organized. As most of the adults are already searching the sandcastle, any delay puts Hunter that much farther away. Plus, you are right, the adults might not just 'let us go' once they learn that Hunter likely took the Key, even if we want too. I guess I am just not sure what to do.

Just as Devin was about to speak, two large Crabs burst back into the chamber, yelling at their top voice, "WE ARE UNDER ATTACK! WE ARE UNDER ATTACK! BLUE CRABS! BLUE CRABS! WE ARE UNDER ATTACK!"

As they finished shouting the warning, the entire audience hall shook, with more than a little sand falling from the top of the chamber roof, as if the entire sandcastle had been hit by something either very large or very heavy.

Crex, returning from another tunnel with a growing number of warrior Crabs following him, or simply coming from other tunnels as well, scuttling into the center of the chamber. There was a lot of shouting and snapping of pincers, with the Crabs all debating what to do next. Rapidly taking charge through the confusion and noise, Crex, in his very direct, calm voice, ordered a few of his closest advisors to go throughout the sandcastle to bring all the adult warrior Crabs back to the front door as fast as they could. They scampered off immediately.

In a booming voice, Crex then addressed the rest of the adult warriors in the chamber, of which there were now at least fifty. "To arms, we must defend the sandcastle, to arms!" Grabbing his great shield from the wall with his smaller pincer, Crex was now wearing the Green Gauntlet, which seemed to appear from nowhere. Crex held up the now lightly glowing Gauntlet for all to see while shouting, "Follow me!"

All the adult warriors still in the audience hall immediately followed Crex's lead. Grabbing their own shields, the entire group sped off toward the front entryway, clacking their raised pincers loudly as they went, to deal with the attacking Blue Crabs.

After all the adult Crabs disappeared for the second time, leaving the two friends alone once more within the audience chamber itself, a strange mood came over both Devin and Cracker. It felt as if a sorcerer had just decided to cast a super strong silencing spell. Shouting suddenly ceased, six seconds seemed sixty, such was the dramatic change that came over the great hall after Crex and the others stormed off to do battle.

For several moments time simply froze before Cracker finally broke the strange silence. He and Devin found themselves alone, without any adults to discuss things with, still not having been able to tell anyone what was likely to have really happened with Hunter and the Key. They just looked at each other for a moment until Cracker spoke up.

Looking directly at Devin, he said with a smile, "Maybe the decision has just been made for us."

"What do you mean?" asked Devin.

"Well, think about it," answered Cracker. "Any of the adults who could go with us to search for Hunter are now busy, having to go defend against the Blue Crab's attack. They are certainly not expecting us to help defend the sandcastle; we are not adult warriors. Plus, no one will be watching the entrance to the water jets for the same reason. An attack by Blue Crabs will have to be dealt with first. It looks to me like we have been given the perfect opportunity to go after Hunter, Orion, and the Key…all on our own. Could there ever be a better time than right now to follow them? Could there?"

Devin, quickly understanding what Cracker was suggesting, started walking toward the tunnel that would take them to the clamming hill. "So, you think we should just go then?" he commented, somewhat rhetorically.

Cracker smiled as he moved quickly to catch up with Devin, who was speeding up his own pace. Waiting a moment, he answered, "Indeed, I do. I think we should pick up our rock swords, some extra netting, new clam shells and get out of here right now…before anyone else finds out what we are doing."

And that, is exactly what they did.

The End

The sandcastle and its various denizens will return soon in the

Treasure of Lafitte's Cove